Shadow

of the

Flag

Milana Dietrich

Shadow of the Flag
by
Milana Dietrich

Copyright © 2023

Putnam & Smith Publishing Company
Cover Design by: Connie Jacobs
Book Design by: Connie Jacobs

Distributed by:
Putnam & Smith Publishing Company
15915 Ventura Boulevard, Suite 101
Encino, California 91436
www.putnamandsmithpublishing.com

Library of Congress Control Number: 2023933995
ISBN: 978-1-939986-38-2

Printed in the USA

For P Y

AUTHOR'S NOTE

1923: In a battle that became known as the Beer Hall Putsch, a rag-tag band of dissidents waving the red and black banner of the newly formed National Socialist Party stormed the Government House in Munich, Germany. Eighteen men died, their blood staining their fallen flag. The survivors were taken into custody, among them an unemployed Austrian named Adolf Hitler.

That blood-soaked flag became known as the *Blutfahne,* the Blood Flag, the most sacred symbol of the Third Reich, confirming their righteous cause: the spilling of pure Aryan blood in sacrifice to the Fatherland.

Thousands of SS swore their blood oaths to Hitler on that flag. In massive dedication ceremonies, waves upon waves of fresh swastika flags were paraded past the Führer as he anointed each new flag with a touch of the old, bloodstained banner. These newly consecrated flags were unfurled over the Third Reich, whose cause and reign were meant to last one thousand years. It lasted twelve bloody years and cost more than 70 million lives.

The Blood Flag, the Holy Grail of Hitler's dream, disappeared in 1945 and has never been found. To this day, those who remain loyal to that dream believe that the Blood Flag has the power to resurrect the Reich from the ashes of defeat.

The Führerbunker-Hitler's Underground Headquarters
Berlin, Germany

Monday, April 30, 1945 - 4:10 p.m.

Amid the stone rubble and blooming jasmine in the courtyard garden above the Führerbunker, a light wind shifted the plume of acrid black smoke from the pyre on the ground toward a small group of men who stood nearby. Reichsleiter Martin Bormann's face contorted, but he did not move out of the path of the smoke. Like a short, squat bulldog, he stood resolute even as ashes from the pyre drifted toward his freshly pressed uniform. Following his lead, none of the others moved.

When the fire began to wane, Bormann ordered more petrol. Flames from the rekindled fire crackled and flashed momentarily illuminating the garden and the sullen faces of the men. Then on Bormann's signal, he and the others snapped to attention and saluted.

With the boom of Russian guns providing a resounding operatic crescendo, the stubborn flames slowly engulfed the bodies of Adolf Hitler and his bride, Eva Braun.

~~~~

Thirty-four hours later under a barrage of mortar shells and shrapnel, a small cadre of men climbed out of the Führerbunker onto rubble strewn Wilhelmstrasse. From there they made their way into the network of subway tubes that ran beneath the city. Their plan: to surface outside Berlin, beyond the tightening Russian noose. Halfway through the city, far short of their destination, Martin Bormann suddenly ordered them to the surface.

Wehrmacht Lieutenant Erich Fromer crawled up the rubble that had once been the granite staircase of the Stadtmitte subway station. A tall man, whose battle-hardened face made him seem far older than his twenty-seven years, Erich emerged from the utter darkness of the tunnel into an inferno.

The Gendarmenmarkt, the picturesque center of old Berlin, lay burning before him. Clouds of sulfurous smoke above the city turned the night sky a sickly orange. The cries of the wounded and dying reverberated around him everywhere as if the city itself was crying out in agony.

The last of his men clambered to the surface behind him with Bormann and their other charges in tow, all four were stinking drunk - General Hans Baur, Hitler's pilot; Ludwig Stumpfegger, his doctor; State Secretary Werner Naumann. Drunkest of all was Reichsleiter Martin Bormann. Most of the soldiers Erich had commandeered from the bunker had disappeared into the darkness of the subway tunnels rather than chance the open streets with these stumbling drunks.

Whether these once high and mighty Nazis had been drinking all night out of grief for their Führer or from simple fear, Erich didn't know or care. The lot of them made him sick. For that matter, he made himself sick. Lieutenant Erich Fromer, the great war hero, leading drunken Nazi scum past the carcasses of smoldering buildings, moving like rats through the sewers of a dying city – to save his own pathetic life.

That's what it was all about now. Staying alive. Gambling on cunning or luck. He was no different from his charges. He would do whatever it took to survive.

A few short weeks ago, Erich had been like any other ordinary soldier who'd had the questionable luck to be decorated for bravery – recuperating from wounds suffered in battle. Everything had changed when he was suddenly ordered into Hitler's suffocating bunker to be shoulder to shoulder with the worst kind of fanatics.

Unnoticed in the background, Erich had seen enough to know how things worked. He had watched as Bormann eliminated the others who had for so long been in Hitler's inner circle – carefully, systematically, creating doubt and suspicion until Hitler trusted no one but the Reichsleiter. Erich saw Bormann for what he was: the snake that lies unnoticed in the grass, until at the precise moment, it strikes. One by one, Erich had seen the others fall from favor - first Himmler, then Goebbels and finally Göring, each one struck down by Bormann's poisonous insinuations.

Hitler's body was still smoldering in the courtyard above them, when Erich's chance came. He cornered Bormann and told him the Führer himself had ordered him to be Bormann's personal bodyguard. It was a brazen lie that, had Bormann suspected, would have cost Erich his life.

But Bormann had accepted it without question. Maybe he thought Erich trustworthy because he was twice decorated for risking his life on the battlefield to save his men. More likely, he simply accepted as fact that another nameless, faceless soldier had been assigned to protect the great Martin Bormann.

Either way Erich's ploy had worked. Bormann was a knock-kneed little bastard, but he was smart, and he was lucky. Smart enough and lucky enough to make it past the Russians alive as few others might. Erich had always suspected that Bormann had a secret escape plan. When Bormann had suddenly ordered them out of the tunnels, Erich became sure of it. Now it was up to him to keep Bormann alive long enough for this secret plan of his to play out.

Crouching low, they headed north on Friedrichstrasse. The stench of death followed them as they moved along the street. It was impossible to avoid. Bodies, or what was left of them, were everywhere – soldiers, civilians, Germans and Russians alike.

As they darted across the once fashionable Unter den Linden, a piercing cry brought them to a halt. One by one they ducked for cover behind a collapsed wall.

The cry repeated drew Erich's attention to a nearby rooftop. Silhouetted against the eerie light of the blazing city, a half-dozen Russian soldiers brandishing bayonets chased a naked woman to the edge of the building. The woman tottered there for a moment; then with a wild scream, she hurled herself off.

It was over in an instant.

Erich's hand tightened instinctively on his sidearm as the Russians above him whooped in triumph. He ached to pick them off one by one; yet he crouched there without moving. He leaned against the concrete wall and fought down the bile that rose in his throat.

Like a man awakening from a nightmare only to find the dream he'd been dreaming was real, Erich knew without a doubt that whatever he had been before, he was now no better than the vermin he was protecting.

A stubby finger poked him in the arm. Erich turned to see Bormann, reeking of stale alcohol, crouched next to him.

"What are we waiting for?" Bormann demanded, "Schnell! Schnell! Let's move!"

Erich looked into Bormann's drink-reddened eyes, but he did not move.

How was he any different from this man, this minion of Satan? Wasn't he sacrificing his soul for the mere chance to survive one more day? Or had he relinquished it altogether the day he'd stepped into the lowest reaches of Hell with the Fiend himself?

Without a word, Erich turned away from Bormann, away from the twisted body of the dead woman and her tormentors and forced himself on.

Shadow of the Flag

CHAPTER
ONE

Los Angeles, California – 1990

Professor Aaron Rosen spotted the first one two blocks back, the second one at the corner. Skinheads, complete with the appropriate tattoos. Had they just singled out an old Jew to intimidate, or was this something more?

He knew he couldn't run. His heart would never take it. He also knew an old man hobbling along with a cane made an easy target. He'd been hurrying home to beat the sun, taking a shortcut down a side street, an otherwise deserted side street. Now the fleeting thought came that he might not make it at all.

The two men behind him closed in as a third stepped out of a doorway in front of him. The disdain on his face twisted his features into an ugly grin. There was no longer any doubt in Professor Rosen's mind who these men were or why they had come.

He had been expecting something like this for a very long time. Still, this wasn't one of the barrios of Los Angeles. This was a well-patrolled neighborhood. He hoped that would be their mistake.

The detached observer in his mind remained oddly calm as he set his feet apart to give himself more stability, his cane gripped tightly at his side. He didn't have to look back; he could feel the two behind him close the gap.

"If you want money," he said as mildly as if they had stopped him to ask the time of day, "I have none."

"You misunderstand, Herr Professor," the English was flawless, but the accent was unmistakable. The man's grin broadened. "We do not want your money. We have come to take back what belongs to us."

The one on his left leaned closer. "*Já, der Greis, Deine Zeit ist um*, your time is up." This one's breath stank of cigarettes, beer and bad hygiene.

"I don't know what you mean," he said.

"Oh, I think you do." The man in front moved a step closer. "And you will give it back now."

Professor Rosen smiled back.

"No," he said in the same even tone, "I don't think I will."

Suddenly, he thrust the heavy tip of his cane sharply up between the man's legs, hitting him hard in the groin. In the same instant, his thumb released the catch at the handle as the man dropped to his knees with a grunt, clutching his crotch. The wooden shaft of the cane fell away exposing a ten-inch stiletto. Before the other two had time to react, the old man's free hand jerked the man's head back by the chin, the blade at his throat.

"One more step and I will hand you his head."

The third man, the silent one, inched forward but froze when a thin line of blood appeared under the blade.

A police siren shrieked behind them.

The two looked at each other, clearly considering their options. They hesitated only a second before they turned and ran. A patrol car skidded after them.

Professor Rosen tightened his grip on the chin, yanking the head back farther.

"You tell him he's too late." The old man said in German, pushed the blade harder against the soft tissue of the man's neck. "Do you understand?"

The man whimpered. "I swear! I swear!"

At the end of the street, the patrol car swung around, heading back toward them.

"He won't be happy with you after this." Professor Rosen released the chin and kicked the man over. "Go."

The man staggered to his feet and stumbled away, clutching his bleeding neck in one hand and his crotch in the other.

Professor Rosen slowly leaned over, picked up the shaft of his cane and slipped it over the stiletto. He bent down once more to pick up his *yarmulke* that had fallen off. Fitting it back on his head, he waited for the police car to stop beside him. A tall young black officer jumped out of the passenger side.

"You okay, sir?"

"Yes," he said, trying to catch his breath. "I am quite well."

"We'll call the paramedics for you."

"No, no. It's not necessary."

A second officer joined his partner - this one older, stockier, with short graying hair.

"Did they take anything, sir?" he asked.

"No. Nothing."

"You were lucky we came when we did," said the first officer.

"Yes. I certainly was lucky. Thank you."

"We'll need you to make a report, sir."

"I'm afraid that will have to wait. You see, *Shabbat*, the Sabbath, is about to begin and I must be home." Yes, he needed to be home. The time had come to finally deal with this. He'd put it off far too long. "Would you be so kind as to take me there? It's not far, but I am quite tired."

They helped him into the backseat of the patrol car and took his name and address. As he watched the familiar streets go by, he struggled to bring his rapid, shallow breath and pounding heartbeat under control. The intensity of the encounter had cost him dearly and had brought his age and his infirmity home to him with crystal clarity.

The driver, the gray-haired officer, glanced back at him in the rearview mirror. "You know, sir, we really ought to do something about that cane of yours. Something like that is considered a concealed weapon and it's illegal."

"I didn't realize," Professor Rosen said, turning the old wooden cane over in his hands. "I've had it a long time."

The other officer shifted to look back at him. "Yeah, well, me and my partner aren't going to do anything about it this time. But you'll need to leave it at home from now on and use something a little less lethal."

"To be honest," said the driver, "neither of us have ever seen anything quite like what you did back there."

"And no offense, sir," said the other, "you don't look like a Karate master to me."

"Karate, no. Not Karate."

"Hey, I know what that was," the driver chimed in brightly. "That was that Israeli self-defense thing, wasn't it?"

"Yeah, that's it," said the other. "I've heard about that. Can't remember what it's called."

"Here's my home, gentlemen. The blue house, second on the right." The car pulled to a stop at the curb in front and he stepped out. "Thank you again. You've been very kind to an old man."

"*Krav Maga!*" the officer said through his open window. "That's it, isn't it? *Krav Maga.*"

"Is it? Perhaps you're right."

Professor Rosen was acutely aware of how weak his legs were as he walked toward the house.

It had always been a matter of time. He'd always known that. And finally, it seemed, time was up.

CHAPTER
TWO

Beth Samuels slammed the serving dish down on the counter, splashing its scalding liquid on her knuckles. It served her right; losing her temper with her father never got her anywhere. She stuck her hand under cold tap water.

He was a stubborn old man. She wouldn't win. She never won. So why was she letting it upset her?

He wouldn't answer a single question about why the police had brought him home. She could have kicked herself for not forcing the issue no matter what he said.

Her head cooled as the cold water soothed her stinging fingers and guilt began to take its place. Clearly, he wasn't feeling well. She knew how hard it had been for him being forced to move in with her after his heart attack.

It had been hard for them both. Her husband had just moved out "to find himself" . . . with a woman young enough to be his daughter . . . and within a month her father had moved in.

Oh, who was she kidding? Their battles had started long before this. If it wasn't this, it would be something else. There was always something.

An observant Jew stuck with a rebellious offspring who'd had enough of keeping Kosher by the time she was ten to last her lifetime. And here she was doing it all again – giving in to her dad and his ways.

To make matters worse, Beth could always count on her daughter Rachel to point out every mistake she made and to be properly horrified when she made them in front of Darling Itzhak, Rachel's fiancé, a third-year rabbinical student and Knower of All Things.

"We're late, Beth."

"Yes, Dad, I know." He must be watching the sun go down. Darling Itzhak was probably timing it.

"We're ready." Rachel grabbed the matches from the drawer. As she did, the telephone rang.

Beth wiped her hands and stretched across the counter to grab it. Rachel's hand on her arm stopped her short.

"Mother, you're not going to answer it." It was not a question.

The phone rang again.

"Of course, I'm going to answer it." She shook off her daughter's hand.

"Mrs. Samuels, *Shabat* has begun." From the doorway, Itzhak gave her the same thin veneer of a smile he used on Rachel when he was annoyed at her childish behavior - imperious, patronizing, and skin deep.

Once more, the phone rang. Itzhak's eyes were humorless.

"It's my phone," Beth said, "and I'm answering it." She grabbed it before it could ring again, ignoring Rachel's expression of disgust.

"Mrs. Samuels," said a man's voice on the other end.

"Yes?"

"Your father is Aaron Rosen, is he not?"

"Yes."

"May I speak with him, please?"

Beth could see her father standing in the living room, watching her. He looked about as pleased as Rachel.

"I'm sorry. He can't come to the phone right now."

"He is there?" asked the voice.

"Yes. But it's after sundown. He doesn't use the phone on

the Sabbath."

"Yes, of course, but I think he will make an exception. I assure you it is quite important. Could you tell him it is regarding Peter Rolf? I will spell it for you, Rolf, R-O-L-F. You will tell him, please?"

Something about the words made Beth feel very, very cold.

"Dad," she said, covering the receiver with her hand, "he says it's important."

"Beth, you know I--"

"He says it's about someone named Peter Rolf."

As soon as the name left her lips, she knew something was terribly wrong. For an instant, her father's face blanched, frightening Beth deeply. He was a tall man, erect in his bearing, yet he seemed to shrink before her eyes.

"Dad?"

Her voice shook him visibly. He squared his shoulders, lifting his head high, as though he had reached down deep within to draw himself up again. He crossed the room and took the receiver from her hand.

"Yes?" he said. "You wanted to speak to me?" As he listened, color rose up his neck into his lined cheeks, until his face became dangerously red. "I don't know what you're talking about." Beth watched a shudder move through his body, but there was no weakness in his voice when he spoke next. "Now, *you*," he said with a force that surprised her, "will understand. This is the Sabbath, and I will violate it no longer." He hung up the phone then stood there, his head bowed, silently gripping the kitchen counter. Interminable seconds passed before he moved again.

"Begin the prayers, please, Beth," he said quietly. "It's late."

Beth put her arm around his thin shoulders. "Dad, are you all right?"

"Yes, yes." He turned to her with a smile. "It was a wrong number, nothing more. Let's begin." He patted her hand.

"But, Dad, please. What's going on? Who was that--"

"Beth! We are already late. Why should God have to wait for our attention? This is His day, not ours."

Rachel had been busy trying to keep Itzhak calm. To Beth, his face resembled a blowfish. With a gargantuan effort, he spoke without exploding.

"Yes, sir. That's exactly why we don't--"

"Of course, Itzhak," Beth said with a pretty large effort of her own, "but there are always exceptions."

"Mother, in Itzhak's position, there can be no exceptions."

"Nonsense."

"It's not nonsense, Mrs. Samuels. It's--"

"Enough!" Her father stopped them all. "God is waiting."

Obediently, they took their places around the dining room table. Rachel draped her grandmother's shawl over her head and struck a match. She lit the candles, covered her eyes and intoned the prayer, "*Barukh ata Adonai, Eloheinu melekh ha-olam bo-re m'orei ha-esh.* Praised are you, *Adonai* our God, Sovereign of the universe, who has created the lights of fire." Rachel's soft voice brought feeling to every word.

The words had lost their meaning for Beth long ago but seeing her daughter as she looked up from her prayers, nearly moved Beth to tears. The depth of Rachel's belief sparkled in her large brown eyes, just as it had with Beth's mother.

Rachel was a duplicate of her grandmother, deep auburn curls surrounding a porcelain doll's delicate features. Beth, on the other hand, was like her father, tall and fair, with his stormy gray eyes. She had inherited his looks, his passion for teaching, but she had not inherited his faith. That seemed to have skipped a generation.

Her father had always been a man intent on fulfilling his obligations as a Jew. Growing up, Beth had felt the pressure of that responsibility. There was no coercion. It was just the way it was. They were observant Jews. Period.

The tension that developed had become a hazy glass

wall between them. Her belief in God had been tenuous at best; and as a teenager, she certainly had no burning need to proclaim to the world, "I am a Jew!" As soon as she could, she had defiantly shed those shackles, only to find years later that her own daughter would fervently embrace them, and her father would be living in her home, a home that had become Kosher, whether Beth liked it or not.

How Fate did enjoy these wicked little ironies.

When it was her father's turn to raise his glass of wine, Beth could hear his voice ringing in her memory, as it had a thousand times, "The wine is our joy, and the full cup shows our gratitude for the bounty we have been given."

But tonight, he skipped straight to the blessing.

"*Barukh ata Adonai*," he began, but his voice broke. He hesitated for a moment, then continued, "*Eloheinu melekh . . .eloheinu melekh--*"

Beth looked up sharply. Something was wrong.

"*. . .ha-olam bo-re p'ri hagafen.*" He finished the blessing in a voice so quiet, Beth hardly heard him. His face was ashen.

"Dad?"

The goblet slipped from his hand and shattered on the table. Blood red wine spread like a grotesque hand across the white tablecloth. He clutched at his left arm and crumpled to the floor.

"Oh, my God! Dad! Dad!" Beth dropped to his side. "Rachel! Call 911!" She loosened his collar. "Quickly!"

Her daughter didn't move.

"Rachel! Go and call!"

Rachel jumped involuntarily and ran to the kitchen.

"Rachel!" Itzhak was right behind her.

"Itzhak!" Beth screamed after him, "Shut up and stay out of her way!" He stopped where he was, his mouth agape. "Rachel," Beth's voice shook, "pick up that goddamned phone and call 911. Now!"

~~~~

Beth had never felt more helpless in her life. They sat in the institutional green waiting room, watching the institutional waiting room television flickering from the wall. Its volume had been turned down too low for anyone to hear, perhaps so it wouldn't disturb the desperate prayers of the families who waited there.

But Beth wasn't praying. Not real prayers, anyway. She wanted to say eloquent words that would shake the heart of a god she didn't believe in, but all that came was begging. *Please, please, please, please, don't let him die, please, if You're even there, if You're even listening, please, please.*

She and Rachel had followed the ambulance in Beth's car. They'd left Darling Itzhak standing at the front door. Since it was the Sabbath, he had insisted on walking.

Silent tears had flowed from Rachel's eyes the whole time, but Beth still hadn't cried. She didn't know if she could. She was too numb. Her thoughts whirled between pleading and wondering what they were doing to her father, and the incessant question, "*Who the hell is Peter Rolf?*" Why had the mere mention of that name caused such a violent reaction in her father?

He had survived the unspeakable horrors of the Holocaust, had fought to bring about the birth of Israel, and had become a respected teacher - a man revered for his wisdom, his spiritual strength, and his generosity. Beth had never seen him lose control. Even in the worst of their battles, it had been Beth who'd had the flashes of anger, Beth who had exploded. Never her father, no matter how disappointed he'd been with her.

But tonight, Beth had seen something she had never seen in her father before. For only one instant, no more than a heartbeat, when he heard that name, Beth had seen cold, paralyzing fear. Then she had watched him steel himself against it.

"Mrs. Samuels? I'm Dr. Hwang."

The young woman standing in front of her with a

stethoscope doubled up in her pocket and a medical chart tucked under her arm should have confirmed that she was a doctor, but Beth's brain couldn't accept it. She looked younger than Rachel. She had to be in high school.

"Your father is asking for you, Mrs. Samuels."

"Thank God," Rachel said. "Then he's conscious?"

"Yes, at the moment, but he's very weak."

"May we see him?" Rachel asked. Beth couldn't speak.

"Yes, but only for a moment and only one at a time."

Beth followed her like an automaton. The child-doctor was telling her something about *Myocardial infarction*, a massive heart attack. His condition was grave. She would only be allowed a few moments before they transferred him somewhere else - maybe it was the cardiac intensive care unit - Beth couldn't hear clearly through the one reverberating thought that resounded in her brain.

Daddy, oh Daddy, please don't leave me.

At first, she thought she'd stepped into the wrong cubicle; it took her a moment to recognize the frail old man on the gurney. The man whose strength had carried her family through so much was barely there at all.

Beth took his cold hand in hers and stood beside him, watching his chest rise and fall in short, ragged breaths. The heart monitor blipped steadily, but his eyes remained closed. Finally, he stirred.

"Beth." His voice was little more than a hoarse whisper.

"Yes, Daddy. I'm here."

"I should have told you before." He was struggling to breathe. "I tried to . . ." His hand gripped hers so hard it hurt. "They know . . .they know . . . they won't stop now--" He broke off coughing, then tried again. "Remember . . ."

His breathing was so labored; she could barely make out the words as he struggled to go on. "'Though He . . . slay me, yet . . . I will . . .'"

Beth knew the words very well. Growing up, she'd been

surrounded by them, printed and embroidered all over their home in Hebrew and in English. They were from the *Book of Job*.

"Though He slay me, yet I will trust Him."

Beth had always wondered why you were expected to trust a god who would slay you for your trouble. It had made no sense to her then, and it certainly didn't now.

"I remember, Daddy," she said. "Don't try to talk now. You need to rest."

He closed his eyes for a moment and then opened them again. *"Liebchen . . ."*

Beth could barely speak for the tears that choked her.

"I love you, Daddy."

He said one last word very softly.

"Anna."

Her father coughed again, then relaxed and closed his eyes. The doctor was there checking him. The blips continued on the monitor, and his chest moved up and down. But Beth knew he was leaving her.

~~~~

While Rachel drove Beth's car, she and Itzhak talked about what needed to be done next. Who to call, who should come.

Beth didn't care. She sat in the backseat, staring out the window at the passing city, surprised somehow that the world was going on about its business as if nothing had happened. But something had happened. Her father was gone. Didn't they know that? How could they not know that?

Four years ago, it had been her mother. But it was different then. Her mother had been ill for so long, suffering, struggling against cancer. Beth had convinced herself it was for the best. She had focused her attention on her father, helping him survive life without his beloved Anna, and that focus had helped Beth get through it.

This was very different.

The sun was brilliant, the day was as crisp and beautiful as any California day, but Beth's heart was gripped by utter darkness.

~~~~

"*Mein Sheyn meydele*," Mrs. Liebowitz urged gently, "you must eat. How else will you make it through *shivah*."

How could Beth argue with logic like that? So, she sat in her dining room, pushing a *matza* around the bowl of chicken soup Mrs. Liebowitz had forced upon her.

The steady stream of visitors, bringing an endless variety of foods with their condolences, started arriving almost as soon as Beth walked in the door. And for the first time in the eight months Darling Itzhak had been around, Beth was thankful for his presence, as long as Rachel and dear Rabbi Pressman kept him busy and out of Beth's way.

The funeral, the burial, all of it had to take place within twenty-four hours. Then there would be the *shivah*, seven days of mourning when Beth and her family were to stay inside and to sit the entire time. Every day, twice a day, the *minyon* would arrive, ten men who would come to hold services and hear the sons of the family recite *Kaddish*, the mourner's prayer. Thank God, Itzhak knew what to do.

In the midst of it all, Brian showed up with Betty Boop in tow. Brian, The Ex. Betty Boop, or whatever the hell her name was, clung to him as if she might be devoured any second.

But between them, Rachel, Itzhak, and Brian arranged every detail without Beth having to think about a thing, which was fortunate, since Beth couldn't decide which shoe to put on first without getting a headache.

"Your papa, such a *mensh*!" Mrs. Liebowitz talked while Beth played with the *matza* ball. "Always he was there to help. A little money here, a little advice there. Look at the time my Maxie was so sick. Polio, poor little thing. And me a widow with three little ones. The doctors they were so expensive, but your papa he says to me not to worry. He saw to it all, the best care. Where should he get such money? He wouldn't let me pay a nickel. Not a nickel. Trust God, he says. Trust and pray. Pretty soon Maxie is playing ball like the other boys." With a sweet smile, she put her hand on Beth's. "A miracle, a real miracle!"

Mrs. Liebowitz went on telling her about her family, the grandchildren and her two great-grandchildren, with Beth only half listening. After a few minutes, she noticed the *matza* had disappeared. This was Mrs. Liebowitz's *mitzvah*, her good deed, to get Beth to eat; and at that moment, Beth loved her for it.

The doorbell rang once again. A moment later, Rachel poked her head around the doorway.

"Mom, the man from the funeral home is here. He says he needs to speak to you and Rabbi Pressman privately. Daddy and Rabbi Pressman said to ask if you felt up to it. Is it okay?"

Beth was able to smile at her. "It's okay, honey." It was amazing what a little chicken soup could do.

She led the two men to her father's room and closed the door. It was the first time she'd been in his room since she'd come home. In fact, she almost never came here. It had become his sanctuary since he'd moved in, and she had respected that. The book he'd been reading lay open on the nightstand beside a photograph of her mother in a delicate silver frame. His reading glasses, a roll of antacids. That stupid sword cane he insisted on using hung on the foot of the bed. It was as if at any moment he would open the door and wonder why they had invaded his room. She wondered that herself.

She noticed that the mirror over the dresser was covered with black cloth and wondered how she'd missed that touch. It was clearly Itzhak's. Who else would have thought of something so excessively proper?

She turned her back on the black shroud and faced Leon

Hassen. He was a sallow young man, who was clearly born to play the part of a mortician. Tall and lanky in his dark suit, dark tie, his head perpetually bobbed up and down, Beth supposed to convey sympathy.

"Mrs. Samuels, I'm so very sorry to bother you at a time like this, but we can't proceed until we straighten this matter out. We obviously want the funeral service to be correct and there's so little time."

"Yes?"

"Well, I had just assumed . . ." He cleared his throat. "That is, we had assumed . . ." He cleared his throat again, with a long, drawn-out effort.

"Leon, whatever you're trying to say," Rabbi Pressman said, "say it."

"Well, you see, Mrs. Samuels, Rabbi, we had just assumed that you wanted a Jewish service."

"What else would we want?" The vice tightened on Beth's temples.

"Oh, yes." The mortician shifted from one foot to the other. "It's just that . . . well, s-since we realized that your father wasn't Jewish, we n-naturally wondered--"

"Excuse me?"

"Since Professor Rosen wasn't Jewish--"

"Have you lost your mind?" The Rabbi took a step toward him, and Leon Hassen shrank back against the dresser.

"But I thought you knew," he squeaked.

"Knew what?" Beth asked. "What are you talking about?"

"Oh, my, then you didn't know? I . . ." His face turned a fluorescent shade of fuchsia. "Oh. . . well. . . You see, Professor Rosen wasn't, um, well, you see, he wasn't actually . . . you know . . . circumcised."

CHAPTER
THREE

abbi Pressman threw up his hands. "Leon Hassen, you're a *schlemiel*! Circumcised or not, Aaron Rosen was a better Jew than you'll ever hope to be. Now, get out of here. And if you know what's good for your reputation, you'll keep this *shtuss* to yourself."

To some disconnected fragment of Beth's mind, the mortician resembled a glow-in-the-dark bobbleheaded turtle, desperately trying to make his bobbing head disappear into his starched shirt collar.

"Of course - so sorry - pardon the intrusion." Suddenly more like a hare than a tortoise, the man bolted nearly tripping over himself trying to get away.

Rabbi Pressman turned to Beth and took her hands.

"He's more than a *schlemiel*, he's a *schlimazel*. What does he know? An uncircumcised Jew - it's uncommon, of course, but it's not impossible, Beth. Remember, a man your father's age, born where persecutions were a way of life, who knows what could have happened? Something must have prevented the *Bris Milah*. Maybe there was no *mohel* to perform the rite; maybe there was a pogrom. Who knows? I was your father's friend for almost forty years, and I am telling you, I have never known a finer, more generous or more righteous Jew than Aaron Rosen."

~~~~

Beth sat on her father's bed until she could trust her legs to hold her. She pushed the black cloth aside, but one look in the mirror almost dropped her back down again. The dark circles under her swollen red eyes wouldn't rub off. No amount of makeup could have helped the pasty white color of her face. There was even less life in her brain. It had turned to stone, unable to think, unable to process what she had just heard.

When she finally went back into the living room, she found that the Betty Boop was still plastered to Brian's side, looking even younger than usual, if that was possible.

Beth's first inclination was to scream at the top of her lungs and throw her out on her tight little glutes. But her head hurt too much to scream, and Brian would undoubtedly follow, lest they be apart for more than five minutes at a stretch. Right now, even if he was the most insensitive oaf on the planet and she hated him for it, Beth needed him.

"What was that all about?" Brian asked, oblivious to her reaction. "Leon flew out of here like the Hounds of Hell were after him."

Beth didn't know what to say. She had always trusted Brian with everything, every secret of her life. She wanted to tell him what had just happened, wanted it with all her heart. But not in front of Betty Boop.

The man sitting there in her living room, looking at her with the same warm brown eyes, the same concerned smile, wasn't the same man she had married when she was still just a kid. This was the tanned, sculpted version, with hair several shades darker than Nature had made it. This man, hanging on a girl almost half his age, was no longer her husband. He was no longer a son of this family, and he had no right to know its secrets.

"Is Mrs. Liebowitz still here?" she asked.

"No, she left a few minutes ago. The kids walked Rabbi

Pressman to his car. Knowing the way Itzhak talks, they'll be awhile. Is something wrong?"

"No, it's nothing. Just some last-minute details."

Genuine concern filled Betty Boop's limpid blue eyes, and she came immediately to Beth's side.

"Are you all right? You've been up all night. You should lie down for a little while and let us take care of these things that come up."

Why couldn't she be a disgusting, infuriating bitch instead of this likable child? Then Beth could hate her and be done with it.

"Maybe I will take a nap." She was too tired to think anymore. Too tired to fight Betty Boop and her perfect face and her perfect body. Too tired to fight the rabbi's flimsy explanations about her father. Too tired and too numb.

~~~~

To Beth, the week of *Shivah* was divided into two separate and distinct parts: the painful haze before David and the rest.

Of course, Brian was there doing his duty, trying to shield her, to keep her cheerful when all she wanted to do was crawl under the bed. And through it all, wherever Brian was, there was Sabrina. That was her name. Beth had remembered it before she slipped and called her Betty Boop to her face. Not that she would have understood the reference. She was too damn young.

Beth couldn't tell where grief for her father began and grief for her lost marriage ended. It was all one dark hole where her heart used to be.

At first, she doubted she would hold herself together at all. Then David came.

Beth was in the kitchen when he arrived. The moment she walked into the living room and saw him standing there talking to Brian, she felt the horrible weight begin to lift. David's eyes - those glistening black orbs that had dazzled two, or was it three, wives - met hers, and as if a magical spell passed across the room, Beth could suddenly breathe again.

He had her in his arms in one heartbeat.

"I'm breaking you out of here," he said so that everyone in the room could hear. Itzhak opened his mouth to protest, but one look from David stopped the words before they could form into more than a guttural croak.

"Okay," she said, yielding to the safety of him. He knew exactly what to do to ease her pain, just as he had always known from the time they were toddlers, their families living together on a *Kibbutz* in Israel. After Beth's parents had immigrated to the States, they had only seen each other on Beth's summer visits. Each time, they had picked up where they'd left off without so much as a breath of hesitation.

He walked her out the door, ignoring the shocked and indignant looks of Rachel and Itzhak and the looks of quizzical concern from the others.

"What's going on with Rachel," David said as he pulled his rented car away from the curb. "I used to think she was a bright girl, but I'm starting to wonder. What do you think of this fellow she's marrying? Seems a bit of a twit to me."

"No comment."

David drove her to Venice Beach where the noise and colors contrasted fiercely with the grief that had been swallowing her whole. At first, it was so painful she almost protested; but after only a few minutes, the sun and the ocean air began to do their job and she started to relax.

The quintessential Israeli, David had a kinetic energy that rippled wherever he went. It had been at least three years since they'd last seen each other. The frosting of gray that had for years crept into his shining dark curls was finally taking over. He looked older and a little more tired, no doubt from the long flight and from the fact that his own father, Uncle Benny, had been gravely ill for some time. But tired or not, David's presence alone filled her up.

Deep down, she supposed she had always had a mean crush on him. They had always thought of each other as cousins, even though the relationship was so remote as not to matter. David's father had always been Uncle Benny and David her cousin. Still, there was a time she'd thought they might have fallen in love. Instead, they simply loved each other - madly and, except for one or two experimental kisses when they were teenagers, platonically.

They sat to watch the ocean and the people. They walked and ate ice cream. And they talked.

She thought about telling him about the police and the phone call that had left her father so upset and Peter Rolf and Leon Hassen and the whole unbelievable idea that her father wasn't Jewish. But she didn't. She just couldn't bring herself to say any of it out loud.

In the end, David didn't say or do anything that the others hadn't already done, but there was a difference somehow - perhaps, because he knew her so well or maybe because he loved her father as deeply as she. She didn't know. She only knew that by the time they returned to the house, her arms and legs were no longer made of lead, her head had once more acquired a functioning brain, and life somehow seemed worth living again.

~~~~

Seven days later, the mirrors were uncovered, the clocks were ticking again, and the constantly changing army of relatives, friends and acquaintances had gone. *Shivah* was over. Rachel and Itzhak had gone. Itzhak back to whatever Kosher hole he called home, and Rachel to her apartment and her roommates across town. And David. He'd come and gone so quickly, the last to arrive and the first to leave, flying halfway around the world and back again just to spend a few hours with her.

Now, Beth was left alone again with a silent, empty house

and a deep aching hole inside.

What she wanted to do was to sit down and have herself a really good cry. Instead, she did the dishes, made the bed and slowly worked her way through the house, straightening, dusting, reading the mail, anything to keep going. Finally, she came to the hardest part, clearing out her father's room. She could have put it off, would have put it off, but what good would that have done? So, she turned on one of the opera tapes he had loved so much, yanked out a dresser drawer and plopped it on the bed.

The first thing she touched was one of his undershirts. It was soft and clean and smelled of fabric softener, and it made her cry. She folded it, smoothing out every wrinkle, and put it back. One by one, she took everything out of the drawer then put it right back. In the end, it had taken her all day, and it was her father who made her go through with it. She could hear his insistence on giving to those less fortunate and not the things you were ready to throw out. Give of yourself, he would say, give the good stuff.

By the next morning, Beth had a carload for Temple Beth Israel's charitable outreach. Then came the bank. Her attorney had already made arrangements for her to begin her job as executor without encountering too many bureaucratic hassles.

The bank clerk checked his computer once again, typed a few strokes, closing out the last of the accounts of Aaron Rosen.

"Well, that appears to be all," the young man smiled cheerfully, "except, of course, the safe deposit box."

"I wasn't aware he had one."

"Let me check again." He tapped away on the computer and then went to a card file at the back of the room to search through the signature cards. "Yes," he said a few moments later, "Dr. Rosen maintained a safe deposit box here since he opened his account in 1963. Your signature is on the card. Perhaps you forgot."

"I suppose that's it." She hadn't forgotten. She never knew.

He must have had her sign the card when she was signing the others, in case anything happened to him. He'd simply kept the box a secret. "Am I allowed to open it?"

"Yes, of course. You're authorized to do so. If you don't have the key, you can make a request to have the bank open it for you, but it might take a while."

"I'll find the key."

Once again, Beth sat on the side of his bed with a small satin throw pillow clutched tight in her arms. There had always been secrets, things he wouldn't talk about, the camps, the war in Israel. So why was this so surprising? A safe deposit box was the logical place to keep important papers, naturally; but why hadn't he mentioned it? Some last pieces of her mom's jewelry, she assumed, maybe a small life insurance policy.

She glanced down at the embroidered pillow in her hands. Her mother's work of course. Beth had never learned to embroider or knit or sew, for that matter. The words were in Hebrew, but Beth knew very well what they meant.

Though He slay me, yet I will trust Him.

"A lot of good trust did you, Dad."

She threw the pillow at a box of his clothes destined for the charity. It missed, skidding across the floor under the desk.

"Great," she said and got up to retrieve it. Instead, she opened the lap drawer of the desk. She had already gone through it before. There wasn't anything resembling a key to a safe deposit box, in fact, no keys at all, just the usual jumble of pens, pencils, paper clips, notepads, junk. She checked the drawers on either side - still nothing.

"Okay, Dad," she said out loud, "if this was so important, where did you put the damn key?"

She reached her hand under the lap drawer and ran it over the rough wood. She found it near the back, attached with a strip of nylon tape.

Old men and their secrets. Good Lord.

~~~~

Alone in the cubicle at the bank, Beth felt guilty opening the box. Her dad had been so independent right up to the end. Now she was sifting through his private things, something she would never have done when he was alive.

Inside the long metal box, she found citizenship papers for her mom and dad, a copy of her own birth certificate, a letter from David Ben-Gurion thanking her father for his service to the new State of Israel. There was also a life insurance policy. When she opened it up, she gasped out loud when she saw the amount - two million dollars with Beth as sole beneficiary. She had expected a few thousand, maybe, to cover expenses, but this? Two million dollars for a retired teacher? It made no sense. Why so much? The premiums must have cost him a fortune - a fortune he didn't have.

A crumpled brown paper bag lay in the back of the box. It was surprisingly heavy. With a sinking feeling in her stomach, Beth reached inside. She pulled out an oily yellowed cloth wrapped around the dark cold steel of a gun; then she poured out eight bullets from the bag. Beth stared at them in the palm of her hand.

She shook herself and dropped the bullets back into the bag. There was nothing unusual about this. It was just a relic from his days in Israel. Uncle Benny had told the story a hundred times. Her quiet, gentle father was a great hero of Israel, having saved an entire *Kibbutz* from the Syrians. It was only natural for him to keep a souvenir.

The last thing in the box was an aging manila envelope. The yellowing tape that sealed it gave way instantly, the glue having long ago disintegrated. Beth pulled out the papers and stared at them in utter disbelief.

The writing was both in English and German, and they were covered with the official stamps of the Department of

War, Occupational Forces. A single word, "de-Nazification," leaped off the page. These were the release papers of a German prisoner of war. The name read, "*Peter Rolf.*"

The face looking back at her from the grainy black and white photograph affixed to the front page was her father.

Shadow of the Flag

CHAPTER
FOUR

Munich, Germany (American Sector) - 1946

Peter Rolf jumped back out of the path of a speeding U.S. Army Jeep and was staggered by its momentum. An old man passing by asked if he was all right.

"Yes, I'm fine," he replied automatically. *"Danke schön."*

But he was not so fine at all. He tried to brush off some of the dust from his ragged Wehrmacht coat. He no doubt looked as wretched as he felt. He'd been on the road for almost three weeks since his release, and it had been nearly two days since he'd tasted food. Now, he was burning with fever.

Still, things were looking up. He'd finally made it to Munich after a brief sojourn into the Russian zone to rescue his belongings. It had been easier than he'd expected; the Russians paid little attention to anyone going east, when hordes of refugees were moving the other direction, trying to escape before they closed it off for good. The rumors said it was inevitable. To get out again, he had simply melted into the human river. Now that he was in Munich, he hoped the worst was over. If he could find his sister, she would help him until he could decide what to do next. He'd also heard of a priest in Munich with a reputation of not asking too many questions.

Since those last days of the war, his only real plan had been to blend in, draw as little attention to himself as possible, and to trust no one. An Allied prisoner-of-war camp seemed as good a place as any to become invisible. No one was very concerned about another lowly Wehrmacht sergeant, not even the Allies.

The trick had been to keep his mouth shut and stay clear of the politics that embroiled the camp. Men who had driven their way to various levels of power in the Reich had been reduced to maneuvering for control of small blocks of internment camp turf. Their names had changed, and certainly their rank, but they were no less dangerous.

He had kept to himself and made a point of avoiding anyone with power. In time, he'd made a few friends, one or two German enlisted men and even a couple of his American captors.

Curious. You're ready to blow each other's brains out without a second thought; then someone yells, "Cease fire!" and you pat each other on the back and become fast friends.

One of the Americans, a captain, had pulled the strings that ultimately got him released. If he had remained much longer, there was little doubt he'd be in far worse shape, perhaps not breathing at all.

He had stayed invisible for months; quiet, pliable, not making waves, or even ripples to bring him notice. Then he'd made the mistake of sticking his neck out. He'd intervened in a beating, a brutal pay back to some pathetic loser who'd stepped in the way of the reigning black marketeer.

Late that night, long after lock-down, one of his barracks mates shook him awake. The camp commandant wanted to see him.

"Now? What time is it?"

"What difference does it make? Those *Amis* bastards want you to report, you report."

Peter was too tired to argue. He pulled on his boots, grabbed his tunic and stepped out into the brightly lit night.

The sharp glare of the flood lamps mounted high above the surrounding barbed wire turned the bare ground silver and cast long black shadows in spots they couldn't reach. It was cold, cold enough that his breath formed white misty clouds as he headed toward the commandant's office, buttoning his tunic as he went.

In his still groggy mind, he wondered why a guard hadn't come to escort him, but he ignored the thought and started trotting past the line of barracks to keep warm.

He was passing the third building when the blow came.

If he hadn't been running, it probably would have killed him. As it was, he was unconscious for a day and a half. The day he was discharged from the infirmary, he was transferred to a high security unit, and a week later he was released.

The American captain told him they'd uncovered no leads, but he'd convinced the camp bureaucrats they didn't want the murder of an inmate on their hands. It was safer to let him out, thus making him someone else's problem.

"Watch your back, buddy," the American had said, then he shook Peter's hand warmly and gave him an extra ration book and two cartons of Lucky Strikes as a parting gift. It was a generous gift, as valuable as gold on the black market.

That was nearly three weeks ago. He was still weak and had begun shivering. He shifted his duffel bag to the other shoulder and concentrated on putting one foot in front of the other. The last thing he needed was to be found collapsed in the street. That would mean questions, and he'd had a belly full of questions. And if he was truly ill, he might not be in control of his answers.

Munich, or what was left of it, was unfamiliar to him. He'd only been here twice before. The river was behind him, so he figured he must be moving in the right direction. But what chance did he have of finding anything even remotely familiar when whole blocks of houses were no more than bombed-out shells?

Out of the corner of his eye, he caught a flash of color amidst the gray, colorless ruins. Daffodils. Five brilliant yellow daffodils trumpeting the arrival of spring in the middle of a barren pile of rubble.

Something inside him came reaching up from a place so deeply hidden he'd forgotten it existed. For the first time in more years than he could remember, he could actually begin to believe that somehow, everything would be all right.

A wet, salty taste reached the corner of his mouth. Standing in the middle of the street, crying over a few daffodils. He laughed out loud at the idea. He must be sicker than he thought.

He wiped his face with the back of his hand and started once again down the street. But suddenly he stopped and looked back, remembering as a small child, proudly presenting a bunch of yellow flowers to his sister, Elisabeth, and the expression of love that had come into her eyes. His little mother, Elisabeth had cared for him after their mother had died. Their father had been too distant, too grief-stricken, so nine-year old Elisabeth had stepped in.

With renewed energy, he cut across the empty property to the daffodils. He set down the duffel bag and carefully broke each stem off so as not to hurt the bulbs. Elisabeth loved flowers, especially yellow flowers. It had been a long time since he'd given her any.

The next few blocks looked more and more familiar; then he saw the street he'd been searching for, Edelweiss Strasse. He remembered that his sister had loved the idea of living on a street with such a beautiful name. He hurried toward her number, but his heart sank as he approached her block. Most of the buildings had been badly damaged and appeared deserted. The only other living thing he saw was a scrawny mongrel dog digging in a pile of bricks for a scrap of food. The little spark of hope brought alive by the daffodils disappeared completely when he found her building.

Number thirty, four stories with eight flats. The right half of the fourth floor was gone, the bricks having caved in, probably from a mortar shell. If Elisabeth had survived at all, surely, she would have found a safer place to live by now. And he had no idea where to begin looking for her.

The frustration, the fever and the hunger welled up in him until he wanted to dash the daffodils to the ground.

Then something caught his attention in the second-floor window on the left - Elisabeth's window. Ruffled curtains tied back with a sash and on the windowsill, yellow daisies. Fresh daisies. He smiled down at the bright yellow bugles in his hand and thought they would go very nicely together.

~~~~

Anna Tauber's swollen knuckles ached as she tied her paisley scarf under her chin. Her hands were those of an old woman, not a girl of twenty-three. Long hours of brutal work in the bitter cold had ruined her fingers forever.

There had been a time when Anna had foolishly dreamed of playing the violin in the Berlin Philharmonic. That dream, along with the violin, had vanished.

The scarf hid her short, dull hair. The doctors said she had severe anemia and that she must eat properly. They said her hair would regain its beauty as she regained her health.

Anything was possible. She forced a small smile at her cracked, distorted image in the broken mirror. After all, she had been given the precious gift of life. She must not squander it on self-pity. Hadn't Mama told her that a hundred times?

It had been almost a year since her camp was liberated. Anna had returned to Munich four months ago with the hope that some other member of her family might have survived and would look for her here. She placed an advertisement in the paper every week and stayed in touch with all the relief agencies, like so many others, hoping, praying someone would still be alive.

Shortly after she'd returned, she'd found this abandoned flat. The bombs had damaged the building, but somehow the inspectors had overlooked it. It still had most of its windows, some furniture, and it had electricity. The old woman on the first floor agreed to let it for twice what it was worth, but Anna didn't care. She'd been lucky to find a flat at all; so many were homeless, spending day after day searching for a place to sleep and a bit of fuel to keep warm.

Anna had found work cleaning for the American officers. She suspected she'd gotten the job because they'd felt sorry for her. She was still little more than skin stretched over bones, even after the enormous amount of food they had fed her at the displaced persons camp.

But food in Munich, in fact in all of Germany, was so terribly scarce. Each person was allowed only a little more than they had been given in the camps. The queues at the shops formed very early every day. When the food was gone, it was gone, and you would have nothing at all. People everywhere were forced to steal just to stay alive.

Anna slipped on the cloth coat the Red Cross had given her and set out for her stroll through the city of her birth, still deeply conscious of the feeling of walking down the street without a yellow star sewn to her coat.

Hopefully, today she would be in time to find something left at the bakery. She even had an extra ration stamp one of her Americans had given her. She had saved it for something special, a meringue. The thought of a little taste of sugar made everything a bit more cheerful.

It was a beautiful day. Spring had taken on a whole new meaning. For all the high walls and barbed wire, for all the grim darkness and horrid death that had surrounded her, the Nazis had not been able to take away the sky, especially the vibrant blue skies of sunny spring days.

She walked toward the Marienplatz at the center of town, down the street where she knew she would see daffodils sprouting through the rubble. She had noticed them the other day, and they'd brought such hope to her heart that she wanted to see them again.

One morning, not long before the liberation of the camp, someone had spotted one lone daisy growing in the barren earth near her barracks. That delicate flower became a symbol that the end of their suffering was at hand, a beacon of hope to everyone who saw it. It had stayed there untouched for three days before an SS guard, a Lithuanian, spotted it and ground it into the dirt with his boot. But he was too late. He could not quell the hope that one flower had stirred in their hearts.

Six days later that guard and the rest of his kind had scattered like cockroaches under glaring light.

Anna looked over to where the daffodils were blooming. There was a man, a soldier. He was picking them, taking them for himself. She wanted to run up to him and shout, "No! They're not yours. Leave them."

But she didn't. She put her head down and kept going. She had learned to mind her own business, even when it hurt terribly.

She passed by the once-beautiful Frauenkirche, the Church of Our Lady, now only ruins, a bombed-out shell. The Town Hall on the Marienplatz with its famous Glockenspiel had fared no better.

Anna looked up to the sky where the clock tower had stood before the bombs had destroyed it. Papa had often brought her and Benjamin here on Sunday mornings to wait for the magical eleven o'clock hour to strike and the animated parade to begin, the dancers and clowns and jugglers, all revolving to the beautiful music.

They were all gone now, the clowns, the dancers, and Papa.

Tears sprang to her eyes. Perhaps some aunt or uncle, some distant cousin would look for her here, would see her advertisements. Then she would not be so terribly alone.

One year - she was determined to stay one year, and four months of that time had already gone by. Then she would find her way to Palestine, as her beloved Benjamin, the teenaged Zionist, had always dreamed.

She turned away from the blackened ruins, forcing herself on to the next minute.

~~~~

"Ah, Fräulein Tauber, you are looking very well today. The usual?"

"Yes, Herr Grüber. *Danke*." The round little baker was always so pleasant to her. If Anna saw him behind the counter, she would join the queue to buy her bread. If his wife was there, she would do without. "And one small meringue, please," she added.

"Ja, ja, of course." He wrapped the meringue and the loaf of bread and held them out to her with a smile. "For you, Fräulein, a special price . . ."

"Nonsense!" The baker's wife appeared from the back room and elbowed her husband out of the way, snatching the package from his hands. "She pays the same as everyone else. We are not running a charity here. We must even stay open on Sundays just to get by."

"But, my pet," He dropped his voice, but Anna could still hear his words clearly. "Those trials in Nürnburg are saying such awful things. And the poor girl . . ."

"That is very unfortunate, I'm sure, but we cannot be held responsible for what happened. We are simple bakers here, not political people." Frau Grüber passed the baked goods across the counter to Anna with a stale smile. "Fräulein Tauber understands that we must treat all our customers the same."

"Oh, yes, I understand." Anna could feel the heat rising in her face. "It would not be fair," she said, trying to ignore the whispers of the other customers in the shop.

"You see, Franz, what did I say? Once again, your soft heart gets in the way of your brain."

Anna paid and left the shop as quickly as she could, but not before hearing someone say, "Jews. Still trying to take whatever they can, while we hardworking Germans . . ."

Anna fled up the street, past the curious glances of strangers, each step pounding the anger and hurt deeper.

Why had she come back to this city that hated her so? It had been a mistake, a terrible mistake. Four months and there had been no word from any of her family. No one was looking for her. She must face the truth. No one was left alive but her. Only her. Only her.

She reached her building and ran up the steps, wanting nothing more than to lock herself away from everything hurtful in the world. A sudden movement in the dark corridor stopped her cold.

A man stepped toward her, out of the shadows at the end of the hall. Anna drew back down to the top stair. He was a soldier. A German soldier.

"Elisabeth?" he said and then collapsed on the floor. Five yellow daffodils fell from his hand.

Anna couldn't move. She stood there, clutching the banister, staring at the man and at the flowers spread on the floor in front of him.

The door across from her flat clicked open a crack. The sound made Anna jump. A small slit of light cut into the darkness of the hallway and streaked across the man's gray woolen coat.

"Who is he?" a voice whispered from behind the open door.

"I don't know."

"Is he dead?" the voice asked.

Anna inched reluctantly toward the man, stretching out her hand to touch him. He moaned, and she almost fell over.

"He is very sick, I think."

"We want no trouble. My mother, she is not well."

"Yes, I know." Anna had known it even though they had never spoken.

"What are we going to do?" The door opened a bit more, and the woman Anna had seen slipping quietly in and out of the flat stepped into the hall. She was older than Anna, perhaps in her thirties - it was difficult to tell - with a pale, thin face, mousy hair and spectacles. "Can you take him?" the woman asked.

"Oh, no. I could not . . ." In her flat? No. She could not, she just could not.

She looked at him, sprawled unconscious on the floor, but what she saw were all the others like him. She saw their mocking eyes filled with contempt as they forced her and her mother to parade naked in a long line of naked, shivering women. She saw them kicking the near dead until they lay still forever. She saw them laughing as they shot children and old women for target practice. The thought of touching this man made her stomach wrench.

The woman knelt down beside her. "If we leave him here, he might die."

"Ursula!" a frightened voice called through the open door. "What's happening? Ursula, please."

"It's all right, Mama. I am just in the hallway." Ursula turned to Anna. "I will help you move him, but then I must go back to my mother."

"Please," Anna grabbed Ursula's arm pleading, "I cannot. I simply cannot. Please, won't you take him?"

The idea filled Ursula's eyes with horror. "Oh, no! You see, Mama, she has been so ill. I can barely leave her alone to go to work. I could never--"

The man moaned. He started to move but dropped down again.

"We must do something. If he dies," Ursula said, "we will have the police."

Anna didn't want the police either, but the idea of a German soldier in her flat, in her bed. It was too horrible to think of. She would rather leave him here.

Then the five daffodils caught her eye - her daffodils. The Elisabeth he had called out for, he had picked them for her.

The angry knot in Anna's heart began to give way.

She would not let herself be like them, filled with hatred and brutality. She would not.

Besides, not all of them were bad. Not all had been part of it. Maybe this man was one of those. He looked so helpless.

"All right," she said. "Perhaps for tonight. Tomorrow, when he is stronger . . ."

"What else can we do?" Ursula said.

It took an enormous effort from both of them to get him off the floor and into Anna's flat, the whole time with Ursula's mother calling for her from across the hall. When they finally had him on Anna's bed, Ursula grabbed Anna's hand and shook it vigorously.

"I promise I will help, but I must go now. I will come back and bring some soup." She stepped into the hall, and a moment later appeared with the daffodils in her outstretched hand. "Oh, I almost forgot. My name is Ursula, Ursula Kahler."

Anna laughed. "Yes, I thought so." She took the flowers. "I am Anna Tauber. It is so nice to meet you."

She closed the door. Deliberately keeping her eyes away from the bed, she put the daffodils in the glass with her daisies. They brightened the whole room. Anna felt brighter, too. Just having met Ursula made such a difference. It was like having a friend again.

If only she didn't have to deal with this . . .

She didn't have a bedroom really, only a cubicle off the main room with a faded flowered curtain to separate it off. She looked across at him sprawled on her bed, still with his coat on and his dirty boots.

She moved to the bed and looked down at his face. His hair was medium brown, close-cropped at the sides, his skin weathered by the sun. And he was so very thin, so ill, his breathing labored. She touched his forehead. He was burning with fever.

What if he died in her bed?

She should have left him in the hall. Why had she ended up with him, anyway? A German soldier. She must be mad.

Well, she had ended up with him, and she was just going to have to do whatever was necessary, wasn't she? She would have to bring the fever down, and quickly from the looks of him. Sponge him off without letting him become chilled. That was it. Besides, he clearly had not bathed in a very long time.

For a moment, she thought of calling Ursula back, but the mother had been so agitated, she doubted Ursula would come. No, she would have to manage on her own.

She tugged his coat over his shoulder and tried to pull the sleeve off the arm that dangled from the bed. She had to push him, then shove him, then crawl over the top of him to get the other side. Finally, she freed the heavy, limp arms, and rolled him off the coat, pulling it free. Next came the boots.

She climbed back on the bed and straddled him to more easily manage the shirt. Once she'd gotten it off, she stared down at the hair that covered his chest.

Without knowing why, she touched the soft brown mat and felt his heart beating under it. There was a terrible scar on his chest, a long gash running up to his shoulder then down the muscle of his left arm, almost to his elbow. Her fingers followed it.

The chest heaved suddenly, sending Anna scrambling off the bed. She stood back watching while his breathing quieted down again and while she built up the courage to continue.

She let out a deep sigh. The pants would have to go, of course. It wasn't as if she'd never seen a naked man before. The guards in the camp had respected neither life nor modesty when they played their brutal games. But this was very different.

She would have to touch him.

Her hands shook as she unbuttoned the pants. He obviously had nothing on under them. Quickly averting her eyes, she pulled the blanket across to cover him. Then from the end of the bed, she tugged and tugged, until the pants came off, first one leg then the other.

With a pan of water on top of her bedside table, Anna gently, very gently wiped his face and laid a cool cloth on his forehead. Even unconscious, his forehead was creased in a frown. His straight dark brows hooded his closed eyes. Were they blue? No, they were gray. She saw a flash of color as his unseeing eyes rolled open, then closed again. His lashes were long as a woman's and dark. She washed over his broad cheekbones, his long, straight nose, down his hollow cheeks and the stubble of his beard to his mouth. His soft lips were relaxed and parted, as if he were about to speak.

She washed his neck and then his shoulders, being careful not to press hard on the awful scars. Trying her best to keep him covered, she washed his chest, and then rolled him as far as she could and rubbed the damp cloth on his back, then down his sunken stomach.

Quickly, she skipped to his feet and his legs.

Feeling things in her body she had never in her life felt before, Anna stopped. She stood back trembling.

If she were a nurse, she would do this and think nothing of it. She would have to do it every day to old men, to young men, even when they were awake and would know.

Oh, dear! That thought hadn't helped.

Her hands were hot, but she was even hotter inside.

She took a deep breath, closed her eyes tight and reached under the blanket.

Oh, dear! she thought.

Shadow of the Flag

CHAPTER
FIVE

Fear gripped him even before he opened his eyes. For a moment, he had the childish idea of keeping them closed so whatever was out there wouldn't find him. He'd been sick, he remembered that. His body felt like a great dead weight, even his eyelids felt heavy as he forced them to open.

A cracked ceiling, yellowing plaster. Where was he? He turned the aching cannon ball that was his head just enough to see the tops of bright flowered curtains hanging near the bed. The effort cost him. He closed his eyes again and waited for the throbbing to pass.

~~~~

He had no idea how long he'd been out. This time he would move in spite of the pain.

The room he saw was sparsely furnished. A divan with an old chair and a lamp. A small kitchen with a table and two wooden chairs in front of a window. Curtains. Flowers in a glass.

Daisies and daffodils.

Elisabeth.

He tried to sit up, but his body was too weak. He and the bed and the room spun round as he sank back down.

Elisabeth. She'd found him. Thank God. Thank God.

"Oh, dear," a soft voice said. A warm hand brushed his forehead. Elisabeth's voice. Elisabeth's hand.

But the face that swam above him was all wrong.

He grabbed hold of the arm and used it to pull himself into consciousness.

"Who are you?"

"Oh, please . . .please, don't . . ."

He was too weak to hold on. The girl twisted out of his grasp. She fell back against the table, terror filling her large brown eyes. She was a mere child, thin, emaciated, with wisps of short auburn hair around her face. It was the face of a porcelain doll.

"Who are you?" he croaked again, pushing himself to one elbow.

The frightened gaze darted toward the door. The poor thing didn't know whether to stay or run.

"No, please, Fräulein. I will not hurt you." How could he? He could barely speak. And sitting up was out of the question. "I don't know where I am."

Those eyes showed him everything. The fear giving way to indecision, giving way to concern. Her shoulders relaxed, and she took one cautious step toward him.

"I found you," she said, "in the hallway. You were very sick."

The voice, as soft as any he'd ever heard; the eyes, large round dark pools; the hand that had touched him so gently. He knew it was the weakness of his body, whatever illness that had brought him down; still at that moment, he thought his heart would break with love.

He lay back against the pillow as she came closer. Just a scrawny child.

"*Danke*," he said and gave himself up to exhaustion.

~~~~

When he awoke again, the lamp was on and the curtains

on the windows were drawn. He watched her moving about the room, a thousand questions moving through his mind. She wasn't a child at all. Round, firm breasts pressed against her colorless shift. Her hips were slim, her arms skinny. Her white neck long and lovely.

He felt his body respond, and for the first time, realized he was naked, and he was clean. He was both embarrassed and intrigued. And he was very glad she wasn't bathing him right then. She'd be even more frightened than before. He smiled to himself at the thought.

She tied a paisley scarf over her head, and for a moment, he thought she was going out, but instead, she crossed to the table and struck a match. She lit two candles then lifted her hands to cover her eyes.

"*Barukh ata Adonai,*" she sang, "*Eloheinu melekh . . .*"

Her melodious voice chanted the words, and his heart shattered into a thousand pieces. The words swam up from his memory as he sank back against the pillow; his eyes closed against an onslaught of such torment that he could hardly breathe.

Aaron's mother had sung that same prayer every Friday evening to welcome the Sabbath. Aaron and he had been inseparable, closer than brothers, until the laws against Jews changed everything, making even their friendship a crime.

But he had defied the laws and his own father's fearful protests in every way he could. In the end, he had helped Aaron and his family to board a train to France and what they had believed would be safety. He remembered the parting banter about the beautiful French girls soon to be falling at Aaron's feet, unable to resist his amorous green eyes.

He had seen those eyes one more time.

Five years later, he lay gravely wounded on a railroad platform in a village west of Krakow, Poland. The ambulance train had been diverted there to avoid strafing by Russian planes as it made its way from the Eastern Front with those few wounded lucky enough to be evacuated from the latest German disaster, the battle of Kursk.

He'd been swimming in and out of consciousness for days. He preferred to be unconscious, at least then he was only vaguely aware of the searing pain.

But that day, the sun felt good on his face and the part of his chest that wasn't swathed with bandages. He'd lain there playing mental games, anything to divert his mind from his shattered shoulder, remembering back to his childhood and the pranks he and Aaron had played on their unsuspecting families. The time they'd replaced Elisabeth's cold cream with lard, and the time they'd dotted Aaron's father's handkerchief with bootblack and watched him wipe his face with it. He imagined Aaron on a shimmering beach in the south of France, surrounded by luscious women calling him "*cheri*." He could almost imagine himself there, too, lying back on the warm sand . . .

From behind him, the shrill whistle of an approaching train extinguished the Riviera from Peter's vision. The train was heading east from Germany, exploding the silence with the power of its massive engine and the screech of its brakes. Its vile stench stung his nostrils before he could see it. Pigs or cattle, maybe. But why were the cars so filthy? This was no way to handle food for the troops.

He caught the eye of a station official and was about to complain about the lax sanitary conditions, when the train pulled into view, slowly crawling past him one car at a time.

His words died in his mouth. It must have been a hallucination. Yes, a hallucination, a nightmare brought on by loss of blood, by the pain.

Human hands reached out from between the slats of the cattle cars, straining toward him. One car after the other inched by him, and behind the hands, sunken eyes pleading for help, like the condemned wretches in Hades.

Slowly, the train ground to a stop, releasing a burst of

steam, as a low, agonizing moan rose from within the walls of the cars. It was the sound of men too exhausted, too full of despair to cry out.

After a moment, a single hoarse voice came, then another, and another.

"Water!" they begged. "Water!" "For the love of God, give us water."

The station official acted as if he did not hear them, as if there was no train there at all. Peter grabbed the man's pant leg with his good arm and held on.

"Give them water!"

The man looked down at him, surprised.

"Why waste water on Jews? They're dead anyway."

The man easily shook his leg free and walked away.

Peter tried to protest, but weakness overtook him again. He lay there helplessly watching the eyes glimmering from the dank gloom of the car in front of him, when suddenly his gaze locked with a single pair of eyes near the end of the car. Recognition registered in those eyes, as it did in Peter.

From the time he was five years old, he had seen those eyes, laughed with them and cried with them. He knew every look, every expression, the way they changed from the color of emeralds when they were happy to the color of a dark pine forest when they were filled with anger. But he had never seen them like this. They were the eyes of a dead man.

"Aaron," he sobbed. "Oh, God, Aaron!" He tried to lift himself, but the pain knocked him back down. The car jerked forward, and he began to scream. As the train slowly pulled away, he screamed after it, again and again, "Aaron! Aaron!"

Finally, when all he could see was the trail of smoke, he sank into a black place and prayed he would never come out again.

But he had come out and he had survived. As soon as he could move from his hospital bed, he had started trying to find out where Aaron had been taken, whether he was still alive. Finally, he learned of a clerk willing to provide information for a fee. Aaron, his father and two little brothers were on one of the lists, their names neatly checked off. The train had taken them to a place called Auschwitz. The check marks meant Peter was too late.

It had been three years; years spent trying to forget, yet never forgetting. Now this beautiful young Jewish woman had bathed him and cared for him, had saved his miserable life.

"Oh, you are awake!" She came to him and touched his forehead. "And your fever is gone. This is wonderful!"

He looked up into lovely eyes that no longer held fear and was swept away from the dark horrible past.

"I did not mean to disturb your prayers," he said. His voice sounded as weak as he felt.

"No, you did not disturb me. There is no wine to bless anyway, or even a proper meal, but I like to pretend."

She smiled and this time the shattered pieces of Peter's heart melted into a puddle.

He pushed himself up a bit. "What is your name, Fräulein?"

"I am Anna. Anna Tauber." She seemed shy, even uncomfortable. Well, why not? He was a perfect stranger, helpless in her bed.

"I am Peter Rolf," he said. "I am afraid I have been a lot of trouble."

"Oh, no. I am just so pleased you are better. I thought for a time that you might . . ." Her eyes dropped, and a small shiver ran through her thin body.

"You have been very kind." Suddenly, he realized if this was her Sabbath, it had to be Friday. He'd been out for days, almost a week. "I cannot impose . . ."

He quickly learned he had a long way to go before he'd be moving far.

"You must not try so soon. Truly. Oh, dear, you must be terribly hungry." With that, she began to bustle around the little kitchen, talking nervously the whole time. "Ursula brought us soup today. It has real carrots. What a marvel she is! On Tuesday, she even managed half a chicken. Can you imagine? Oh, it was lovely. Real chicken soup. We even got you to take some. That is probably why you are better. Mama always said there is nothing like chicken soup."

She ended up in front of him with a steaming bowl in one hand and a spoon in the other. He pushed himself up as far as he could and took the bowl. She pulled a chair close to the bed and sat down with her hands folded in her lap.

It was the first time he had noticed her hands, and they made him wince. They were hands that didn't belong on so beautiful a girl.

She had seen his reaction and quickly hid them under the folds of her apron, her color heightening. Peter felt as though he had just slapped the kindest person he had ever known.

"The soup tastes wonderful," he said, desperate to say something, anything. "Who is this Ursula?"

As she told him about her neighbor, Anna became more animated and, for a moment, even forgot her ugly hands in a gesture.

"I still have not met her mother. It is silly, is it not? And Ursula has not told her about you. She is afraid, you see. Ursula's stepfather was taken away by the Gestapo. Then with the bombings, the strain has been too much for her. She is like a frightened rabbit."

Anna took the empty bowl and filled it again.

"After the Americans came," she went on, "Ursula and her mother found this place, as did I."

"My sister lived here once," Peter said.

"In this flat? Oh, is she Elisabeth?"

"How do you know about Elisabeth?" Did she know her? Did she know where she'd gone?

"You said her name quite a lot when you were sick."

Dumkhopf, he thought, what else had he said?

~~~~

Over his fervent protests, Anna again spent the night on her divan. The next morning, when she left for work, he used the opportunity to get himself to his feet. He didn't last long the first time, but after a bit, he managed to move around by holding onto the wall and convenient pieces of furniture, the whole time certain Anna would come back and find him stumbling around stark-naked hunting for his clothes.

He found them finally in a cupboard, washed, ironed and neatly folded. He dressed then hunted for his duffel bag. It was under the bed with everything exactly as he'd left it; he doubted she'd even opened it to look for his ration card.

The image he saw in the cracked mirror of her tiny lavatory gave Peter a shock. His gray eyes were dull and bloodshot, sunken behind dark circles; a thick growth of beard covered his hollow cheeks. Even after he shaved, he looked more like a skeleton than a living man. And he was voraciously hungry.

Another search turned up a thick slice of bread and a piece of cheese on a plate waiting for him. He sat at the table with the wilting flowers and ate half of what she'd left. He was still hungry, but he left the rest for her.

The room around him carried the sweet scent of her. Where she moved, where she slept. He could close his eyes and see her face, hear her nervous chatter. Why wouldn't she be nervous? Yet she had touched him so intimately. He'd been unconscious, but some part of him remembered that touch, remembered being caressed and nurtured by it. And aroused.

How long before she would come home?

The thought shocked him. What kind of cad was he? Lusting after her as if she were a whore on the street begging to bed his Aryan manhood.

To Anna, he had to symbolize every foul thing she'd had to endure. To her, he was the enemy.

Even with his mind muddled, he knew he couldn't stay here. As soon as he was strong enough, he had to move on. He had to find Elisabeth.

My God, had she gone back to Berlin to look for him?

~~~~

The sound of the door opening jolted him awake. Anna stood in the open doorway, smiling, her arms loaded with potatoes.

"You are out of bed. I am so pleased."

A tall, thin woman in spectacles peered past her, and Peter felt a flash of disappointment that they weren't alone. He pushed himself unsteadily to his feet.

"This is Ursula Kahler, Herr Rolf," Anna said. "We could never have managed without her help. And now look what she has brought us."

Ursula unwrapped the plate she was carrying and proudly displayed two large fat sausages.

"They are beautiful, neh?" she said.

Sausages! Good God, how long had it been since he'd tasted one?

"You are indeed an angel, Frau Kahler. *Danke, danke.* How do you manage such miracles?"

She blushed a rainbow of reds and giggled.

"It is Father Josef who works the miracles. I only deliver them. When he heard there was a soldier who was ill, he insisted that I bring enough good food to make you well."

A priest supplying black-market sausages to a German soldier? It was too much of a coincidence. It had to be the same man he'd heard about in the camp.

"I am very grateful to both you and your Father Josef. You have been most kind."

"Oh, yes, Ursula," Anna said, "you have been so wonderful. Please join us for a few minutes. We will leave the door open so you can listen for your mother. And you must have half of these beautiful potatoes. A truck turned over and potatoes rolled everywhere. We all ran as fast as we could to catch them. Oh, it was lovely!" Balancing potatoes and sausages, Anna went into the kitchen and quickly found the food he'd left. "Herr Rolf, you ate so little."

"I ate all I wanted, Fräulein. The rest is for you."

"Then we will have potatoes and bread, you with your sausages and me with the cheese." Anna's sweet laughter rang out. "It will be a feast."

Of course, Peter thought, she would not eat sausage. Even with so little, she was trying her best to keep the Kosher rules. Why that pleased him so much, he didn't know, but it did.

He stood there watching her, mesmerized by each movement, by the water running over her hands, the curl of her hair at the nape of her neck, the small mole behind her ear that she probably didn't realize was there.

She was humming.

Bach. Yes, Bach, but what was the piece? He couldn't place it.

"You do not look at all sound, Herr Rolf," Ursula's voice broke the spell. "Perhaps you should sit down."

Peter had completely forgotten anyone else was in the room. Nothing had existed for him but Anna in her kitchen and the sound of the melody she hummed. If he had stood there much longer, he likely would have toppled over.

He sank down into the chair and smiled at Ursula.

"I think I have heard of this priest of yours," he said. "Does he often help soldiers?" With a little luck, if this was the same priest he'd heard about, he might have just found his way out of Germany, away from this lunacy that was rapidly possessing him. And not a moment too soon.

"Oh, yes. Father Josef helps everyone. He was in a concentration camp himself, you know, like poor Anna, and not the least bitter about it."

"Could he help me find a place to stay?"

"I am sure he will. When you are better, I will take you to him."

"If you could tell me where he lives, perhaps I could go there this evening. I've imposed on Fräulein Tauber's hospitality long enough."

A plate crashed to the floor, and Anna bent to pick up the pieces. She looked up at him, deep alarm in her eyes.

"Please, you cannot go yet," she said. "You're not well enough."

"Anna is right, Herr Rolf." Ursula motioned for him to stay seated while she went to help Anna. "I doubt that you would make it to the end of the street, and then how would we get you back up the steps?"

Anna stood up, the broken shards of the plate still in her hands. "You would only make yourself sick again, Herr Rolf," she said. "Please be reasonable."

With her every feeling flashed on the clear screen of her glistening brown eyes, he was helpless before them. Some logical corner of his mind whispered that he had no right to stay. But the throbbing in his heart and in his groin drowned out the words.

He threw up his hands. "My dear ladies, I surrender. I will wait a day or two, until I am stronger."

Anna visibly relaxed, and then she laughed. "Good. We will feed you full of sausages and send you off to Father Josef, who will feed you even more sausages. And then you will be quite fat." She arched her back and puffed out her cheeks, then laughed again.

He was a fool to think he could go on being so close to her. A bloody fool.

"Ursula!" came a cry from across the corridor. "Where are you?"

"Oh my," Ursula said. "I must go." Abruptly, she left them, closing the door behind her.

He stared after her, then for a moment, his eyes met Anna's.

The expression on her face left no doubt that their discomfort was mutual. They had been living together behind that closed door for a week, but this was entirely different. He was no longer an unconscious invalid with Anna the nursemaid. He was a man, and she was a woman, and they were about to spend the night alone.

As he watched her prepare their "feast" and lay it out on the table, he was also keenly conscious that every part of him ached to touch her.

He would not touch her. He could not. He would walk away from here with his honor intact.

Anna served their meal as if she were playing house, making the table as attractive as she could. Her delight in this small thing instantly vanished the gloom that was fast settling over Peter's heart, but it did not vanish the tension between them.

They sat across from each other chatting about the ordinary things of life, the amusing quirks of the people she'd met since she'd returned to Munich, the kind Herr Grüber and his shrew of a wife, the Americans, and the queues, the endless queues.

She called him Herr Rolf and he called her Fräulein, and the inevitable discussion of sleeping arrangements hung unspoken between them to the end.

With the last morsel of food gone, Peter helped her wash up. He put the last dish back on its shelf and hung the towel up to dry.

"Fräulein Tauber, I must insist that you take back your bed tonight." She blushed scarlet at the mere mention of the bed, but he plunged ahead before she could protest. "I cannot allow you to give it up one more night."

"But you have been so ill."

"I am well enough now, thanks to your wonderful care. I will be most comfortable on the floor."

"At least, the divan . . ."

He laughed. "I am afraid I am too long for the divan, Fräulein."

"Are you certain you--"

"I'm quite certain."

Finally, after several small logistical embarrassments with neither making eye contact, the lights were out, Anna was safely in her bed behind the flowered curtain, and Peter was on the floor wrapped in two blankets.

He undressed in the dark in his makeshift bedroll and tried not to think of her lying in the bed where he had been, her body warm and soft, her breasts . . .

He had to get a grip on himself.

"Good night, Herr Rolf," she said from behind her protective curtain.

"Good night, Fräulein." He rolled over on the hard floor and tried to fight the images out of his mind.

~~~~

In the darkness of the night, a terrifying cry woke Peter with a start. For a moment, he thought his nightmares had returned; but as he became more aware, he realized the cry hadn't come from any dream of his. It had come from the cubicle where Anna slept.

He heard her tossing about in the bed, mumbling and crying out "No! No!" over and over again.

He wanted desperately to throw open the curtain and take her in his arms, to comfort her, but he didn't dare move. He would only frighten her more. Instead, he lay there trying to close his ears to the terror of her dream, hating the butchers who had brought it into her life.

Long after Anna became quiet again, Peter continued to stare up into the dark room. He was no better than they were, and as much as he hated them, he hated himself more.

Shadow of the Flag

CHAPTER
SIX

He must have fallen into a fitful sleep, because when he awoke again, it was morning, Sunday morning. He could hear Anna moving about in her minuscule lavatory.

She was humming.

He grabbed his pants and pulled them on quickly under the blankets. When he stood up to put on his shirt, she stepped out.

He heard a small intake of breath as her eyes went first to his bare chest. After a moment's hesitation, she brought them up to his face. That moment and the blush that followed not only cheered him as nothing else could have, wiping away the self-recriminations of the night, it brought out something very primitive in him.

"Good morning, Fräulein Tauber." Meeting her eyes, he smiled, and slowly, very slowly, he pulled on his shirt.

"I . . .oh . . .Good morning," she stammered. "I was about to take a walk. I mean, we have very little for breakfast, and I thought . . ."

"May I join you?"

It was his first time out since she found him, and the morning sun felt marvelously good, but he was far weaker than he'd thought. They walked slowly toward the heart of the city, resting often. Part of the time he had to lean on her arm for strength, and part of the time, he did it just to touch her.

When they came to a sidewalk cafe, one of the few still operating in a city of desperate shortages, he insisted they stop.

Most of the clientele were American soldiers sitting with flirtatious Fräuleins. Who could blame these young girls, who had to struggle for every mouthful? Besides, most of the German men were either locked away as he had been, or too pathetic to bother with. Like him.

At least he had ration stamps and the best currency in Germany — Lucky Strike cigarettes.

When he told Anna to order whatever she liked, her eyes lit up. Her delight in every morsel of her pastry made him feel as if he had just bought her the moon. He savored watching her even more than the taste of his own food.

Anna told him of her childhood in Munich, her father and mother, and Benjamin, the darling little boy her family had taken in when his own parents had died. She spoke of them in happy times and avoided anything else, except to tell him of her hope that one day one of her relatives would see her advertisements. He told her of his own father and his sister, Elisabeth, and the mother he barely remembered. And then he ordered her another cocoa and another pastry, and one for himself.

Like the other couples around them, they talked and laughed, as if there were no ugly ruins just across the way, as if there had been no war, no camps, no horror. Only springtime and flowers and love.

On their way back, they bought what food they would need, and then stopped to sit on a green patch of lawn in a park and watch the children playing in the sun. Farther on, Peter bought her a bouquet of fresh yellow flowers from a street vendor.

By the time she helped him up the steps to her flat, Peter was exhausted, but he was also as happy as he could remember being in his life, as long as he didn't think about leaving.

Anna closed her eyes, feeling strangely warm inside. The day had been perfect, sunny and sweet. The pastry, the flowers, the adoring eyes of a man, a man she found shockingly attractive. She snuggled down, cozy in her blankets, hoping to dream sugary dreams.

But she was there again, among the mountains of rags. Piles and piles of rags, reaching to the sky. She was to sort the rags, coats and dresses and stockings and shoes - those in good condition in one pile, those no longer usable in another, and those that could be repaired in the third. Clothing, most of it beyond repair, piled as high as she could see.

Anna was not alone. There were others sorting through the rags, too. All of them skeletons, living, moving skeletons, their faces hideous skulls, covered with thin, sallow skin, with deep hollow holes for eyes and only short stubble for hair. Anna was not frightened or repulsed. She worked on mindlessly, feeling nothing.

The woman next to her leaned closer and spoke in a hoarse whisper, "We've got the best job in the camp, you know."

Anna knew she was right. Rummaging through the mountains of clothing, there was always a chance of finding a bit of bread, a morsel of cheese hidden away in one of the pockets. Or the odd piece of jewelry, sewn in a seam perhaps, that you could use to bribe the *kapo* for an extra portion of soup, enough to keep you alive one more day.

Off in the distance, another group of emaciated prisoners shuffled into the compound. None of them suspected what awaited them, the gas chambers, the crematorium. They clutched their parcels to them, clung to their children, the sick, the elderly. Anna felt nothing for them, not even pity. She watched them, living cadavers walking to their deaths, and she felt nothing at all.

A whistle blew and Anna joined the other workers as

they shuffled outside into the bitter cold to form an endless line of colorless skeletons waiting to receive their one meal of the day. As she waited her turn, Anna watched as a woman's corpse was dragged from one of the barracks. The prisoners pulling her, barely alive themselves were too weak to lift her, even though she must have weighed very little. The dead woman looked like all the other women, gray skin on bones.

Anna watched the woman's head bump down the stairs of the barracks. She heard the hollow sound it made as it hit each step. Bump. Bump. Bump. But she felt no pity, no horror, no loss. She simply turned away and held out her bowl, ready for her watery soup and crust of stale bread.

The whistle blew again, and the line shuffled back inside to the mountains of rags, and Anna began sorting again through the ripped dresses, the dirty, frayed coats.

Suddenly, her hand felt the cold touch of metal deep in one of the pockets. A square gold-plated compact. Powder. A silly thing to keep, she thought, when all else is lost. What good is it? The guards wouldn't want it. She was about to stash it in her pocket, just in case, when she noticed the delicate engraving on the top.

She rubbed the yellow metal against a bit of cloth, bringing it to a brilliant shine, and then she clicked it open. The soft fragrance reached her, wafting to a secret place hidden away inside her. She closed her eyes to try to hold it there just a moment longer. When she opened them again, she was looking at the small square mirror mounted inside the compact, at a decaying cadaver of protruding bones and hollow eyes reflected back. At herself.

Soon, it would be her body dragged bumping down the steps of the barracks. Soon, it would be her turn.

~~~~

Again, Peter was torn awake by tormented moans.

He tried to lay still and wait them out, but he couldn't.

He threw off his blankets, pulled on his trousers, and went to her bedside. Behind the curtain, he could hear her thrashing about.

He couldn't bear the sound. He pushed the curtain aside and crawled onto the bed beside her.

"Shh, Anna, shh," he whispered, gently touching her tear-streaked face.

She jerked back from his touch, opening her eyes in horror, but he didn't pull away. He stroked her auburn curls, pushing them away from her face.

"Anna, shh, it was only a dream." He wrapped her trembling body in his arms. "They will not hurt you anymore. I won't let them."

He kissed the top of her head and held her tight against him.

She clung to him, until she fell asleep in his arms. When the first light of morning began to seep through the windows, he slipped quietly back to his place on the floor.

~~~~

He had stationed himself by the window to watch for her. She would come around the corner in seven minutes, minutes that had become an agony of waiting last night and the night before. He had told himself he wouldn't do it again, but here he was doing it again.

Their outing on Sunday had nearly done him in. That and the sleepless night that followed had left him severely weakened. There was no way she would let him leave as long as she sensed he was still not well. Yesterday, he'd felt somewhat better, weak, but he could have left. He didn't leave today, either.

He was as bad as a lovesick schoolboy. Worse, because the carnal need he had for her was driving him as much as his bursting heart. He wanted to possess her, to take her. He wanted her so badly he ached. And yet, when she was in the room, he was content to sit and listen to her voice, to watch her smile, to make her laugh. He would not have dared to touch her.

He was driving himself mad.

The shadows of late afternoon were muting into dusk. She would turn the corner any moment. The warmth of expectation made him smile as he waited for the first glint of her auburn hair.

Instead, he saw a furtive movement behind a collapsed wall near the corner. Then he saw it again. Street thugs. One. Two. No, three of them, maybe more. They were waiting for Anna. She was walking into their trap.

He was out of the flat and halfway down the steps when he heard her scream. He ran, stumbling, falling, then bounded up again, yelling at the top of his lungs, "Stop! Get away from her!"

The largest one had her pinned against the wall. His filthy hands were on her, groping her. The other two had seen Peter and were waiting for him, one with a knife, the other with a club. They were nothing more than scrawny boys, fifteen or sixteen, starving from the looks of their sunken cheeks. Boys like these were everywhere in Germany, lost, alone; and these were itching for a fight. He could see it in their eyes. The other one, the one with Anna, was older, the ringleader, no doubt.

Peter sidestepped toward a pile of debris and grabbed a loose board. He came at the boys swinging with a strength he didn't know he possessed. The board connected on his first strike. The knife skidded across the street. He brought the board back. The blow landed on the side of boy's head, dropping him to the ground. The other boy threw aside his club and scrambled over the rubble to get away. Peter plunged at the one with Anna, knocking him down. The bones in his face cracked under the first blow. Peter kept pounding him, until Anna's voice broke through pleading with him to stop. He yanked the whimpering boy to his feet and held him against the wall.

"Fräulein, are you all right?"

He could see that her dress was torn, and she was sickly pale, but she forced a weak smile.

"Yes, Herr Rolf, I am now. Thank you."

He turned back to the sniveling coward in his hands. "You're lucky I don't kill you. Now, get your friend and get the hell out of here. *Mach schnell!*" The boy stumbled to the other one in the street, who was trying to stand. The two quickly vanished into the mountains of rubble.

"*Scheisskerl*," Peter muttered, "bastard." He waited for the sounds of their retreat to disappear completely before he turned back to Anna.

"Fräulein," he said and collapsed at her feet.

~~~~

Anna sat in the dirt, cradling Peter's head in her lap. She was far more frightened for him than of the thought that the men might return.

"Peter, Peter," she repeated over and over. After an awful moment, his eyes opened. "Thank God! Oh, Herr Rolf, you're all right."

She saw his gray eyes clear as they blinked. He struggled to stand, but she had to help him.

"That was stupid of me," he said. "They could have come back."

"I think they have gone. We will go slowly."

With his arm around her shoulders and hers on his waist, she helped him cross the street to her building.

"Are you really all right?" he asked.

"Yes, I'm all right. When I saw you, I knew I was safe."

"Some hero. I fainted at your feet."

"I thought you very brave."

As she struggled to help him move up the steps, she

glanced up at his profile, so concentrated as he pulled himself up each step. Her cheek lay against his chest where she could feel his muscles straining with every movement. She could also feel his ribs through his shirt. He wasn't eating enough. She'd seen him stop when she was certain he was still hungry so that she would have more.

Anna helped him to her divan and set about making him comfortable. Then she fixed their meager meal, making certain he would have the larger portion and was pleased to see he ate every morsel.

Later, as she stood at the sink washing up, the terror she'd felt on the street came back suddenly. The thought of those hands on her repulsed her so much she dropped a pan. It clattered against the sink.

Peter was at her side in an instant. He wiped the tears from her eyes and spoke to her gently. Then he made her a cup of tea, and they sat and talked. On into the wee hours of the morning, they talked, never for one moment realizing how late it was.

Finally, she fell asleep against his shoulder. She awoke the next morning, still fully clothed, tucked in her own bed.

CHAPTER
SEVEN

"Father Josef?"

From his shoulders up, the priest looked like any balding man in his fifties, but with eyes that sparkled like those of a child and a body so bent he might have been ninety. He peered over his spectacles at Peter, who stood on the front steps of the neat half-timbered house on a street that had somehow miraculously avoided the bombs when all around had fallen.

Peter had gotten the priest's address from Ursula over a week ago. Every day he had sworn he would come here, and every day he'd put it off. First, because he wasn't strong enough, then after the incident with the street thugs, to make sure they didn't return.

Each day that passed his madness grew, until his longing for her crippled his every thought. Now, he was seeing that passion in her eyes, too. The two of them, turning, moving in that tiny flat, brushing up against each other, wanting each other, yet denying the desire that was consuming them. Today, he knew he had to get away.

"Ah, yes. You must be Sergeant Rolf. *Guten Tag.* Frau Kahler told me about you. Come in. Come in."

"*Danke schön.* I appreciate your seeing me on such short notice, Father."

"Not at all." He shook Peter's hand warmly in both of his and showed him into the parlor. "Please sit down. Let me just . . .Oh, there you are. Frau Hauptmann, would you be so kind as to bring us the schnapps. I think the Sergeant would enjoy it." The dour woman glared suspiciously at Peter, nodded curtly to the priest, and walked away muttering under her breath.

"Pay no attention to her, Sergeant. She sees herself as my watchdog. I think she would bite any thief who had the bad luck to choose this house to rob." He lowered himself into an overstuffed chair that seemed to have been hollowed out to fit his body. "I am pleased to see you are doing so well. I understand you have been quite seriously ill."

"I was, but I am feeling much better. *Vielen Dank,* many thanks. I believe I am very much indebted to your kindness."

"Sometimes God provides healing in very practical ways. Like chicken soup."

"And sausages."

"And schnapps." The priest laughed. Mrs. Hauptmann brought in a tray with a decanter and two cut crystal glasses. With one last sniff of disapproval, she left the room and closed the door quietly behind her. Father Josef poured a glass for Peter and one for himself. He raised his glass.

"*L'chayim,*" he said and took a sip.

"To life." Peter did the same, the sweet liquid warming him as it slid down his throat.

"Ah, you know Hebrew?"

"Some."

"There are few in this country who would admit it even now."

Peter felt heat rising under his collar, and it had nothing to do with the schnapps.

"I am not a Nazi, if that's what you're getting at. I was conscripted into the Wehrmacht. I was not *SS.*"

"Of course. One wonders how the National Socialists

ever took over a democratic country like Germany when so few were party members." The priest's bright eyes studied Peter over his glass.

"Perhaps I've made a mistake coming here." Peter set his glass on a small, polished table and stood to leave.

"And why did you come here, Sergeant? To thank me for sausages? Or to find a way out of Germany without a passport and travel papers?"

Peter stared at him. The kind Father Josef was not at all what he had expected.

"Sit down, Sergeant. Finish your schnapps. Perhaps I can help you. Perhaps I cannot."

Peter sat back down. He emptied his glass, and the priest poured him another.

"Let me tell you my story." The priest leaned back in his chair. "And doesn't it seem that all of Germany has a story these days." He slowly rolled the crystal glass between his hands. "I was arrested in 1944. You see, it wasn't until then that I began to complain about the deportations. Unfortunately, by that time, most of the Jews, poor wretched souls, had already been taken away. I am afraid it took me that long to find the courage to speak out. Speaking out in those days exacted a terrible price, and until then I was not willing to pay it, I suppose. Ironically, it was in the confessional that I had heard something I could no longer ignore." The sparkle of the man's eyes had become an intense fire. "Fortunately for me, I was released a few weeks before the war ended. It seems there was a clerical error." He leaned forward. "So, Sergeant Rolf, now it's your turn. Tell me why you think I should help you."

"I have no idea why you would want to help any of us."

"I am not your judge, Sergeant. I have given absolution to men who have done things far more horrible than anything you could imagine. God is the ultimate Judge of us all."

Peter stood up again, anger filling him up, anger and uncertainty. He hated this.

"You want my confession, is that it?"

"That's up to you, of course. Confession can cleanse the soul."

"I'm not a Catholic."

"Do only Catholics have souls, Sergeant? What about Lutherans? What about Jews? For that matter, what about Nazis, Sergeant? Do Nazis have souls?"

"Perhaps like Faust, they have sold theirs."

"And you? Have you sold yours?"

Peter walked to the window and looked out on a tidy little garden, on a street of tidy little gardens, sitting smack dab in the middle of the ashes of Hell.

"I have killed a great many men, Father," he said without turning away from the window. "I have no idea how many." He hesitated there for a moment while a robin hopped across the grass below him. Then he turned back, placed his glass on the table and sat down to look the priest in the eyes. "But I swear to you I have never knowingly killed civilians, certainly not women and children. I can't say I didn't know it was happening. It was impossible not to. But I am not a war criminal, nor am I wanted by the Allies. I can't prove it, of course. Either you believe me, or you do not."

"It may surprise you to know that I do believe you. At least I believe what you have just told me. I'm also quite certain you're not telling me the whole story."

"It would be better if you didn't know."

"Yes. I'm sure it would."

"Father, I must get out of Germany, and I don't very much care where I go. Although, I don't think I would last long in South America." He laughed at the thought. "Can you help me?"

"Possibly. But it will take time."

"I'm afraid time is one thing I do not have."

"Then you are in imminent danger?"

"No, I don't think so. But, you see, there's a young woman

. . ." Peter looked down at his hands, but what he saw were her hands, her poor disfigured hands.

"I assume you mean the Jewish girl who has been caring for you. Does it offend you so much to be cared for by a Jew?"

"No! Of course not. It's just that . . ." Peter was up again, this time pacing between the window and the door. "You see, she's . . .she's very lovely, Father. Very lovely. And I find that I'm . . ."

"I see."

"No, I don't think you do. I've fallen in love with her. Quite hopelessly, I might add. And every minute I'm with her, my resolve . . . I don't know how much longer I can. . ."

"Does she feel the same towards you? It makes a difference, you know?"

"I don't know. She's lonely and vulnerable. Her family is gone, probably dead."

"And with you ogling her every move, which I'm sure you have been doing, she's no doubt flattered. Sergeant, you must not take advantage of this girl."

"You think I don't know that? I know perfectly well I'm no better than the swine who brutalized her in that camp."

"You are wrong there. Quite wrong."

"How? What makes me any different from them, wanting to use her up and toss her away when I leave?"

"Simply put, you have a conscience, my boy, and they had none."

"I hope to God you're right."

In a painful process to watch, the priest pushed himself to his feet.

"I'll contact you through Frau Kahler as soon as I can. That will be the simplest, I think."

"There's one more thing, Father. My sister. I don't know where she is."

"Yes, this is a problem so many face these days. So difficult. Well, give me what information you have, and I'll see what can be done."

"Her name is Elisabeth; her married name is Schreiter. She lived here in Munich during the war, but I heard that her husband was killed in France, so she may have gone back to Berlin to find me. I don't know."

The priest went to his desk and made a note of her name.

"We must trust God to guide us." He patted Peter warmly on his shoulder. "He does, you know, if we let Him. But sometimes He takes us in directions we may never have imagined we would go. There's a passage in the Old Testament that says, '*Though He slay me, yet I will trust Him.*' That's what Job had to learn, and I have come to understand that it is ultimately what we each must learn in our own way."

~~~~

Peter opened the door to her flat and found Anna sitting at the table, still in her work clothes, her face streaked with tears. She rushed toward him then stopped in the middle of the room.

"You didn't go," she said. "I thought you had gone."

"Of course, I didn't go. Look, my duffel bag is still here." The flowered curtain had fallen over it, but only partially blocked it from view.

She wiped her eyes with the back of her hand. "I didn't see it. I just saw that you weren't here and thought--"

"Silly goose." Peter came to her, taking her in his arms. "I wouldn't leave without saying goodbye."

He pulled the scarf from her head and rested his cheek on her auburn curls, then his lips. Her arms were around his waist, holding him tight, her body trembling against his.

He brushed his lips on her forehead, the scent of her filling his lungs, intoxicating him. The touch of her soft skin against his lips made him dizzy. He tilted her chin up and wiped the tears from her cheeks.

"See now, there's no reason to cry."

He kissed away the tears that still clung to her lashes, and then he kissed her lips. Gently, at first, but as she responded, his kiss grew more intense.

Finally, somehow, he took a breath, but it only served to fill him with more fire. His lips followed her long, graceful neck, while his hands found her breasts. She moaned in his arms, meeting his urgent touch.

The sound of her passion stopped him cold.

Peter pushed her away from him. He tried to breathe but couldn't. He held her at arm's length with his eyes closed and did battle with the demon that was possessing him.

When he opened his eyes, she was staring at him as if he were a mad man. No doubt he was mad. He had to stop this before the demon took him over completely.

"I must go. I'm sorry." He left her standing there and lifted his duffel bag from the corner.

"Go?"

"If I stay . . ." He turned back to her and touched her face, running his hand slowly down her velvet skin. "If I stay, I won't be able to stop myself. I'd be no better than the rest of them. Don't you see that?"

"What do you mean? I don't understand." Tears brimmed her lovely eyes and spilled in streams down her cheeks, driving him insane with pain.

He grabbed her by the wrist and pushed up the sleeve of her sweater, exposing the line of numbers tattooed on her thin white arm.

"No better than the ones who did this to you." He took her hands, her ugly raw hands and held them up before her wild eyes. "Or the ones who did this. I can't be one more monster who hurts you, Anna. I can't."

He dropped her hands, grabbed his bag and banged out the door. He rushed down the stairs so quickly that his feet slipped; he nearly fell the rest of the way. When the cold air hit him, he slowed down, hoisted the bag to his shoulder and crossed the dark, empty street.

Then he made the mistake of looking up. The light was in her window, the curtain still open, and yellow flowers were in the glass on her table.

His soul, who had it now? God or Satan himself?

~~~~

The door to the flat slammed shut. Anna couldn't move. She stood still trying to breathe; the room spun around her. She reached out for the wall to steady herself, but slid down it to the floor, her body wracked with sobs.

There were no thoughts, no logic, only the tears and the pain twisting her tighter and tighter. The passion she had felt rising in her body only moments before had become the cruel torturer that had torn open her heart and left it to be devoured by her desperate aching loneliness.

"Peter," she whispered. "Oh, Peter."

She had fought the feelings inside her from the very first. She had intended him to stay only one night, but he had been so ill she couldn't turn him out.

As she nursed him, something darkly hidden began to awaken within her. In the camps, to allow yourself to care for anyone, even those dearest to you, was to die of sorrow. But when Peter came, so helpless, needing her, Anna began to care again. At first, she wanted only that he would be well enough to leave. But as she gave him back his life, life returned to her as well.

The days flew by, and she saw the way his tormented gray eyes looked at her. They were hungry and savage and soft and gentle, the color of the North Sea in a winter storm. They followed her as she moved about the room and they made her feel beautiful, feel alive. They made her taste his desire. As he wanted to touch her, she longed for his touch, until the thought of him made her throb inside, as if her heart had dropped into the pit of her stomach. Then, beyond all reason, beyond shame, she began to know that she loved him.

And now he was gone, and she was alone again. Alone.

She started to push herself off the floor, pushing against the weight that was crushing her, when suddenly the door opened. He stood framed in the doorway.

She must be dreaming him. It couldn't be true.

Then she felt his hands in her hair, on her face, lifting it, his lips on hers.

"I couldn't go," he whispered. "I couldn't leave you." His cheeks were wet, his eyes red, rimmed with pain. "If you tell me to go, I swear I will leave right now."

She grabbed hold of him and pulled him to her. She would not let him leave again. Not ever.

"I beg you, Anna, tell me to go."

"I will not," she said with all force she had left in her.

Peter's eyes held hers as he lifted her into his arms.

"Then God help us both," he said, and he carried her to the bed.

Shadow of the Flag

CHAPTER
EIGHT

Los Angeles, California - 1990

Beth sat in the cubicle of the bank, staring at the name typed across the yellowing page. The face in the photograph was her father's face. The eyes, hooded by a dark frowning brow, had been startled by the flash of the camera. They were her father's eyes, but the name was Peter Rolf.

The words, the picture swam up in front of her sending her thoughts crashing in upon themselves like waves breaking in a violent storm. Beth was drowning in them, being swallowed up by a tempest of confusion and disbelief.

She wanted to run out of the bank, bolt and run. Tear the horrible papers up, leave them. They were a lie. They said her father was Peter Rolf and Peter Rolf was a Nazi.

She dragged in a breath.

She didn't believe it. She couldn't believe it. It couldn't be true. Her father was Aaron Rosen. Aaron Rosen. A Jew, not a Nazi. My God, he was a fabulous Jew! The kindest, most generous, most devout. He didn't do it by rote. He said all those prayers meaning every word. He meant it all. She knew he meant it.

How could it have been a colossal lie?

The collar of the uniform showed clearly in the picture. It and the soft cap that he wore were unmistakable; she'd seen them a thousand times in movies. Movies about Nazis.

No! This could not be her father. The face was his, but it wasn't him. There had to be another explanation.

"*. . .your father wasn't Jewish. . ."*

No! It was a mistake. A hideous, obscene mistake.

"*. . .he wasn't circumcised. . ."*

She didn't care what the papers said, what anyone said. She knew her father. She knew him. She would never believe it. Never.

She laid her head down on her arms in the dark little cubicle, and his face flashed before her closed eyes. His face that night when he'd heard the name Peter Rolf. It wasn't just fear she'd seen in his eyes. There had been something else, but she didn't understand it then.

She did now. And it made her want to vomit.

She'd seen guilt in those eyes. Guilt and fear twisting together.

Beth was caught in the vortex of the storm now. Everything she'd known, everything she'd believed was being sucked out of her, like the breath that was being sucked from her lungs.

"*They know . . ."* he said it as he lay dying. "*They know."* Those words were her proof. Not the papers. His own words.

Everything she had ever known about her father told her none of this could possibly be true; but suddenly now, somehow, she knew it was true, and it was strangling her.

Daddy, Daddy, was your whole life a lie?

Rage began to fill her up, starting in the pit of her stomach, rising through her like red-hot lava, exploding out in burning tears.

I loved you and you lied to me! Why did you lie to me?

Now she was cold, shivering, struggling to breathe, to think past the confusion, past the rage. She gathered together the papers and shoved them back into the envelope, stacked them with the other things, including the crumpled brown paper bag with the gun and the bullets, and left.

Everything inside her was shaking as she stumbled across

the lobby of the bank, almost tripping over a small child who darted into her path. The mother muttered something about her rudeness, but Beth kept moving. If she stopped, she would explode.

Once in the car with her father's things on the seat beside her, she had no idea where to go.

What exactly was she supposed to do now? Did she go home, put all of it away in the bottom of a drawer and forget about it, go on with her life?

If her father wasn't Jewish, what did that make her? A German? Funny, Beth had always thought of Germans as the enemy. No. Worse. She'd considered them beneath contempt. When she and Brian had toured Europe, she'd refused to set foot in Germany. When Brian's business started doing well and he wanted to buy a Mercedes, Beth pitched a fit. He finally relented and settled on a Lexus. She knew all the names of all the companies who had participated so willingly in the annihilation of so many innocent lives and now sold things as innocuous as aspirin and coffeepots. She refused to own any of them.

Now, was she a German?

No, no matter what, she was Jewish. It doesn't matter what your father is. If your mother's Jewish, you're Jewish.

A sudden horrible, horrible thought jolted her as if lightening had just seared right through her.

What about her mother? Was that a lie, too?

No! No! No! Her hands, her gnarled, ugly hands. The tattoo on her arm. That couldn't have been a lie.

Beth saw those hands every time she thought of her mother. She remembered the day she first knew they were different. At school, she had noticed another woman's beautiful thin tapering fingers buttoning her child's coat. Beth had been so ashamed, ashamed of her mother's ugly hands. She'd said something horrible; she couldn't remember what. But it had made her mother cry.

That evening, her father had taken her on his lap and explained. Beth could hear his soft voice now and see the tears that filled his eyes as he told her how her mother had suffered in a terrible place. And that once, she'd had beautiful hands like other women, but something had happened in that terrible place, and now her hands carried the scars.

"Is that why Mama has a number?"

"Yes, *Liebchen*, that's why. Very bad people put that number on her arm."

"Did it hurt?"

"Yes, it hurt very much."

"And they hurt her hands, too?"

"Yes, they hurt her hands, too."

But you didn't tell me that you were one of them, Daddy. You didn't tell me you were one of the bad people.

Beth started the car and drove. She didn't know where she was going, she could barely see through her tears, but she drove anyway. After a long wandering route, she found herself on Pico Boulevard. She pulled the car to a stop beside the Simon Wiesenthal Center.

The same unseen force that had driven her to this place dragged her out of the car and shoved her into the building. At the desk, she asked the young man wearing a faded "Cats" tee shirt and a *yarmulke* how she could find out if a name was on their list of known war criminals. She was shown to a room where she could search their files.

Beth's heart stayed embedded in her throat and her stomach in a knot as she went through the names. But there was no Rolf listed, or any spelling close to it. She left her name and number, just in case anything turned up later, anything on a Nazi war criminal named Peter Rolf.

Then she went home.

~~~~

Rachel and Itzhak were coming to dinner. Thank God

they were bringing it with them - Kosher take out. How was she going to tell them? And how was she going to get through the evening without falling apart?

She picked up the phone to call Brian. He would know what to do. He always knew.

"Hi!" two cheery voices said in unison. "You've reached Brian (his baritone) and Sabrina (her squeak). We can't come to the phone right now . . ."

That's right. They'd gone to Cabo San Lucas for a week. Cabo San Lucas. Sun, fun, sex, and margaritas. He might as well have gone to the moon.

She stood there holding the phone, needing to call someone. She tried Rachel. Maybe they hadn't left yet. Beth was surprised when she answered.

"Oh, hi, Mom. What's up? Did you want us to pick up something when we pick up dinner?" she said. "We'll be there around 6:30."

"No, honey, it wasn't important. I'll talk to you when you get here."

"Sure. See you later. Love you, Mom."

"I love you, too, Rachel."

What would she have said, anyway? Oh, by the way, your grandfather was a Nazi.

She took a shower, scrubbing herself furiously, as if she could scrub it all away. Then she lay in the tub sobbing, with the water running over her body, until it turned so cold it hurt.

Shivering, her teeth chattering, she dried herself and began to dress. Suddenly, one clear thought sounded in her head as if someone had broadcast it there.

Uncle Benny must know the truth.

My God, yes! Uncle Benny was probably involved somehow. He had often recounted their clandestine arrival in Israel, how the *Hagana* had brought them in under the noses of the British while they were busy holding the *Exodus* hostage in Haifa.

Uncle Benny would know.

~~~~

"But, Mrs. Samuels, you can't be serious!" Itzhak's cheeks were already starting to puff.

Beth got up and poured herself another cup of tea.

"Yes, Itzhak, I'm quite serious. As a matter of fact, I've never been more serious in my life. So, you'll excuse me if I don't ask your rabbinical advice about my decision."

The cheeks puffed rapidly now; his face turned a vicious burgundy. If he opened his mouth, he would probably fly around the room like a ruptured balloon.

The image gave Beth the first relief she'd had all day.

"Mother, I'm sure Itzhak is just trying to point out that it's *Shloshim*. It only lasts thirty days. Can't you wait a couple more weeks to make your trip?"

Itzhak muttered something about *Shloshim* being a year for the loss of a parent, not thirty days. Even Rachel ignored him.

"Honey, I can't wait. This is very important. I'm sorry if it offends you, but there's nothing I can do about it. I have to go. I have to. I just need you to water the plants, pick up the mail. If that's too much . . ."

Rachel put down her cup and came to her. Beth hadn't even realized she was crying until Rachel wrapped her arms around her and held her.

"Mom, of course, it's not too much. I'm just concerned about you. This has been so hard on you, Papa's dying. I just thought it would be better if you waited until you're a little stronger."

Beth patted her daughter's cheek and forced a smile.

"You're right. It has been hard, very hard, but I'll be surrounded by family there, too. I'll be all right."

"When will you go?"

"Tomorrow, if I can make arrangements." Beth blew her

nose on a paper napkin. "I can take another week or so off at school, I'm sure. Hopefully, David can pick me up at the airport in Tel Aviv. If all that works out and I can get a seat, I'll need a ride to the airport."

"Of course, we'll give you a ride. Won't we, Itzhak? Itzhak? We'll give Mom a ride to the airport, right?"

Beth had the distinct impression Darling Itzhak was about to spout steam from both ears as well as his nostrils.

~~~~

El Al's flight left at 12 Noon to arrive in Tel Aviv at 2:30 the following afternoon. Beth made it business class, which cost a fortune, but at least she wouldn't be miserable for sixteen hours.

When they were airborne and the man seated beside her was safely absorbed in his own work, Beth pulled the manila envelope out of her bag and looked through the pages. Her father's birthday was listed as March 26, 1921. Interesting. They had just celebrated his seventieth birthday on December 18th - last year - 1989. Why on earth lie about such a simple thing?

Born Peter Josef Rolf in Feldenhausen, Bavaria. A sergeant in the Wehrmacht. De-Nazified and released April 1946. How lovely.

A smaller piece of paper shook free. Unlike the others, it was entirely in German. It was a certificate of marriage. Peter Josef Rolf married Anna Rachel Tauber on July 25, 1946, in Munich, Germany.

Beth had heard the story a hundred times. They'd met, fallen in love, and married all in a span of a few weeks. In Munich. A Catholic priest, who'd also survived a concentration camp, had performed a Jewish wedding ceremony for them. That part may actually have been true. But Beth had always believed her mother had married a man named Aaron David Rosen, not Peter Josef Rolf.

Beth pulled out the German travel guides she'd picked up that morning and tried to find the village of his birth. She couldn't. It must be too small.

Then she looked up Munich. The Glockenspiel, the Marienplatz, Oktoberfest. Lovely place, Munich.

Beth slammed the book closed, startling her neighbor, who by now was clicking away on his laptop.

"Sorry."

"Not a problem," he said and went back to his computer.

She turned out her overhead light and closed her eyes.

Her father was there before her, as he had been in the photo, young, handsome. He was smiling at her, calling her *Liebchen*. It was a German word, but after all, German was his first language, wasn't it?

He had played her child's games with her whenever she'd asked, helped her with her Hebrew studies. At her *Bat Mitzvah*, he had beamed with pride, as if she had just been crowned queen. And he had cried at her wedding, cried openly in front of everyone.

She could see his hands. Making a spider with his fingers and chasing her until she shrieked. Tying a bow for her, touching her cheek. His hands on her mother's shoulder, on the small of her back. Strong hands, masculine hands. She had always been in love with her father's hands.

Beth opened her eyes and looked at her watch. She had fifteen hours to go before she reached Tel Aviv.

Berlin - 1945

At the Weidendamm Bridge, a tank barrier blocked their way. To make matters worse, the Russians were now shelling the area south of the bridge. Erich was about to turn the cadre back when the ground beneath his feet began to shake. Five German Tiger tanks rumbled toward them. In two thunderous shots, the tanks destroyed the barrier and started moving across the bridge.

With a series of deafening explosions all around, Erich and the others darted across, using the tanks for cover. By the time they reached the other side, it was clear they had landed themselves in the middle of a tank battle, and they were trapped.

Erich saw a flash. A split second later, the tank closest to him exploded in a fiery ball, hurling Erich like a rag doll into the air and crashing him to earth. Badly shaken, his ears ringing, he pushed himself up and stumbled away from the flames.

Ahead of him, Bormann was on his knees, trying to stand. Erich grabbed the leather satchel Bormann had dropped and pulled the Reichsleiter to his feet. They scrambled into a bombed-out tenement, joining the others to catch their breath and regroup.

After a few minutes, Bormann took the lead, heading west along Schiffbauerdamm, following the course of the Spree River toward the Lehrter Bahnhof rail station.

The first hint of dawn began filtering through the smoke bringing the full extent of the devastation into focus. On both sides of the Spree, as far as Erich could see, nothing was left whole. The clean, orderly city of stately, historic buildings had become a vast field of scattered bricks and mortar and smoldering debris.

Ahead of him, a body swayed slowly back and forth from a lamppost. It was a boy, a mere child, no more than fourteen years old, wearing the uniform of the Hitlerjugend, the Hitler

Youth. On his chest hung a crude placard reading, "Traitor, Deserter, Coward, Enemy of His People."

Traitor? Traitor to what? My God, traitor to what?

Russians had not done this. Germans had. Erich had heard of bands of savage SS roaming the countryside summarily executing anyone they suspected of desertion.

The boy's wild, bulging blue eyes bore through to Erich's soul, exploding a rage in him that nearly buckled him at the knees.

Suddenly, rifle shots rang out sending Erich and the others clambering down a railroad embankment into the courtyard of a smoldering building. The sniper was across the river on top of the Reichstag, or what was left of it. He was firing at them like ducks in a carnival shoot.

As Erich tucked himself into a sheltering doorway beside Bormann and Stumpfegger, he heard a scream. General Baur lay directly across from them, clutching at his legs, pleading for help. The sniper's bullets exploded into the ground around him, playing with him before the kill.

Instinctively, Erich started toward him, but then he remembered Stumpfegger. He looked back at the good doctor, all six feet, six inches of him, cowering in the darkest corner of the alcove.

"No! I won't go," Stumpfegger answered the unspoken demand. "Why should I? He knew the risks like the rest of us."

Erich lost what little control he had left. He grabbed the doctor by the collar and shoved him against the wall.

"You sniveling coward, he's your friend."

Stumpfegger's white face turned red as Erich squeezed.

"Leave him!" Bormann pulled Erich away. "You're here to protect me, not play hero."

"He'll be killed!"

"I said leave him!" Bormann bellowed, as Baur's pleas grew more desperate.

Erich shook free.

"You're safe enough here until I get back." Without waiting to hear Bormann's response, Erich slipped out of the alcove and ran toward Baur.

Shadow of the Flag

CHAPTER
NINE

Geneva, Switzerland - 1990

A toadstool in the midst of towering tree trunks. He saw it there, reflected in the polished brass doors of the elevator, a shriveled old man, bent with age, surrounded by tall young attendants.

Few men reached his age, fewer still with their wits intact. His mind remained sharp, even if his body had deteriorated. His eyesight was nearly gone, his hearing impaired. A lesser man would have given up long ago, let the younger generation take over. But a lesser man would not have survived at all, would not have defied the odds all these years under the very noses of his enemies. No, he would not quit. Not now, even when all seemed lost.

He had one thing left to do, and after waiting almost half a century for his chance, he was determined to succeed. A few days ago, victory had seemed so close he could taste it, taste its sweetness, feel its seductive warmth in his grasp. Then suddenly it had been snatched away. He must move quickly to get it back.

Quickly! He laughed at the very idea. Nothing at his age was done quickly.

On the top floor, the usual circle of sycophants tripped

over themselves to greet him. He looked past them to his secretary, who stood to one side. With a swipe of the hand, he dismissed the others, who melted back into their holes. He had neither the time nor the inclination for civilities, but the sight of his pretty young secretary pleased him.

She fell in with his turtle's pace as he inched his way down the corridor to his office.

"He's waiting for you, sir," she said, anticipating his question. "Shall I tell him you've arrived?"

"Yes, by all means."

She opened the double doors to his office and closed them behind him, leaving him alone. He shuffled across the expansive room to take his seat behind the massive mahogany desk.

The best years of his life hung around him in this room. Photographs, medals, his ceremonial dagger, even a watercolor by the Führer himself, a gift from one of his many nephews. The focal point hung on the far wall in an ornate gold frame, glowing below two spotlights mounted overhead: a life-sized portrait of the man who had inspired a nation, Adolf Hitler, so young and vital that if suddenly he took a breath and stepped from the painting, it would seem the most natural thing in the world.

Ten or twenty years ago, few would have had the courage to display such a portrait openly, but that had changed – at least across the border in Austria. Small private shrines that had been secreted away in closets and back rooms were slowly being replaced by bold statements like this one, even in the finest of homes. People were no longer afraid. The time for Austria to reclaim her birthright was at hand.

He had seen his long efforts begin to pay off with the spectacular takeover of the Austrian Freedom Party. Its new leader, Jörg Haider, a young man dedicated to the Führer's dream, had proven that the people of Austria yearned for a return to the Old Ways. They had spoken clearly in the last election in Carinthia. Only one state, but clearly, the Freedom Party was on its way. The old coalitions were quickly crumbling as history again stood poised to repeat itself, so like when the Führer had seized the Chancellorship in 1933.

Goebbels had shown the way seventy years ago. The right moves had to be orchestrated at precisely the right moment. No matter how much time it took.

That is why I have lived so long, the old man thought with a chuckle. The baton has passed to me alone. I am the conductor of this orchestra! I am the only one left to see it through to the end. He longed to be there to see it firsthand, but he was safer here protected by the Swiss. They were so good at keeping secrets.

The side door opened, and his breath caught. With all the setbacks, the idea that this search was almost over sent an electric charge through him, even to his fingertips. Victory after so long! The power of it made him tremble.

"It's true, then?" he asked.

"There is no mistake, *mein Herr*."

The young man, blond and beautiful, a perfect Aryan specimen, spread a newspaper over the polished surface of the desk and offered a magnifying glass, pointing it at a picture in the center of the page under the headline, "Jewish Community Mourns One of Its Own."

"You're positive?" The old man moved the glass up and down, focusing on one face in the middle of the page. "It's not very clear."

"*Ja, mein Herr*, we have it confirmed."

The old man's throat began to constrict, his heart race. He closed his eyes trying to control his breathing. Slow steady breaths, he told himself, but the excitement was rising in him of its own volition, threatening to explode like a geyser from his chest.

In that moment, he was young again, standing in front of a massive fireplace in an ancient monastery high in the mountains of Italy having this same conversation. It was 1946. Two men dressed in simple monastic garb, fugitives like so many others hidden by the Mother Church.

"Are you certain it was him?" Bormann asked as he paced back and forth across the stone floor, impatient as usual - impatient with the austerity of life forced on him here; impatient to have a woman, any woman. Bormann had never been particular about that. But now his wife was dead, and his mistresses - God alone knew where they were. The few prostitutes that had been smuggled in to keep him quiet had not satisfied him. He wanted to move on.

"Yes, there is no doubt. We've tracked him to Munich. He will show himself again." This time, I will take no chances, he thought bitterly; but to Bormann, he said, "It's only a matter of time, Martin."

"Time?" Bormann exploded, stopping in his tracks. "Time is running out."

The old man opened his eyes. Bormann was gone. Eichmann, Mengele, Wolfe, Rauch, his loyal Viktor - they were all gone now, but the struggle survived. He had made certain it survived. Over the years, even when the power he had amassed in some quarters had dwindled as various *juntas* fell, new alliances had been forged. Old enemies had become friends.

The Führer had met with them, befriended them. Races beneath his contempt. And he had used them. No one was happy about it back then; few were now. But necessity had won out.

The Palestinian Grand Mufti had found a haven in Berlin during the War; and in return for that kindness, he had arranged safety for the SS and the other survivors in plain sight of the Zionist-loving world - in Syria, Egypt, Libya, Afghanistan, wherever Muslims fought their Holy War, their *Jihad* - good, solid Nazis had fought beside them and, even more importantly, had funded them.

Together they had the strength, the courage, the determination to destroy their common enemies - Israel and anyone who supported it.

Nothing could stop the reawakening now.

Bormann had been right. Time was running out. His time. He could not afford to waste any of it.

The young man fidgeted uneasily. "I know this looks bad, *mein Herr*, but I'm sure it will work out."

The doctors who had told him not to shout had no idea what it was like dealing with imbeciles.

He lowered his voice to a deliberate whisper.

"The daughter. Tell me about the daughter." As long as he had the girl, there was no need to give up hope.

"We have a man on it now, *mein Herr*."

There was a time when I would have had your head on a pike, you incompetent piece of dog dung.

"You have a man on it. How clever of you." He closed his eyes again and counted his breaths. In and out. He sat there for a long time, waiting for the muscles to relax, waiting for the pacemaker to do its job.

"He's been dead a week!" he suddenly bellowed. The young man jumped. "Over a week! And you have a man on it?"

"*Jawohl*! One of our best. You see, with Jews--"

"Jews!" The old man laughed. "How droll."

"They have seven days of seclusion after a death, so you see--"

"I will not tolerate any more mistakes. Do you have that? Is it clear?"

"*Jawohl, mein Herr*!" The blue eyes were wide with fear, desperate for escape. "Perfectly clear, sir."

"Then get out of here and do what I expect for once."

. . . or I will gut you myself.

In and out. In and out. The idiot retreated quickly. In and out. He was alone again.

He picked up the magnifying glass and stared at the photo for a very long time, then smashed his fist down on the blurry black and white face.

"I will win yet, you bastard. One way or another, I will win."

He buzzed his pretty secretary to come in. Steno pad in hand, she took her seat. Crossing her shapely legs, she deliberately turned in such a way that he could see farther up her thigh.

"I want to send a message to my nephew."

"Herr Kemp or Herr Vogler, sir?"

"I suppose I will have to bring them as well. But first, you will contact Johann. Satellite phone, I believe."

"Johann, sir? I've not heard you mention him before."

"I have many nephews in many corners of the world. Johann is . . .hmm, yes . . . He's special and he has been away far too long. It's time he paid a visit to his uncle, neh?"

He would need all three. Werner the Smug, Otto the Reckless, and without question, Johann. Johann the Magnificent? Johann the Inscrutable? No. He knew exactly. Johann the Terrible. A force to be reckoned with, a terrible, mighty force. The others would do well not to underestimate this one.

The old man leaned back in his chair to enjoy the view his secretary offered him. Old he may be, dead he was not.

CHAPTER

TEN

Tel Aviv, Israel – 1990

"*Shalom.*" A pretty, dark-eyed, olive-skinned flight attendant greeted Beth as she stepped out onto the ramp at Ben-Gurion Airport. Beth was home.

She had always thought of herself as an American, but the truth was, she was Israeli. The moment the dry desert air hit her face that fact was brought back to her. She'd been born here during the tumultuous birth of this nation, and every time she returned, she felt as though she were returning from her own exile, like the 2,000-year exile of her people.

Eretz Israel, the Land of Israel. Home.

"Beth!" She heard her cousin's voice coming from a crowd of expectant faces as she emerged from Customs. Then she saw him pushing through toward her. He was casually but impeccable dressed, in perfectly creased jeans, a charcoal gray sport jacket (designer, of course) and a crisp white shirt - all in the heat of an Israeli spring day.

"*Shalom!* My God, it's good to see you." David kissed her on both cheeks. A second later, she was enveloped in his arms. Even when he released her, he kept one arm around her shoulders, as if to keep her in his cocoon of safety. "I can't believe it. I don't see you in what? Three years? Now, twice in a blink of an eye."

"I really appreciate you coming to pick me up. I hope it wasn't too much trouble."

"For you, my lovely cousin, I would drive to Baghdad and back, but why not simply speak to the Old Boy by phone? We do have such things in Israel, you know? Not the best service in the world, I must admit, but I hear it reaches all the way to Los Angeles."

"I couldn't do this by phone, David, I'm sorry."

"No apologies necessary, love. Your slightest wish is my command."

He picked up her luggage and led her through the crowded terminal, teaming with every kind of human being, dressed in every kind of costume imaginable, speaking a thousand different tongues. And of course, the ever-present soldiers, the Israeli Defense Force, armed to the teeth. Rather than giving Beth a sense of safety, they always made her more nervous. No one was ever truly safe in Israel, and the soldiers were a glaring reminder of that fact.

In the parking lot, David headed straight to a silver Mercedes. When he opened the door for her, she nearly laughed out loud at the irony. No doubt, he was making a statement of some kind, but she was too tired to bring it up. It would have meant a debate, and oh, how David did love to debate. If they started, there was also no doubt Beth would lose.

"The Old Boy's excited about seeing you," he said, as he got in beside her, totally unaware of her reaction to his choice of cars or ignoring it.

"Is he any better? You were hoping--"

"False hope, as it turns out. I don't think it will be long now. Perhaps a month. Perhaps two."

"I'm so sorry, David."

"I am, too." He paid the parking attendant and swung the Mercedes out into the snarl of traffic. "He's a hard old man, but I think he's afraid."

"I hope you didn't say that to his face."

David laughed. "You know me better than that. I'm the confirmed coward in the family. And he's still the General through and through. He may have been retired for years and nearly dead, but he can still bark out orders as if we were his seasoned troops. And believe me, his bark gets louder as his body grows weaker. The poor nurses take the brunt of it. He abuses them, and it's left to Rivka to fix it up again."

He went on telling her about the family and Rivka, his stepmother, the mother of his five young half-brothers and the one burdened with the unruly invalid. Most of the time, he gestured with both hands at once, giving Beth more than a few heart-stopping moments in the heavy traffic of Tel-Aviv.

They drove through the city, passed a long stretch of resort hotels and high-rise apartments. Like the rest of Tel Aviv, most were painted white. The traffic stayed heavy until they left the city, driving north toward Herzliya along the shimmering blue Mediterranean to their left.

As they drove, Beth sipped a bottle of water and listened to David complain alternately about Yasser Arafat, the Likud party and various religious extremists, both Arabs and Jews, all of whom he considered determined to catapult Israel into all-out war. David was a political animal down to his DNA, exactly like his father. Although, they would both deny any similarity to their last breath.

The rift between them, which had begun when David was a small child, had grown to cavernous dimensions over the years. His father's career had kept him away from the family most of the time, but more than that, Benjamin Klaus tended to treat his soldiers with greater affection and understanding than his first-born son.

When he was a young man, David had rebelled openly, thumbing his nose at everything the "Old Boy" expected of him. It had been Rivka who had prevented a complete split between father and son.

And somewhere along the line, perhaps as he grew more comfortable with himself, David had begun to follow his own heart, which, though he wouldn't want to admit it even to Beth, beat very much in unison with that of his father. But he did it quietly, covertly, keeping every success a secret, lest his father have the pleasure of being proud of the son he had so loudly condemned for so long.

"So, what's the big secret?" he said.

"Secret?"

"I know you too well. Impulsive you are not. At least, not to the point of flying halfway around the world for no good reason. Therefore, I assume there's a reason, and I want to know what it is."

"Oh, David, I don't know if I can--"

"If that son of a bitch Brian--"

"No, it's not Brian. Oh, maybe it is. Maybe if I didn't have to deal with him, I could think clearly about everything else. I don't know."

"I never liked Brian."

"You did, too. You always liked him."

"No, I didn't. The man's an ass. Always has been. And he proved it when he failed to recognize what he had in you, love." He reached over and took her hand. "We're getting you something to eat. If you feel like talking, we'll talk."

"I'm not hungry."

"When did you last eat?"

"I don't know. On the plane maybe." Or had she? She remembered the tray. She'd tasted something. Was it chicken? Whatever it was, she hadn't finished it.

"On the plane maybe? Beth, I hate to say this, but quite frankly, you look like shit."

"Oh, thanks a lot."

"I'm serious. Look at you. You're far too thin. You look haggard."

"Give me a break! It was a sixteen-hour flight."

"How much do you weigh?"

"None of your business."

"Bloody hell! You certainly are my business."

They had reached the outskirts of Herzliya, the most exclusive city in all of Israel, where the rich hobnobbed with the even richer, where Major General Benjamin Klaus's family compound overlooked the azure sea.

"Here's our turn." David swung off the main highway and followed a narrow dusty road to an old-style *shuk,* a marketplace that must have been there long before Herzliya became Herzliya. He stopped the car in front of a questionable-looking establishment. "It's Kosher, in case you're into that these days, and the food's quite decent."

~~~~

David ran his hand through his hair, shaking his head for the umpteenth time.

"I'm sitting here listening to this, seeing it in black and white, and I still can't fathom it."

"How else do you explain it?"

They were sitting in a back booth, whispering. This was not a conversation either wanted overheard. Fortunately, they had missed the lunch crowd; and except for a middle-aged waitress, who wore the modest garb of an orthodox Jew with a particularly unflattering wig, they had the place to themselves. She told him everything—everything that happened that horrible night and everything she found in that bank.

"Perhaps he was a spy. An uncircumcised Jew going undercover as a German soldier. Perfect cover."

"David, how many uncircumcised Jewish men do you know?"

"That's beside the point. Beth, this was your father. He was practically a rabbi. If Jews had saints, he'd already be canonized."

"I listened to all that stuff at the *Shivah*, about what a great Jew my father was, the great war hero. Then I opened that envelope . . ."

Beth looked down at her plate, baked fish wrapped in crisp shredded potatoes served with steamed vegetables. It really was delicious. She'd eaten part of it while David chatted about bright and happy things, but when the conversation had turned to the only thing that twisted around in her mind and her heart, her throat had closed, refusing to allow another bite.

"Your father knows," she said, pushing the plate away.

"Yes, I imagine he does. And your mother obviously knew. Amazing. It's hard to believe in all those years, someone at a urinal didn't happen to glance over and think, 'Jesus! Aaron Rosen isn't circumcised!'"

"Thank you for that, David."

"I'm quite serious. How the hell do you keep something like that a secret?"

"I don't know, but they obviously did. What I want to know is why. I keep coming back to the same thing. He must have been a war criminal, hiding . . ." David reached across the table to wipe away the tears from her eyes.

"You're making a big leap, love. It says here he was a sergeant, just another slogging foot soldier."

"Then why the charade? Regular slogging foot soldiers went back home to their lives after the war; they didn't have to hide who they were. Why live that way if there wasn't a very good reason?"

"You can't tell me you seriously believe your father was a Nazi. Now, if you were suggesting my father had been a terrorist, I'd agree with you completely. He would have done anything to drive the Brits out of here, including murder. Even mass murder, if he thought it would work. So would I, if I'd been around. But your father a Nazi? There was something so intrinsically moral about him. Good God, Beth! It couldn't have all been an act."

"No. I don't think it was an act. That's why I want the truth. Do you think I'll get it from your dad?"

"If it suits him. He's old. He's dying. Maybe his conscience will bother him, but I wouldn't count on it." He handed her back the papers. "I don't know why your parents kept this a secret from you, but I'll wager a guess at the Old Boy's motives."

He broke off when the waitress brought their bill, waiting until she'd walked away.

"How far do you think he'd have gotten in this country if it had become known his brother-in-law had this nasty little secret?"

~~~~

David turned the Mercedes down another nondescript dirt road, this time toward the high white stucco walls of the Klaus villa. They were stopped at the gates by an armed guard who glared in the window at Beth, then waved them through.

"Don't you get tired of this?" she asked.

"Immensely. But I'm far too fond of my own safety to be stupid about it either. I can't even guess at the number of threats the Old Boy's received over the years."

"I didn't know."

"No reason you should. He'd like to have every one of the family followed about by an army of bodyguards, but he can't sell the plan. Even Rivka thinks it's excessive."

David pulled the car up the broad circular drive and stopped in front of the massive three-story villa with large Roman columns on either side of the main entrance. It had been built at the pinnacle of Uncle Benny's career and reflected his extraordinary success, not only in his faithful service to his country, but also in his shrewd business investments. After his retirement from the army, Major General Benjamin Klaus had ultimately become one of the most powerful men in Israel.

Protected from the outside world by a high wall on three sides and by the tranquil sea on the fourth, the compound had always had a retreat-like atmosphere about it, as if nothing, even time, could touch you here. But not now, not anymore. Beth felt as if she had entered an armed fortress. There were armed guards everywhere, including the rooftops.

There had been a change in David as well. He made no move to get out of the car. He sat there, looking straight ahead with an expression Beth had seldom seen on his face. He was serious. Deadly serious.

"My father's been making enemies for a long time, Beth," he said finally. "And not all of them are Arabs."

CHAPTER
ELEVEN

"How is he?" David flung the question at the tanned youth with a head of shining black curls and large black eyes who bounded down the sweeping marble staircase. He was dressed in tennis garb complete with a racket on his shoulder. Beth knew he was one of the younger brothers, but which one she had no idea. She always got them mixed up.

"He's asleep now." A smug grin played on the boy's handsome face. "But he was ranting. You poor bastard, you're in for it. He expected you an hour ago. Leave me your car and that gray Armani, won't you?"

He deftly dodged the hand David directed at his ear.

"Watch your mouth, you insolent pup, and say hello to your cousin."

"*Shalom*, cousin." The grin expanded, lighting the boy's face with the same irresistible charm so evident in his older half-brother. "I'm Moshe, the middle one." He kissed her warmly on both cheeks.

"My goodness, you've changed." What she remembered was a brooding, gangly teenager, not this spirited young pretender to David's throne.

"Tall," David said. "He's grown tall. I swear he's added another inch since I left this morning."

"Superior gene pool," was the response.

Moshe Klaus stood still long enough to politely express his condolences over her father's passing, but his black eyes darted repeatedly toward the side patio doors and the tennis court beyond, where a small group of young people were gathered, including one particularly attractive long-legged brunette. Finally, Beth put an end to the boy's misery.

"David, why don't we let Rivka and your father know we're here so Moshe can get along to his tennis game?"

It was all the boy needed. "Good luck," he called cheerfully as he made his exit. "You'll need it."

Beth laughed. "Do you get the feeling you're watching yourself in a mirror?"

"And it scares me to death."

"He'll be going in the IDF soon, won't he?"

"He turns eighteen in another month. Rivka's not going to like it; he's got his heart set on the paratroopers."

It was paternal pride Beth caught flickering in David's eyes as he watched the boy join his friends, not that of an older brother. Perhaps because his five half-brothers were young enough to be his own sons, or perhaps because of the years of unhappiness he had endured as a child, David had always been driven to give the boys what he had never had himself, the interest of a father.

Whether things had changed in recent years, Beth wasn't sure. But no doubt if she stayed here long enough, she would find out. This was a Middle Eastern family, with the same volatile emotions that had kept the Sons of Abraham at each other's throats for thousands of years. Hostilities did not boil long under the surface.

With her luggage in both hands, David led her up the stairs to his father's room.

A large swarthy man in an ill-fitting suit leaned back in a chair beside the door. He sat up as they approached.

"My cousin, Mrs. Samuels." David addressed him in Hebrew.

The guard nodded.

"Rivka is probably in the kitchen bullying the cook. I'll drop these off in your room and let her know we're here. I'm trusting you'll have the Old Boy eating out of your hand by the time I return."

"If he hasn't bitten it off."

Beth took the manila envelope out of her bag and stared at it.

"Are you okay with this?" he asked.

"Yes. I'm okay."

"All right, then. I'll join you directly." He kissed her lightly on her forehead and headed off down the long corridor.

Beth tried to take a deep breath, but it didn't work. She couldn't even remember the last time she'd been able to breathe deeply. The knot in her chest was too large, too overpowering to allow such things.

Maybe she should wait a while to bring this up. She could relax, visit with Rivka. After all, she wasn't going back for a few days. There was plenty of time.

No. There was not. This need to know the truth was consuming her like a slow burning fire that started in the center of that knot and was devouring her from the inside out, one cell at a time. She couldn't wait. She had to know the truth. She had to make her uncle tell it to her. Then she could breathe again. She was sure one deep breath would quench the fire and let her live. She just needed the truth.

Beth suddenly became aware of the guard staring at her. At the very least, he was questioning her sanity. She tucked the envelope under her arm and walked in.

The smell struck her first. Not the disinfectant, which was prevalent, certainly. It was the odor of the slow, unrelenting approach of death. She recognized it instantly; she had smelled it before with her mother.

The room was large and sparsely furnished, with only a few simple utilitarian pieces, a dresser, a book-laden nightstand

and two straight-backed wooden chairs, one of which was occupied by a uniformed nurse absorbed in her knitting. The walls of the room were covered with the awards, medals and photographs of a national hero. Opposite the oversized hospital bed, a bank of windows looked surprisingly not at the sea, but at the desert.

"To remind myself of one thing, each morning when I rise and each night when I close my eyes," he had told her when she'd asked why he hadn't taken a room on the opposite side of the house facing the spectacular Mediterranean. "I live for Israel, only Israel."

The robust man Beth had known all her life was now unbearably thin with the gray pallor of ebbing life. He looked so small, so frail, dozing in the center of the bed.

The nurse put down her knitting and rose when she saw Beth enter.

"Mrs. Samuels? We've been expecting you." She addressed Beth in English.

"I don't want to disturb him—"

"No, no. He's been quite agitated. I wouldn't dare let him sleep." She crossed to the bed and touched his arm. "General Klaus," she switched to Hebrew. "You have a visitor, sir."

Two intense brown eyes snapped open. Clearly, he had been feigning sleep, waiting for the exact moment to pounce.

"It's about time." The voice was as strong as ever. "I suppose that idiot son of mine took you sightseeing while I lay here dying." He spoke in Hebrew, the language he had adopted when he came to Israel in 1946. Hebrew and Yiddish. If he spoke anything else, it was occasionally English, but never his native tongue, never German.

"No, Uncle Benny, David brought me straight here." Which was technically true. Admitting that they'd stopped to eat would have served no purpose whatever. "You know how heavy the traffic is these days. Besides, I knew you'd be too stubborn to die before I got here." She took his hand and bent down to kiss him.

He may have been a lion to everyone around him, but to Beth, he had always been a pussycat. Maybe because she was the only girl of her generation, or maybe because she reminded him of her mother, she wasn't sure. But even as she'd watched him make grown men tremble in their boots, he had never intimidated her. And that seemed to please him very much.

"I'm a dying old man. I'm allowed to be impatient. Sit. Sit."

Beth sat on the edge of his bed and continued to hold his hand.

"Your papa, *alav hasholom*, he should rest in peace, it was a blessing he went so fast. Dying by inches is hard, even for me."

He nodded his head as Beth told him about the funeral, about the tributes from so many.

"I said *Kaddish* for him." His eyes had filled with tears.

"Oh, thank you, Uncle Benny."

"He was my friend for over fifty years. I should have been there."

"But David came."

"What does he know? Twice your papa saved my life, once from the Nazis and once from the Arabs. David. Pah!" He pounded the bed with his fist. "I should have been there."

The nurse rushed to the bedside.

"General Klaus, you must remain calm, or I'll have to ask Mrs. Samuels to leave."

"Calm!" he roared. "Who are you to tell me I can't grieve for my dead friend, you incompetent bootlicker? Get the hell out of here before I have you carried out!"

The woman's face blazed a dangerous shade of red, but she stood her ground, brave woman that she was.

"General Klaus, sir. You know Doctor's orders. I will have to give you a sedative if you insist on—"

The explosion of curses that followed, most of them Arabic from the sound of them, clearly shook her resolve. When the old man started to get out of bed, Beth grabbed her by the arm and pulled her away.

"Why don't you wait outside? I promise I'll calm him down."

David appeared at the door and took over scooting the nurse out of the room.

When Beth turned back to her uncle, he was lying against his pillows completely relaxed, with a self-satisfied smirk on his face.

"You old devil. You enjoyed that."

"She deserves it. She treats me like an idiot child, and I can't abide that. Never could. Besides, getting her goat is about the only pleasure I have left."

"You're impossible."

The old man giggled. He patted the bed for her to sit down again. "Now that we're alone, you can tell me why you had to come all this way in such a hurry."

"How do you know I didn't just come to pay you a visit?"

"You don't survive as long as I have by ignoring the obvious, child."

David stuck his head in the door.

"Is everything okay in here?"

"Goddammit!" his father erupted. "Can't I have five minutes alone with my niece without half the State of Israel checking on me?" A green plastic pitcher flew past Beth and splashed against the wall.

"Good shot," David said coolly, brushing water from his sleeve. "I'll give you a few minutes. But if you keep this up, Old Boy, you'll answer to Rivka."

He ducked out as a plastic cup sailed at his head, hitting the closed door.

Uncle Benny winked at Beth. "Now, tell me. And you'd better do it fast before Rivka shows up. She'll have my hide for this."

Beth had no idea if this mood of his would work in her favor or not but putting it off was no guarantee either. Her mind had been screaming her need to know the truth ever since she sat in that cubicle in the bank, and now that she was here, looking into his expectant eyes, she didn't know if she could speak at all.

Beth handed him the envelope and forced the words out.

"Tell me about my father, Uncle Benny. I have to know the truth."

He held the envelope for a moment, and then laid it down beside him without opening it.

"I've already told you the truth, Beth. Your father risked his own life to save mine, not once but twice. For almost fifty years, he was like a brother. There's nothing more to tell."

On the outside, Beth was freezing, shivering, while the fire inside had flared into a white-hot inferno.

"What do you mean, there's nothing more to tell?" She opened the envelope with her trembling hands and pulled out the papers. "It says here my father was a German soldier named Peter Rolf, not the Jew Aaron Rosen."

Her uncle's eyes were immutable with no hint of what was going on in that stubborn mind of his.

"You knew this, didn't you?" she demanded. "You don't even have to look at these papers. You know what they say."

He said nothing. Nothing.

Beth crossed the room to the wall of photographs. One stood out from all the rest. Two handsome young men sitting on a tank in the desert, one fair, one dark, her father and Uncle Benny smiling at her from the past. She turned back and found him watching her.

"At the very least, you owe me an explanation. You owe me the truth."

Her uncle looked away, out at the desert. When he finally spoke, he did so slowly and deliberately, without looking at her.

"Your father was a good man, Beth, a good man. That is the truth. Now, leave it at that. I'm tired. Go away."

"Please. I have to know."

"Go away and get my nurse." He closed his eyes tight and didn't move.

"You can't do this. You can't. Uncle Benny, please!"

He continued to lie there with his eyes closed, ignoring her.

Beth stared at him, willing him to look at her. He didn't move. She wanted to shake it out of him, shake him until he gave her what she wanted, until the truth fell from his lips. Instead, she grabbed the papers and her bag and turned to leave. She stopped at the door, so full of rage it threatened to explode from her very pores.

"You stubborn old man, they're both dead. You're dying. What harm could it possibly do to tell me the truth?"

~~~~

David watched as Beth ran past him and down the stairs before he entered his father's room. He crossed to the end of the bed and observed his father's chest slowly rise and fall. It wouldn't be long now. His breathing had become more and more labored over the past few weeks.

For all their differences, he loved his father, and it broke his heart to watch him endure the thousand ignominious humiliations this disease had brought him.

But at that moment, David understood him less than ever. Why was he so determined to keep this a secret, even to the grave? It made no sense.

"Why not just tell her the truth?"

The old man opened his eyes and scowled at him.

"Why let her suffer just to protect your reputation?"

There was still no answer. There wasn't going to be, and David knew it. After a minute, he threw up his hands in frustration and walked away.

"Is that what you think?" His father's voice stopped him at the door.

"What else could it be? You can't be protecting Uncle Aaron. He's dead."

"Maybe I'm protecting her. Did you ever think of that?"

Shadow of the Flag

CHAPTER
TWELVE

Austria – 1990

At precisely 11:00, Johann Schmidt rang the doorbell at a stately townhouse in an elegant section of Old Vienna.

Elsa opened the door. Fat, ugly Elsa. In five years, the only thing that had changed about her was that she appeared to be fatter and uglier, like a grotesque frog squatting on a lily pad, all cheeks, jowls and double chins, with no neck whatsoever. Seeing him standing on the doorstep, her beady eyes filled instantly to overflowing.

"Herr Schmidt!" she squealed and leaped at him, throwing her fat arms around his middle, hugging him for all she was worth, painfully squeezing the air out of him.

"My goodness, Elsa, it is good to see you, too," he said as he peeled her arms from around his waist.

She pulled back, snuffling loudly, trying her best to compose herself.

"I beg your pardon, Herr Schmidt. But it has been so long."

At the first sign that she might lunge at him again, he stepped back out of her reach.

"Elsa, I am here to see your mistress. She is expecting me."

He could see her tiny brain working this one over. She was clearly torn between wanting him all to herself and the certain knowledge that keeping her mistress waiting would bring a particularly painful retribution. After only a moment's hesitation, fear won the day.

"I will tell her you have arrived."

"Thank you, Elsa."

When she returned, her fleshy cheeks were burning red. Even that short delay had drawn a sharp rebuke; no doubt a tongue lashing that had found its mark in Elsa's spineless bulk.

If he could feel for anyone, he would have felt for poor, loyal, weak-brained Elsa. She had been the one who had sneaked him sweets, had covered up for him when he played one of his nasty little pranks on the wrong person. But as it was, he found her discomfort mildly amusing. He had little tolerance for the weak-minded and even less for the weak-willed. None at all if that weakness led to disloyalty.

She ushered him into a large bookshelf-lined study dominated by an impressive portrait hanging above the fireplace at one end. SS General Wilhelm von Ströben dressed in his full-dress blacks. An extraordinary man to look at, tall, ramrod straight with silver hair and a monocle poised in one of his piercing steel blue eyes, clearly an aristocrat. It was to General von Ströbon and men like him that Johann Schmidt owed his very existence.

Lebensborn, the Fountain of Life, had been the brainchild of Heinrich Himmler, but it had been von Ströben who had brought it to life. Every SS man, whether married or not, had been ordered to impregnate as many women as possible before going off to the front. Von Ströben had insisted the *Lebensborn* farms were not brothels. They were pleasant, safe environments where the finest German women could couple with the most superior German men. Johann Schmidt was the product of such a union.

Johann had always hated the nameless cow who had given him birth then dropped him into the waiting arms of strangers to raise. Yet somehow, the faceless image of his father had remained heroic, offering his seed before laying down his life for the Fatherland.

In the end, it had been Gertrude Bräden, von Ströben's daughter, who had saved Johann's young life and had become his surrogate mother. With defeat imminent, Gertrude had chosen the healthiest, the most promising, the most Aryan of the *Lebensborn* children. The others she placed with anyone who would take them. With the Russians at her heels, she had spirited her brood over the Alps into Austria, where they could be raised to walk in the footsteps of their illusive fathers.

"Johann, you have come!"

Gertrude glided into the room, so regal in her manner he was almost tempted to bow. She was a tall woman, only slightly bent with her seventy-eight years. Never a great beauty, still she had the power to turn heads, like a goddess with mere mortals. Her shimmering silver hair was pulled back in a chignon, her face perfectly made up, creating the impression that not having wrinkles was somehow inferior. She wore a soft gray dress that spoke modesty yet moved suggestively against her well-formed figure letting the world know this woman was still desirable.

"Yes, Auntie, I have come." He kissed the fingertips of each of her outstretched hands. "It has been five years, and yet you remain as beautiful as ever, and as seductive."

"Who would be seduced by such an old woman," she said. "No one. Even far older men demand young beautiful bodies."

"Any man who would choose youth over you, Auntie, would be a fool." He could see her chin tilt up ever so slightly.

"Such charm, Johann. I have missed you so! Your brothers are such louts. How you could stay away from me so long in those horrid, horrid countries, I will never understand."

"It suited me."

"But, darling, you! However could you bear it?"

"It has its rewards." He kissed her hand again. "Besides, the world offers few morsels as enticing as you."

She giggled. "Don't tell me you did without altogether! Surely those harem girls--"

"If you don't want my answer, Auntie, then don't ask." He waited for her to take a seat in one of the high-backed wing chairs. He sprawled on the settee. "As the Americans so adroitly put it, let's not beat around the bush. I have come a long way and, if you please, I prefer to skip the interrogation."

"But I haven't seen you in so long, Johann. I only want to know how you have been. If you care for me at all you will at least be civil."

"I have come, that should prove that I care. What I do not care for is being questioned as to what I do and why I do it. That should also be clear to you by now."

The flash of fear he saw in her eyes pleased him. He laughed out loud.

"No, no, Auntie, you are quite correct. My deepest apologies. Civility is important. Tell me all about you and Elsa. How are you getting along these days?"

She smiled, but it was a cautious smile. That also pleased him.

"We have been managing," she said. "Elsa is old and very nearly useless, but she is loyal. I must say that. She has always been loyal to me and to the Cause.

"I have always wondered how you can bear looking at that face of hers year after year. And that body! She is revolting. Although . . ." He leaned back, remembering. "There was a time I enjoyed those rolls of flesh, but that was when I was young and had an insatiable appetite." He laughed again at Gertrude's horrified stare.

"Not really! Not Elsa!"

"Since you seem determined to know the details of my sexual exploits, I will tell you. I bedded Elsa by day and you by night, and the chauffeur in between."

"Johann! You are indeed wicked!"

"No doubt." He stood up and crossed to mantel. "Perhaps now you will stop this nonsense and tell me what is behind this cryptic summons you sent. I received it less than an hour after the one from Uncle."

She watched him for a moment, her gaze moving from him to her father's portrait above him. Her eyes filled with tears as she spoke.

"Was it not enough that those cowards should escape while the *Amis* bastards sent my poor Papa to the gallows? Those men who claim to carry the mantle of our beloved Führer. Cowards and scoundrels, that is what they are. Not one of them good enough to clean my dear Papa's boots."

"Which men, exactly? If I recall, there are quite a number who fall into your description."

"Enough of your flippancy!" Gertrude was on her feet, angrily meeting his eyes. "This is not a joke."

"You have my deepest apologies." He bowed dramatically. "Forgive my insensitivity. What exactly has happened?"

"Rolf has been found. Peter Rolf. And they have tried to hide this fact from me, hoping, I am certain, to prevent me from taking my rightful place in the new Reich."

"Ah, I see. Am I to assume that I am to deal with this Peter Rolf for you before anyone else can?"

"He is already dead."

"Dead?" He laughed. "That makes it easier all the way around. Why do you need me?"

"He has left a daughter who will no doubt be the object of your uncle's attention." She stepped close to him, looking up into his eyes as she once had long before she was old. "I have called you to ask that you help me. You must help me, Johann. I can trust no one else."

"And what is it you would have me do? Force this woman to do your bidding? Is that it?"

"Yes! Yes! Promise me you will. Promise me. You must

find her and retrieve what is rightfully mine."

"Ours," he said vehemently, grabbing her by her thin wrist. "What is rightfully ours." When she cried out in pain, he shoved her away and laughed.

She fell back into her chair, clutching her wrist. "My God, Johann," she sobbed, "you are cruel."

"Yes, and who made me that way, Auntie dear?"

"Now, Johann, don't be so hard on our Auntie."

Johann turned to see Otto Vogler and Werner Kemp, his *Lebensborn* brothers, standing side by side in the doorway.

Otto strolled across the room and kissed Gertrude on her cheek. "I'm quite sure she has always had our best interests at heart. That is, as long as our interests coincided with her own." Heavier than Johann remembered him and flabbier, and totally bald, Otto had shaved what little hair he had left no doubt thinking it made him more attractive to the ladies.

Otto perched himself on the arm of her chair and took her hand. "Now, what do you suppose our dear Uncle has in mind for his three favorite nephews? I'll bet anything you know all about it, don't you, Auntie dear?"

"Don't be an idiot. Of course, she knows." Tall, serious, and as always, impeccably dressed, Werner crossed to shake hands with Johann. "It's been a long time, brother. The Sudan, or was it Afghanistan? That's where you've been, isn't it? Training our dark-skinned comrades in your special skills?"

"As usual, dear brother, it's none of your fucking business what I do or whom I do it to."

"Touché!" said Otto. "Family reunions do so warm the heart, don't they? Oh, by the way, Uncle sent us over here to collect you, Johann. He said something about Gertie being up to her old tricks again. What do you think he meant by that, Auntie dear?"

"You're hurting me, Otto!" Gertrude snatched her hand out of his grasp.

Otto laughed.

Berlin - 1945

Bullets exploding all around him, Erich ducked from one doorway to the next, working his way to where Hans Baur lay. Through another burst of fire, Erich heaved the general up and carried him out of the courtyard into the shelter of a bombed-out flat.

Baur was bleeding heavily. He'd been hit in both legs and the abdomen and had lost consciousness. Erich looked around for something to stop the bleeding, but all he could find was an old tablecloth covered with plaster. Then he remembered he still had Bormann's leather satchel. He unbuckled the flap and dug inside for something he could use as a bandage. He pulled out a shirt, but there was something else, a bundle wrapped in brown paper and tied with twine.

Erich tore it open, exposing a heavy red cloth covered with deep brown stains. He knew what it was immediately. What German would not recognize Hitler's precious Blood Flag? Erich tossed it aside in disgust and focused on the shirt.

He did what he could to stop the bleeding from the hit to Baur's side. The bullet went straight through, and there was a chance it missed anything vital. When he'd finished making a rough splint for one leg and bandaging the other, Erich sat back in the debris, staring at the bundle that held the Blood Flag.

Bormann wouldn't keep something like this as a souvenir. Then why was he going through the trouble of carrying it at all? Erich could see only one reason. Even with Hitler dead, these bastards would perpetuate this madness. The Blood Flag had been their rallying point once, and they meant it to be again.

Outside, the sniper fire had become sporadic. He could hear Bormann yelling impatiently for him to hurry up. They would be moving on soon. If Erich lost them now, he may lose his one chance to make it out alive.

Baur moaned next to him, his eyes opening for the first time. "My legs," he said.

"Yes, General, you've been hit. I did what I could."

"Thank you, my boy."

Baur passed out again before Erich could respond.

The general's brief return to consciousness came just as Erich had decided what he must do. He checked to make certain no one could see him before he untied the knot that held the bundle together and set to work.

CHAPTER
THIRTEEN

Herzliya, Israel - 1990

hrough one half-opened eye, Benny watched the guard reach in and close the door behind his departing son. The impudent upstart, what did he know? Not a damn thing.

Beth had spunk. She reminded him of Rivka in that. Give her time, she'd figure it out herself. Something like that can't stay hidden forever. Aaron had been a damn fool to think it could. A damn fool.

Benny would have helped her if he could. But he couldn't, and that was that. His hands were tied. Aaron had tied them tight nearly fifty years ago. The whole thing frustrated the hell out of him.

He shifted in his bed under the torturous weight of the sheet that covered him. Dying and useless, that's what he was. He had always been a man of action – decisive action. He'd had to be. They all had been in the early days. Israel had been forged by men like him, not fancy pants like his son, sitting around on their backsides negotiating with the likes of that Nazi-sympathizer Arafat, who would happily blow you to kingdom come.

This disease had reduced him to nothing more than a helpless mass of flesh who couldn't even piss without a woman helping him. Christ! He wanted action. He yearned for action. He wanted to grab his niece and tell her the whole bloody story. She had a right to know.

He pushed himself up on his pillow and sat there for a moment; then slowly, painfully, he swung one withered leg off the bed, then the other. Using the bedside table for support, he stood and took a step to his walker. As he did, his hand brushed against the gold pocket watch and chain curled on the table. He picked up the watch and turned it over in his hand.

Funny how after all these years the feel of it in his hand could still invigorate him. Hatred could do that, even hatred long since satisfied.

He clicked open the lid and checked the time against the clock across the room. It was running slow again, like it had the night his train had shuddered to a stop inside the gates of Auschwitz.

Benny closed his eyes against the desert outside his window, against the warmth of the room around him, letting in instead the blinding glare of floodlights as the door of the cattle car slid open.

Half dead from starvation and frozen to the bone, crammed in reeking stench for five days, unable to lie down, unable to move, he still couldn't believe he was anything less than invincible. At sixteen years old, death happens to the other guy.

The noise around him was deafening, but the rumbling train was merely a backdrop in a scene that stretched out before him, a scene that seemed staged by a demented motion picture director. Bursts of steam billowed around the moans and cries of men, women and small children being shoved out of the train, barked orders and barking dogs, and above it all, Ludwig von Beethoven's Symphony No. 7, played by an orchestra of living skeletons in striped pajamas. It would have been ludicrous had it not been obscene.

Benny lost his footing and tumbled through the open door of the car onto the platform below. He righted himself before an SS boot could connect with his ribs. The man behind him wasn't so lucky.

With his pathetic bundle of rags clutched to his scrawny chest, Benny maneuvered toward a queue of men, but a guard grabbed him by the shirt and shoved him into another queue of old men and boys.

Across the platform, Benny could see the women and children being sorted into two lines as well. The oldest, the sickest and the smallest in one line. The stronger, healthier ones in another. He wondered which queue Frau Tauber and Anna would be in, or if they were sent somewhere else altogether. He hadn't seen them since they'd been separated more than two weeks ago. It had been even longer since he'd seen Herr Tauber, coughing and hacking, hardly able to stand.

Just then, the music stopped. An SS officer mounted a raised platform and began to speak into a microphone. His voice, coming over a loudspeaker, was gentle and conciliatory. A large black German shepherd sat obediently at his feet.

"Welcome to your new home, my friends. I am SS-Sturmbannführer Hausser. You have been assigned to one of the Reich's most modern facilities. Here at Auschwitz, if you work hard, you will be treated well."

Suddenly, the dog at his side erupted in ferocious barks, straining at his leash, teeth bared. A small child had wandered out of line. The mother snatched it back into her arms. Hausser quickly yanked the dog under control then calmly continued.

"I know you have had a long journey and would like to freshen up. We have arranged for you to have hot showers, and then you will be shown to your new quarters."

The music began again as a whisper of relief swept through the lines. A hot shower. It was almost as welcome as a feast. The lines began slowly inching forward.

As he waited, Benny's eyes searched past the revolving glare of the searchlights, past the sign above the gates that read, "*Work will set you free*," and into the black night that enshrouded the camp. He could just make out four towering smokestacks, each of them belching out billows of putrid smoke.

As he shuffled forward, a snatch of words he had overheard somewhere gnawed at the back of his mind.

Never go to the left.

Two lines for women and two lines for men shuffling forward. One strong, one old and weak. Too weak to work. On the right, the strong. On the left, the weak.

Benny was in the wrong line.

Suddenly, a woman screamed. Hausser's black shepherd had the child. The same child. No one moved to stop him.

The man in front of Benny vomited.

The hideous screams ripped through Benny's soul as he swallowed the bile that rose in his own throat. He had swallowed his anger for so long, he had learned to survive on a diet of pure raw hatred. He averted his eyes, trying to close off his senses until the screams died away.

He would find a way to live through this; and one day, he vowed, one day, he would pay back.

Out of the corner of his eye, he saw Hausser, still on the platform. He had opened his pocket watch and was frowning down at it. He rapped it against his hand and held it to his ear.

In that instant, Benny saw his chance.

"I can fix that for you, mein Herr," he yelled out.

A guard rushed toward him with his rifle raised, ready to bring the butt down on Benny's skull.

"I'm a watchmaker's apprentice, mein Herr," Benny yelled again.

Hausser lifted his hand and the guard backed off. "Take him to my office."

The guard yanked Benny out of line.

It took him thirty years to find SS-Sturmbannführer

Hausser. When he did, there was no trial, no appeal. Benny killed him with his bare hands. He kept the pocket watch as a memento.

Benny dropped the watch into his pajama pocket and started his trek. Slowly, painstakingly, he inched across his room to the door, rolling the walker forward and taking a step to meet it. Step by grueling step, he moved out the door. Shooing the startled guard out of his way, he crossed the hall to his wife's bedroom. He had to stop in the doorway to rest. His goal might as well have been miles away. He had to rest two more times before he reached the balcony.

He knew Beth would be down there. The sea was the place he would go to escape, if he could. He could see a flash of her hair amongst the rocks. She wanted to run away, and he didn't blame her.

"You could have stopped this," he said out loud. "You had to know you couldn't protect her forever."

He shifted his weight from his walker to the balcony railing and watched the dramatic little scene unfolding below him. David gesticulating wildly at two of the guards, the alarm sounding, the mad search was under way.

"Fools, all of them. And you, you were the biggest fool of all. If I tell her the truth, she will go home, go back to her nice life in America, and that would be that. But you have prevented that. You have made the next step inevitable."

"And what will that be, my husband?"

Benny was too old and too tired to be startled by Rivka anymore. He answered her without turning around.

"There are times, my love, when what makes the most sense is the most impossible."

"Like you being out of bed? Like you harassing the nurses? This makes sense?"

She kissed his cheek and turned him back to his walker as easily as if he were a small child. He would yield to her as he would to no other woman.

~~~~

Beth sat at the edge of a large rock formation that jutted out to the sea, the water lapping at her bare feet.

Her daughter had discovered this spot the first time they'd come here. It had taken them nearly an hour to find her that day. The only thing that had kept Beth from panicking was the sure knowledge that Rachel was too good a swimmer and far too levelheaded to get herself into serious trouble. She had just wanted to get away from the boys for a while, and she'd found the perfect spot. It was hidden from the beach and, save for one or two windows on the upper floors, hidden from view of the house.

Now it was Beth's turn to use it as a sanctuary. She could hear David calling her. She fully expected to be discovered at any moment, but she needed the time alone.

She wasn't thinking about her father or her uncle or even herself. She was thinking about her mother. Thinking about this woman she had obviously never really known. This woman who had quietly taken a back seat to the husband she adored and had kept his awful secret for so long.

What had made her do it after all she'd been through? How could she have protected him like that? How could she have possibly loved him?

Beth had known many other Holocaust survivors. Some never spoke of what happened in the camps, others talked of little else. But there was one common thread that ran through them all: the driving need for justice and the sure knowledge that they would never know it. She'd heard families of crime victims talk about the need for closure, but Holocaust survivors would never have it. Never. Even if a few of the monsters were caught, tried and convicted, the horrors were too great to be laid to rest. What they had seen, how they had survived, the ones they had lost, would haunt them forever.

So how was it this woman, this gentle woman who had

endured the same horrors as the others, would choose to live her life with one of the monsters and allow him to pretend to be one of her own?

The sun had become a fiery ball of vibrant orange sending flaming streaks across a purple canvas when David finally found her.

"Goddammit, Beth! Do you have any idea what you've put us through?"

"I'm sorry," she said. But she didn't feel like moving, and she didn't want to take her eyes off the sunset. In fact, she didn't want him or anyone else to share it.

"Isn't it obvious if we've got guards stationed every twenty feet around this place, there just might be a reason?"

"All right. You've found me. Now leave me alone."

"*Vay iz mir*! You sound like my father." He sat down on a rock beside her, pulled off his shoes and socks and rolled up his pant legs. "For what it's worth, I tried to talk to him."

"I always thought he loved me." Beth hugged her knees; she was shivering again.

"He says he's protecting you."

Beth stared at him. "From what? From the truth? It can't be any worse than what my imagination is dreaming up."

"No, I don't suppose it can. But he's not budging. He's never been the most reasonable of men."

"I can't leave it like this, David. I must try again. What about Rachel? What the hell am I going to tell her? She has to know."

"Why? What difference does it make? Her mother is Jewish, and her mother's mother."

"And she's about to marry a future rabbi who has about as much understanding as Jerry Falwell on the subject of gay rights. What exactly would you have me do? Follow in my father's footsteps and lie?"

"So, what are your options?"

"I don't know. But I'm not giving up. At least, not yet.

Maybe I'll go to Germany and track down his family. I've got his name and his birthplace. Someone must know something."

"Little Beth goes to Germany. I never thought I'd see the day."

"Believe me, neither did I."

David stood up and held out his hand. "Come on, love. Let's go let the Captain of the Guard know he's not sacked." He took her hand and pulled her to her feet. "Then you can explain to Rivka why we're late for dinner." He helped her down off the rocks onto the sandy beach. "If you think the Old Boy is formidable these days, wait till you tangle with Rivka. She's the only person alive who can still make my father cower in fear."

They were halfway to the main house, when Beth came to a stop.

"David, who was after him?"

He turned around.

"He told me at the hospital. He said, 'They know.' My father wasn't just hiding the fact that he wasn't Jewish. He was hiding from someone, someone who'd been hunting him all this time, and that call meant they'd found him. Who are they?"

"I wondered when you'd look at that side of it," he said as he turned back toward the house.

She grabbed his shirtsleeve.

"Don't you see? Someone else knows the truth about my father. I've got to find them."

"Not so fast, love. First, we find out who they are."

"Of course--"

"You know nothing about these people. I don't want you charging into something that might be dangerous."

"I have a right to know who my father was."

"Yeah, you do. But in finding that out, you may be digging up things that are best left buried."

"Nonsense."

"It's not nonsense. Beth, these people may not want to be found."

"I don't care whether they do or not. I am going to find out the truth about my father."

"And in the process, love, you may just stumble onto something you hadn't bargained for. That's what worries me."

Shadow of the Flag

CHAPTER
FOURTEEN

Geneva, Switzerland - 1990

"Send them in," the old man replied to his secretary's announcement that his "nephews" had arrived. He'd wanted them there immediately, but it had taken time to bring Johann back. It always came back to time, didn't it?

They trooped in and stood at attention before him, side by side, as they had done as youths. Otto, Werner and Johann. There was no question which was his favorite. It had always been Johann.

He was as magnificent as ever – thinner perhaps, darker - face and hands tanned and weathered by harsh climate – but magnificent, nonetheless. Compared to his two *Lebensborn* brothers, he was quite a specimen. Taller, handsomer, brighter, with a cruel streak that tickled the old man's fancy. Simply put, the others lacked his cunning, his shrewdness. Werner nearly had his height but had let himself go. Always the shortest, stoutest of the three, Otto's years of debauchery had diminished him in every way save his towering ego.

"Sit down, my boys. Sit down. You need not stand on ceremony with your uncle."

As they sank down into their chairs, the other two showed their innate smugness, each in their own way – Werner arrogant and Otto cocky, but Johann took his seat reluctantly – his eyes wary, suspicious. Johann trusts no one, not even me, the old man mused. Especially not me.

"Something amuses you, Uncle?" It was Otto who spoke. Typically.

"Only the delight of seeing my three favorite nephews. It has been far too long, has it not?"

Otto and Werner glanced at each other.

"We saw you only last month, Uncle. Don't you remember?"

Is the whelp drooling over the idea that I am losing my memory? How fascinating.

"Has it really only been a month, dear Werner? I had forgotten."

"*Ja*, Uncle," Otto said, catching on a little slower, "don't you remember? The Führer's birthday party. We were here."

"Not Johann," Werner threw in snidely.

"Of course, you are correct. I had forgotten. An old man does so occasionally. Johann, my boy, you were forced to miss our little celebration, were you not? Perhaps you would like to share with your brothers and me what you were doing that kept you away? Perhaps I have forgotten that, as well."

Johann smiled shrewdly. "I am quite sure you have never forgotten anything in your life, Uncle."

The old man roared with laughter. "You are so right, my dear Johann. I have a very long and very accurate memory.

Werner squirmed for a second before chancing to speak. "Why exactly have you called us here, Uncle?"

"All in good time. All in good time. But first, a report on your activities, Johann. It is important for your brothers to understand the vital work you have undertaken for the Cause."

"Very well." Johann leaned back in the seat and crossed his long legs. "As you requested, Uncle, I have spent the past two years and three months cultivating a close working relationship with certain elements currently operating with impunity in the mountains of Afghanistan and most recently Sudan. I have been quite successful. The promise of financial support has overcome their initial reluctance to deal with an infidel such as myself. Once they understood that we are working against a common enemy, they were more than willing to accept the aid I offered. And the training.

"Do I trust them? No. Nor do they trust me. But they more than trust the twenty million Deutsche Marks I promised, especially when I was able to deliver on a sizeable portion of that amount."

Otto let out a whistle. "Twenty million Marks! I'd trust you with my sister for that kind of money."

"If you had a sister," said the old man with a chuckle.

Otto laughed, but Werner did not. "Who exactly is funding this venture, may I ask? That is a great deal of money."

"Not to worry, Werner. The money is coming from private donations especially earmarked for this purpose. We still have a few wealthy friends who find the Cause worth supporting."

"Yes," Werner said, leaning forward in his seat. Money enticed Werner's interest like no other intoxicant. "But what are the chances that any of these groups will do anything worth that kind of investment?"

"That's right! By God! Twenty million Marks. Shit, it wouldn't take twenty million Marks for us to fuck up half of Europe."

"Clearly, Otto," the old man snapped, "you have been fucking half of Europe on far less." He pushed himself painfully to his feet. His voice was raised now, and he loved it. "If we are serious about bringing the Zionists and their sympathizers to their knees, it will not be done by screwing every woman in sight."

He felt even more energized by what he saw in their eyes. Fear. Werner's first – always. Then he watched the cockiness melt out of Otto's. Yes, he loved to see that happen. His eyes met Johann's. Those did not flicker. Satisfied, he lowered himself into his chair once again.

"It will be done by the kind of dedication I see manifested in your brother Johann. This money is an investment that will pay off in the long term.

"Clearly, he is not one to boast of his exploits, but I am certain that they have been harrowing, knowing the men he has had to deal with. Living in such rugged conditions with these foul beasts could have been no treat. Have you had a treat, my dear boy? Perhaps your brother Otto can provide one for you. He seems to think his exploits are legendary."

Johann laughed. "Surely, Uncle, you did not bring me this far just for R and R, as the Americans so aptly call it."

"You are quite correct. I have a little job for you. For all three of you. I will leave the planning to Johann. He is in charge. Do you understand? I no longer trust just anyone to handle this situation, and I certainly don't trust either of you two dimwits to do it right."

Werner stood up, outraged. The old man ignored him.

"Sit down, Werner, and listen for once. You two will report to Johann, and Johann will report directly to me. You will do whatever he asks of you without question, and you will do it without fail." He leaned forward and fixed both men with his stare. "If I think for one moment that this is not the case, I will personally see to it that you will wear your balls around your neck in a bag, Otto. And that your pretty little daughter, my haughty friend," he skewered Werner with one glance, "will not be so pretty anymore. Is that perfectly clear? Now get out of my office while I talk privately to Johann. Get out!"

He waited as Otto and Werner snapped their arms out in salute and left, watching Johann all the while. The old man assumed his nephew had enjoyed that little scene as much as he did. At best, Johann appeared bored; certainly, he hid his thoughts well.

"I assume your dear auntie has brought you up to date on all of my secrets."

"She has certainly tried, Uncle."

"No doubt."

"I understand there is a daughter."

"Yes! Then you know about the fiasco that's taken place. I am surrounded by idiots and incompetents. With you here, Johann, my boy, I finally feel hopeful. It's been so long." He felt the weight of it all pressing on his chest. "I've been so close so many times only to be foiled again and again. You must not fail. You must not."

"I won't fail, Uncle." Johann stood now beside the old man's chair. "You know I won't."

"Yes, yes. I know you won't. You are the one man I know will not fail me." He reached out and took the Johann's hand. "There's one more thing. Your auntie."

"What about her, Uncle?"

"Keep your eye on her, Johann. She cannot be trusted. She has never held the Cause as close to her heart as her own ambitions. I fear there may come a time when she will outlive her usefulness."

"I thought that myself, Uncle."

"Good. I will leave it to your discretion."

Shadow of the Flag

CHAPTER
FIFTEEN

Herzliya, Israel - 1990

Rivka Klaus, the daughter of Yemenite Jews, had been a sergeant in the IDF when she turned then Brigadier General Benjamin Klaus, a man more than twice her age, into a love-struck loon. He had defied not only every military rule but every convention to have her.

He was married; she rejected him. He divorced his wife; she ignored him. He pursued her for over a year, finally breaking down in tears at her feet. She dismissed him. Then, for reasons known only to her, she showed up at his headquarters shortly after the Six-Day War and announced that she would marry him, but he had better not treat her as shamelessly as he had his first wife.

To Israel, he was a general, a war hero, a business magnate, but in his own home, there was only one ruler. Rivka. And only one law. Rivka's law. Even Benjamin Klaus was not fool enough to defy it. He loved her too much. As did his sons.

Beth fully expected to feel the Wrath of Rivka when she and David arrived so late for dinner. Instead, she was embraced so warmly and so affectionately, that she longed to remain wrapped in those strong, comforting arms. Nothing bad could reach her as long as she stayed there.

"Look at you, my poor darling." Rivka took Beth's face in her hands and kissed both cheeks. "*Shalom, shalom.* It's too much sadness, your poor papa. *Alav hasholom.*"

Rivka Klaus was no more than five foot two, at least six inches shorter than Beth, a fact that always surprised Beth. When she pictured Rivka, she somehow always materialized tall. Tall and beautiful. She was neither. Deeply tanned, with large round eyes and shining black curls like her sons, she carried the noticeable scars of teenaged acne. Her face was often serious, intent with interest, with a little line between her brows, but just as likely she would erupt in laughter that lit her all over.

When she walked into a room, heads turned as if a great beauty had entered. It was that aura that had mesmerized her husband and captivated everyone who crossed her path, man, woman and child. Beth had never been able to find just one word to describe it. Self-assurance, an indomitable power that was unshakable, but also there was kindness, generosity of spirit, and unwavering loyalty.

"David!" Rivka boxed David on the shoulder. "You should be ashamed, bringing her so late to dinner. Look at her, she's skin and bones."

"Don't blame me, darling." He kissed her cheek. "She's been hiding."

"No wonder. Such *chozzerai.* David won't tell me a thing. He just runs off looking for you. And my Benny, he's impossible. He talks in riddles, if he talks at all." She hooked arms with Beth and led her into the dining room. "Whatever it is, it will wait. Now, you eat. Boys, where are your manners? Say *shalom* to your cousin."

Conversation at the massive oak table ceased just long enough for Rivka's five sons, Chaim, Shmuel, Moshe, Yitzhak, and Shimon, all named for the great heroes of Israel, to stand and greet Beth. Two of them had their young wives at their sides. The conversation erupted again as soon as she sat down.

Like Mrs. Liebowitz with her matza soup, the joy of life served at that table began to seep into Beth, filling the deep emptiness within her. Listening to the parade of subjects bantered back and forth, whether it be politics or horses or soccer or women, with opinions varying in extremes moment by moment, Beth was being swept away by the sheer force of their love.

Tears sprang to her eyes as the answer she had sought came to her unbidden. It came when she realized the deep root of the pain she felt was not shame or even the sense of betrayal, but rather the love that ran beneath it all.

The reason her mother had been a willing accomplice to her father's lie was the same reason Beth had come to Israel. They both had loved this man to a depth she could not fathom. Her search for the truth was ultimately a need to vindicate the man she adored. And at that moment, she knew it.

~~~~

"May I come in?"

Beth stood in front of the open doors of her balcony, staring at the glittering moonlight on the black sea, when Rivka tapped and peeked her head in the room.

"Yes, of course," Beth said.

"Aaah." Rivka's eyes quickly surveyed the room, landing on Beth's suitcase. "You haven't unpacked."

Before Beth could react, the suitcase was on the bed and Rivka was fumbling with the locks.

"Please don't bother. I'll--"

"Nonsense. You have the keys? Good. Give them to me." Obediently, Beth dug in her purse and handed over the keys. "You'll see how much nicer it is. No, no. You sit. I will hang them up."

Beth sat while one at a time her clothes were shaken out, examined, commented upon, and hung in the tall oak armoire.

"Such dark colors! Poor darling, you think you must be in mourning, but these don't suit you. Not at all. Tomorrow, I will take you shopping. David will drive us."

"I really--"

"Sh-h. Not another word. Tall and thin like you, you need the European designs. Couture. They're much more for you. We have such lovely shops."

"Really, Rivka, I can't possibly--"

"Of course, you can." Rivka closed the empty suitcase and set it in the armoire. When she turned around, a wicked smile danced across her face. "My Benny hates to spend money. Like poison, he hates it. So, if he won't talk, he will pay. Before we're through with him, he will beg to tell you whatever you want to know." She kissed Beth on each cheek. "Besides, it will be such fun. Good night. Sleep as late as you like."

The door shut, and Beth dropped out of the eye of the tornado.

Not for the first time did she understand why the dictatorial Major General Benjamin Klaus had succumbed so completely to this woman.

~~~~

She didn't know which she enjoyed more, shopping or watching David follow them around loaded down with bags like a liveried servant.

Rivka's enthusiasm for the moment swept away all the problems of the world. She wouldn't let Beth pay for a thing, and she spent a small fortune. Half of it on Beth and half on herself.

The shops were way out of Beth's comfort zone. No racks, just a few headless mannequins artfully displaying the most elegant designs. The staff at each shop greeted Rivka as if she were their most valued patron, which she probably was, and Beth as her heir apparent. They were only too pleased to drape her in one gorgeous creation after another. It only took a few minutes of this to expand Beth's comfort zone dramatically.

They stopped for lunch at a very chic sidewalk cafe, where Rivka settled back, squeezed lemon in her tea, and cheerfully announced, "Now, you will tell me all about this husband of yours."

"Ex-husband," Beth said.

"I say good riddance. So, who's the bimbo? He parades her around your home at the *shivah*? What a *shtunk* he turned out to be."

"That's not quite the word I would have used," David said as he dug into his salad.

While Brian's character was being quite thoroughly shredded, Beth felt just a little guilty, but not so much that she was tempted to put a stop to it.

After lunch, Rivka herded them on to yet another shop. While she continued to try on everything the attendants brought her, David found an excuse to disappear for a while and Beth, still groggy from jet lag, kicked off her shoes to rest her feet.

She was mindlessly wiggling her tired toes, packages piled around her, when a young boy with a mop of black curls and huge brown eyes came into the shop and walked straight up to her. About seven or eight, in bright blue shorts and a clean white shirt, he was too well dressed to be a street urchin, but still he had that look about him.

"Madam," the urchin said, obviously proud of his English, "are you Bet'?"

"Yes, I am."

"Madam. Daveed sayz you must come to meet him. You know thees man Daveed?"

"Yes, but--"

"He sayz to come now." The boy laughed as he grabbed hold of her arm with his brown little hands and tugged her to her feet. "He has a beeg surprise for you. Come quick."

"Leave it to David to plan an adventure when my feet are killing me. All right. All right." She slipped on her shoes, and as the urchin pulled her through the door, she called out to the salesclerk that she'd be right back.

Outside, the boy let go of her hand and bounded ahead, motioning for her to follow him as he disappeared into the crowded street. She caught a glimpse of the black curls rounding the corner half a block ahead and hurried after him, dodging the other pedestrians who all seemed headed in the opposite direction. As she reached the corner, she heard someone call her name.

A balding little man with a red face and a wrinkled linen suit stepped out of a dark blue Volvo idling at the curb.

"Mrs. Samuels?"

"Yes?"

The little man wiped his face with a large handkerchief then smoothed a few long strands of dyed black hair over the top of his perspiring head.

"Please, may I have a moment of your time?" His beetle eyebrows looked dyed, too.

"How do you know my name?" she demanded. Inside the Volvo, she could make out the sunglasses and bushy mustache of another man behind the wheel.

"I have been asked to speak with you, Mrs. Samuels. I hope you'll excuse the intrusion. Perhaps we could talk in my car." He opened the back door. "It's air conditioned, you see."

They were in broad daylight on a crowded street, but Beth felt completely alone, completely vulnerable. And David was nowhere in sight.

"You sent that boy, didn't you?"

"The boy? Ah, yes. I do apologize. There are times, you know, when one must use methods, methods that are not always above the mark. You understand."

"No, actually, I don't." She'd had enough. She started to push past him, but he sidestepped in front of her.

"A few minutes is all I ask. I assure you, Mrs. Samuels, it will be worth your while."

She stood nearly a head taller than him and could probably outrun him, but she wasn't so sure about the one behind the wheel. She backed away a step.

"What do you want?" Where the hell was David?

"My client has authorized me to make you an offer, Mrs. Samuels. But it's so hot out here." He wiped his face again to prove the point. "Can't we talk about it in my car?"

She stepped back another step. Just then, she heard David call her name and turned to see him rushing down the street toward her. The little man saw him, too. He slammed the back door of the car shut.

"Call me, Mrs. Samuels." He fumbled in the inside pocket of his jacket and pressed a business card in her hand. "It will be worth your while." He jumped into the car.

David reached her side as the car lurched away from the curb.

"So? Who was your friend?" His voice was calm, but his gaze was grimly fixed on the blue Volvo as it disappeared from sight.

"According to this, he's Jacob Smith, Business Agent." She handed him the card.

He glanced at it. "Jacob Smith? A good Jewish name." He casually slipped the card into his pocket, while his eyes scanned the street around them. "Let's get back before Rivka wonders where you are." He took hold of her elbow, propelling her back through the crowd, his grip a vice on her arm.

"Ow! You're hurting me." She twisted out of his grasp. "What's going on, David? Who was that man?"

"You just told me. Jacob Smith, Business Agent."

"That's not what I mean, and you know it. He knew me. He knew my name and he knew I was with you. He had a little boy lure me out here to meet him. And you obviously know who he is."

"I recognized him, yes."

"And?"

David took her arm again, gently this time, coaxing her to walk with him. It struck her then that he very much wanted her off the street.

"His name changes frequently, but it's true, he's been known to act as a business agent from time to time, for any lowlife who pays him enough."

"Lowlife? You mean criminals. What would criminals want with me?"

He slowed his pace for just a second, then said thoughtfully, "I'm not quite sure."

Beth pulled her arm away again and stopped. They were in front of the dress shop where they'd left Rivka.

"In other words, you have a pretty good idea, is that it? It's about my father. What else could it be?"

"Can't we walk and talk at the same time? I'm not willing to discuss this in the middle of the street." He pushed open the door and made an elaborate bow for her to enter. "If you please."

"Oh, all right."

"Besides," he said as she walked in ahead of him, "if we leave Rivka alone much longer, she's likely to bankrupt the Old Boy. I have my inheritance to consider."

CHAPTER
SIXTEEN

In the end, David either wouldn't or couldn't tell Beth anything more. His excuse was the lack of privacy. Too much chance to be overheard by the wrong people, and they had Rivka to contend with. As soon as they returned to the compound, he managed to disappear completely.

Later, after Beth awoke from the nap, she'd taken to shake off her jetlag, he was still nowhere to be found. Instead, the Captain of the Guard told her that David had imposed a few new safety rules, just in case.

He had arranged that she not be left alone at all, except in her room with a guard stationed at her door. She would be able to relax, read, walk on the beach, go anywhere in the compound she wanted, all under the watchful eye of the sharpshooters on the roof. Furthermore, a guard with an Uzi submachine gun strapped across his chest was to follow her everywhere. And if she left the compound, a bodyguard would be with her constantly.

Having been explained the rules of her imprisonment, Beth returned to her room with every intention of calling the mysterious Mr. Jacob Smith to demand some answers. Then she remembered David had pocketed the phone number.

Instead, she headed to Uncle Benny's room dressed in her new, extraordinarily expensive Crepe de Chine pants with matching shirt, a deep gray that Rivka insisted matched Beth's eyes exactly. After all, Uncle Benny had paid dearly for them, he might as well see where his money went.

Beth got as far as his door. Rivka blocked her way.

"My poor darling, are you rested? Dinner will be soon." Rivka linked arms with her and pointedly steered her away from her uncle's room.

"Actually, Rivka, I want to speak with Uncle Benny. Is he awake?"

"He's resting, darling. Later, we will see how he feels. This outfit, on you, it's perfect. Wasn't I right? Even here, I can see it light your eyes."

Beth was quite sure the light in her eyes had nothing whatever to do with her clothes. She let herself be led away, but it wasn't going to stop her. Uncle Benny wasn't going to stop her. All the guards in his armed fortress weren't going to stop her. She was going to learn the truth one way or the other.

~~~~

She was walking into the sanctuary of a church, a cathedral with marble pillars and statues of saints lining the walls, her footsteps echoing on the marble floor. A crucifix hung above the altar, its larger-than-life marble Christ twisted in agony, painted blood dripping from his hands and feet, from his side and down his face.

In front of the altar ten rabbis stood, all chanting different prayers in Hebrew, creating a cacophony of sound that jarred the air around her.

Only then did she notice the coffin before the altar. She couldn't see inside; she was too far away. She inched forward, unable to stop herself, yet terrified of what she would see.

As she drew closer, she realized the coffin held the body of a woman in a white dress, her arms folded across her chest, a white lily in her hands. It was her mother as she had once been, young and beautiful, yet white and cold and dead.

Suddenly, from the other end of the coffin, her father sat up. The two of them together in the same coffin. He was an old man, wearing a Nazi uniform, a swastika on his arm. He looked at her and smiled.

"Trust God, Beth. Always remember to trust God." Then his arm shot out in salute. "Heil Hitler!"

From behind her came the booming response, "Heil Hitler!" Beth whirled around. The church was full of Nazis, all with their arms raised, all shouting those hateful, awful words over and over. "*Sieg Heil! Sieg Heil!*"

Beth shot out of bed and switched on the light, awake but with the vivid images of the nightmare still hanging before her eyes. Her logical mind told her it was just the jet lag, but the dream had left her shaken. She got a drink of water and stepped out onto her balcony, hoping the cool night breeze would wipe the pictures from her mind. The sound of tires crunching on the gravel drew her attention toward the back of the building.

Light streamed from an open door, illuminating a guard with his automatic rifle and the back of another man immerging from the passenger's side of the car. He was dressed in a dark suit and *khaffiya*. A blue and white Palestinian *khaffiya*.

For a moment, she thought she might still be dreaming, but the feel of the glass in her hand, the touch of the cold tile under her feet told her this was no dream.

The man shook hands with the guard as the car glided away, the only sound she heard was the gravel under its tires and the soft lapping of the sea in the background.

The man pulled off the *khaffiya* and ran his fingers through his hair. At that moment, he looked up and his eyes met hers.

His knock came so quickly, she assumed he'd run up the stairs. When she opened the door, she heard him telling the guard to take a break. The expression, rather the smirk, on the guard's face made it clear what he thought as he left his post.

David ignored him. He walked in, locked the door and turned off her bedside lamp. The room was now dark except for the moonlight filtering in through the windows.

"All right, love." He sat down on her rumpled bed and leaned back against her pillows. "What do you want to know?"

"Why were you dressed like a Palestinian?"

He didn't answer.

"Did you go to the West Bank dressed like that?

"I went to visit friends, actually."

"Friends? How silly of me. I should have guessed. I suppose I'm not supposed to ask what it's all about." With David, it was probably something shady, covert, something to do with spies and intrigue. "Not that you'd tell me anyway."

"No doubt, you're right. I probably wouldn't."

"Just tell me this, these *friends* of yours, are they terrorists?"

"It depends on your perspective. I prefer to see them as peacemakers. After all, isn't someone supposed to be blessing the peacemakers?"

"God, I hope so, for your sake. Does your father know what you're up to?"

"Knows and objects loudly. He holds a grudge longer than any man I've ever known, but he lets us try. Someone's got to. Otherwise, it will be a matter of who's left standing. I don't want to see that and neither does the Old Boy, I think. But if you want the truth, tonight they were giving me information about your friend Jacob Smith."

Suddenly, Beth felt like Alice, having just hit bottom after plummeting through the looking glass. She had to sit down. David moved his feet to make room for her.

"Jacob Smith? David, what . . .? Why would you . . .? Oh, what difference does it make? Do these friends of yours know who this client of his is? And what does he want with me?"

"You forgot one. How the hell does whoever it is know you're in Israel?"

"Well?"

"It seems Mr. Jacob Smith is nowhere to be found. The number on the card has been disconnected."

"He's disappeared?"

"As if into thin air. I presume he panicked when he saw me. He will probably reappear in the West Bank at a less critical time as Abdullah Smith, but for the moment, he and his mysterious client remain just that - a mystery."

She wished she could see enough of David's face to make out his expression. Despite his flippancy, he sounded worried. Suddenly, he leaned forward and took her hand.

"Beth, I want you to tell me again everything you remember about the night your father died." Despite the darkness, she could see the intensity of his eyes.

"Why? I was right. This is about my father, isn't it?"

"Possibly. Most probably. The phone call, man or woman?"

"A man. There was an accent, but I'm not sure what kind. Maybe German, I don't know. European, for sure."

"What did he say?"

"He asked if my father was there. I remember that he knew my name. He called me Mrs. Samuels, exactly like Jacob Smith did today."

"Same accent?"

"No. And the voice was different. Deeper, more sure of himself. Jacob Smith was kind of whiny."

"Go on."

"I told him Dad couldn't take the call because of the Sabbath." As she spoke, David moved behind her on the bed and began massaging her shoulders. "He said something like 'I think he'll take this call.' I was to say it was about Peter Rolf. He spelled it, R-O-L-F, as if he didn't want me to make any mistakes."

"And you told your father?"

"Yes. There was something about the voice; I don't know what, it made me uneasy. And when I told him . . . Oh, David, if you could have seen his face. He went absolutely white. I remember thinking this is fear, cold fear. You always read about it, but I was actually seeing it in my father's face. It only lasted a split second."

"And he took the call?"

"Yes. He said they had the wrong number, and he hung up. A few minutes later he collapsed." David's hands on her shoulders, her bizarre dream, the dull ache inside, it all suddenly propelled her off the bed. "I've told you all this before. I don't see--" She started pacing.

"What did he say later, before he died?" His voice had become gentle. "Try to remember exactly. Any detail might help."

"He was unconscious at first, and after we got to the hospital, he said very little. He quoted Scripture. You know the one, '*Though He slay me, yet I will trust Him.*'" The image of her father sitting up out of that coffin flashed itself in Technicolor across her mind. It made her shiver. "I hate that verse. I suppose he thought it would comfort me. It didn't. It just made me angry. Why the hell…? Oh, never mind, you don't want to hear this."

"It's okay to be angry, Beth. It's part of grieving."

"Not this angry, David. Not this angry."

He stood up and pulled her to him. They clung to each other for a long time. His closeness was unsettling.

Then suddenly he seemed to stiffen. He released her, kissed the top of her head and walked to the door.

"Get some sleep, love," he said finally. "We'll talk about it later." His hand on the doorknob, he turned back to look at her.

"Damn dirty shame, you know, our being cousins. Damn dirty."

Then he walked out of the room.

Beth leaned against the door.

"We're not cousins, David," she whispered to the empty room. "We're not."

~~~~

The next morning, on the patio overlooking the sea, Rivka laid out her plans for Beth's day over croissants and fruit.

"Then we'll drive into Tel Aviv," she said while buttering her last bit of croissant.

"No, Rivka," Beth suddenly blurted out, "I have to speak with my uncle."

"But darling, you must understand; my Benny is very weak. Any excitement--"

"I know, Rivka, but I've come all this way."

Suddenly, fire flashed in those large black eyes. "Your only concern is for what you want. Mine is for my husband's life! Which do you think will prevail?"

Beth felt her own anger flame up, ready to engulf her again. She struggled not to lose control. That would get her nowhere with Rivka.

"Please, Rivka, someone knows an awful secret about my father. Something that upset him so badly it killed him. Uncle Benny knows it, too, and he's refusing to speak. Don't you see? I have to know the truth. I have to."

Rivka's eyes had not moved from Beth's face, but they had softened, if only slightly.

"I cannot have him upset like he was before. But I will speak to him. *I* will speak to him, not you. That is the best I can do."

~~~~

Beth sat on her rock, her feet dangling in the water, waiting. Rivka had basically told her to get lost. She would work on Uncle Benny in her own way, and she didn't want Beth anywhere around. The guard with the Uzi sat on a rock not far away, skipping pebbles over the sea. Beth envied him. At least, he was enjoying this.

~~~~

Her soft, warm hands moved over his aching bones,

gently massaging the pain away, taking Benny back to the first time she had unbuttoned his shirt and run her fingers over his chest and down his stomach into his pants.

Too bad there wasn't enough blood left in him for one more time with her, to feel her from the inside, to possess her.

Ha! Possess Rivka? Never. She had possessed him from the first time he had seen that fire in her eyes. Eyes like the Yemenite girl fighting next to him in Galilee in 1948. There were times when he thought he would go mad from wanting that girl. Her round breasts bursting the buttons on her uniform, brushing against him.

All he wanted was to take her, so instead he took the Arabs with bullets. He'd killed more Arabs that day than anyone else. After the Yemenite girl was hit, killed instantly with a bullet through her pretty head, he shot so many of the enemy, the bastards had retreated, at least for the moment.

Years later, when he saw Rivka with those same fiery eyes, he knew he would have her. He had to have her. Even now, when his life was slipping away, he wanted her.

"So, what have you done to make Beth so upset with you, my husband?" Rivka poured more of the oil, warming it for a moment in the palm of her hand, and smoothed it over his shoulders. "She says she must know the truth about her father, and you refuse to help her."

"I cannot help her."

"David is angry with you, too."

"Let him be angry." Why was she telling him this when all he wanted was her hands on him?

"It's such a big secret you should upset them like this? You upset them, they upset you. Round it goes."

"I cannot help her. She should go home and forget it."

Rivka laid him back and moved her hands to his legs. But her touch was not so gentle. She was getting angry.

"You're a stubborn man, Benny, but you're not a fool. This girl will not forget so easily. Why do you do this?"

"I told you I cannot--"

"Pah!" She threw her hands in the air. "Then why will you not tell me? Me! When have you kept a secret from me, Benjamin Klaus?" She furiously wiped her hands on a towel then threw it down. "You treat me now like you treated your other wife, eh? Then perhaps you prefer the nurses to care for you instead of me? Is that it?"

"Rivka, please, I cannot--"

"You cannot? No, my husband, you can help her. It is that you will not." She turned her back on him.

"Rivka." He reached his hand out and took hers. "I swore an oath."

"An oath?"

The words came from the doorway. Beth stood there, her fists clenched, tears gleaming in her angry eyes.

"You honor an oath to my father and deny me the truth? An oath to a liar?"

"An oath to my friend, Beth. To my friend."

She glared at him; her mouth clamped shut as if to hold in a barrage of words. She turned and stalked away.

Rivka still held his hand.

"He is dead, Benny, surely now--"

"I cannot. He made me swear."

Shadow of the Flag

CHAPTER
SEVENTEEN

Beth reached the staircase, shaking so badly she thought for a moment she might lose her balance. David was waiting for her at the bottom. He held out his arms to her and she ran down into them.

"Let's go," he said, and without waiting for an answer, he led her out to a Land Rover parked in front. He helped her in and handed her his handkerchief. "Blow your nose," he said and closed the door.

Obediently, she blew.

He climbed in next to her, started the engine and took off, spewing a shower of gravel behind them.

Beth quickly buckled her seat belt.

He didn't say a word as they bumped over the road. The muscles in his jaw tensing again and again, he drove like a madman. Swerving onto the highway, he barely missed an oncoming truck.

"Where are we going?"

"I want you to see something."

"Oh."

They rode in a tense silence for several kilometers, but the farther they drove, the more they both relaxed. He wasn't scowling anymore, and she had become truly captivated by the landscape around them. He drove them north along the coast to Hadera then swung off into the desert.

Beth lost all awareness of time, and she didn't care where they were headed. Even her anger seemed to have been lost somewhere back behind them. Rocks and sand and nothing all around. The emptiness of it soothed her soul.

David finally began to talk, describing various hills and rock formations like a tour guide. He didn't mention his father or her father or any of it, which was fine with Beth.

As they drove out of the forested Samarian foothills, to the ancient city of Megiddo, he pointed out that according to the Christians, this would be the sight of the last battle of mankind.

A second later, he added cheerfully, "How about some ice cream?"

"Great. Ice cream and Armageddon," she said. "Why not?"

"My point exactly. Why not?"

Twenty minutes later, they were eating ice cream and driving across the lush green and gold patchwork of the Jezreel Valley and back into another desolate expanse of bare rock. As the purple-brown mountains beyond the Sea of Galilee came into view, David turned the Land Rover off the main road onto an invisible track along a wadi. After a few bumpy minutes, he pulled to a stop.

"From here we walk."

He took her hand and led her, pulling her in some places, up the banks of the wadi and on from there to the top of a rocky hill. A magnificent valley stretched out before her. Olive groves, gardens, green fields, poppies and scarlet acacias. Willow trees and eucalyptus draped along the banks of the Jordan River, all laid out against a backdrop of jagged mountains and turquoise sky.

"This *Kibbutz* was one of the earliest, formed soon after the first Jewish settlers came from Russia in the early 1900's. It's still fully operational and still run by the old rules, common ownership, communal living down to child-rearing. Beautiful, isn't it?"

"It's stunning."

"I wanted you to see it from here. The mountains there are in Jordan." He pointed at the fringe of peaks on the horizon; his shirtsleeves were rolled up, his arms bronzed by the sun, like the rest of him. "And those are in Syria."

The sun was warm, and the breeze was cool, as he led her to a perch on a pile of giant rocks.

"You don't know this place, do you?" he asked.

"Should I?"

"Funny how we Jews relive our history at every opportunity, every holiday, over and over again, but the things that really shape our own lives, no one speaks about."

"All right. What's so important about this place?"

"This is where it all happened. Your father became the big hero and my father nearly died. Down there in that *Kibbutz*."

"David, I really don't--"

"I wanted you to see it from up here," he said, ignoring her interruption, "so you could get a clearer perspective of what happened that night." He leaned on one denim-clad knee; the other leg dangled over the rock.

"You know, if it hadn't been for your father saving the Old Boy's life, I wouldn't be sitting here. Mother was one of the nurses who took care of him. That's how they met. In fact, knowing my father, that was probably where I was conceived, in his hospital bed."

She laughed. "Knowing your father, you're probably right."

David relaxed back on one elbow beside her. "How much do you know about that battle?"

"I've heard the story enough times, David. My father single-handedly saved a dozen stranded settlers from certain death by the Arabs. It was a great moment. He was a great man. I don't get the point of this."

"Ever wonder where your mother was, where you were, when all this was happening?"

"I assume we were wherever women and children go when their men are out killing each other."

"Ever wonder if it was true? One man against the entire Syrian Army?"

"Actually, yes, I have."

"That's why I brought you here. Before you go off digging up deep dark secrets about your father, I want you to see what he did here. Then, no matter what else you learn about him, you'll at least have this. Okay?"

"Do I have a choice?"

"No. First, you get the history lesson."

"I had a feeling."

"Indulge me. Imagine what it was like in May 1948, forty-two years ago almost exactly. The British were in a desperate situation. Their war debt was immense. The Empire was crumbling before their eyes. They'd just lost India, the Jewel in the Imperial Crown. What Hitler couldn't finish with the Blitz, the war debt surely would.

"Then the UN stabs them in the back by ending their mandate in Palestine. You have to remember, the British promised the Jews a homeland in the Balfour Declaration, but they had also promised the Arabs to keep the Jews out. Which promise do you think they were going to keep? The Jews had been a royal pain in the ass for 20 years and the Arabs had the oil. The British figure, what the hell, if they get out of the way, the Arabs will clear out the Jews, and they can move back in and get on with rebuilding Britain with Arab oil. They've got Lebanon on the north, Syria, Iraq and Jordan; it was Transjordan back then, on the east, and Egypt poised to take the south, most of them puppets of the British government, and all of them with troops already amassed inside Palestine ready to strike.

"So, on May 15th, the Brits pull out and the Arabs attack

on all fronts. And where do they strike? At the heart of the Zionist dream, the *Kibbutzim*."

"Lovely history lesson, David, but I don't see--"

"Shhsh! I'm just getting warmed up. Now, go back about a year, to three pitiful refugees trekking across the Alps into Italy, then crammed on a fishing trawler to Lebanon and finally smuggled across some pretty nasty mountains into Palestine in the dead of night. Your parents ended up here, living on this *Kibbutz*, farming during the day, learning Hebrew at night. It must have been paradise compared to what they'd left behind. The Old Boy, on the other hand, joined the Palmach, a militant offshoot of the *Hagana*, who had been hitting the British every time they took a breath. He just happened to be here visiting when the bombardment started, so he stayed."

Beth, who had been only half listening to his rambling lecture, suddenly sat up straight.

"Bombardment?" Just the sound of the word shook her. She could hear the shells exploding, feel their impact, seeping up from deep in her past.

"Yes. Syrian heavy artillery pounded the settlers, softening their defenses. The Arabs believed the *Kibbutz* had been amassing arms for years. The truth was the *Kibbutz* had almost nothing. They were hammering women and children, old people, the sick, who had nothing but a few rusty rifles, a couple grenades, and one Bren gun. One."

"The explosions. I remember them. I remember the fear. No, not fear, terror in my mother's face. David, I was there."

"Yes. You were there. But you were less than a year old, Beth."

"I don't care. I remember it. No wonder I've been afraid of thunderstorms all my life. It's the same sound. Why would they have infants in the middle of a battle zone?"

"The leaders of the *Kibbutz* couldn't believe they would be attacked. They were farmers, after all. The few newcomers, like your parents, couldn't convince them. These people had been peacefully plowing fields when the Nazis were throwing Jewish babies out of second story hospital windows. They had no idea what a living hell life could become."

David was sitting up now; his legs crossed, looking out at the mountains across from them. He picked up a pebble and tossed it as far as he could, then another. They flew out into oblivion, too small to send even a breath of sound back up to them.

"The Arabs had been robbing and murdering them for years, but I suppose they just accepted that as part of life. By the time the bombardment started, it was too late for a safe evacuation. Our fathers, yours and mine, started organizing the defenses with what little they had to work with. Digging trenches, stringing barbed wire, setting booby traps, whatever they could think of to slow the bastards down. The Syrian tanks were less than 150 yards outside the perimeter fence, sitting like huge black beetles waiting to devour the place. Over there, where the olive trees are now."

He pointed to a peaceful grove of perfectly spaced trees - no black beetles, no tanks, but they were beginning to take shape in Beth's mind's eye. The explosions, the frightening weight of someone's body covering her to protect her from falling debris. She could smell the fear, the panic, all around her. Beth sat on the rock, hugging her knees, the present spread out before her in the neat orderly lines of an olive grove, but she was seeing the past.

"Then word came that Samakh and the two Degonia settlements to the north were under attack, and two nearby settlements had already been overrun by the Syrians. They knew they would be next."

"This time, when your father demanded they evacuate the elderly, the sick and, most of all, the children, everyone agreed. The oldest men drove them out in three trucks in the dead of night with no lights. You and your mother were in one of those trucks."

"I doubt my mother went quietly."

"No, probably not, but for your sake, she went."

"The first attack came before dawn, only a couple hours after the last truck pulled out. The defenders repelled that attack, forcing a retreat, but they were hopelessly outnumbered, running out of ammunition, and the casualties were mounting. The Old Boy was in a trench firing the Bren gun. He'd been hit in the first wave but refused to leave his post. The second attack came very quickly, and this time the tanks began to break through. One of them perched itself squarely on top of one of the trenches and was spraying the entire area with its guns.

"That's when your dad stuffed a grenade down his shirt and grabbed three Molotov cocktails, one in each hand and one under his arm. His rifle slung over his shoulder, he scrambled along the trench, over the bodies of people he had lived with for months, making his way within yards of that tank.

"He lobbed the first bottle, then the second. Both hit, engulfing the tank in flames. The first Syrian climbed out of the turret, firing his pistol as he leaped to the ground. He hit one of the defenders, a sixteen-year-old boy, before your father stopped him and the others.

Then, with his one grenade followed by his last Molotov cocktail, your father knocked the next tank off its tracks. As it ground to a halt, he jumped onto the turret and waited for the Syrians to open the hatch. He struck the first one with the butt of his empty rifle. He yanked the man out, grabbed his handgun and took out the rest of the crew before they knew what hit them. He climbed inside, turned the turret around and fired, blowing the tank behind him to smithereens. Then he turned the machine gun on the Syrians, mowing them down in their tracks, driving them back beyond the perimeter.

"That night, while the Syrian Army regrouped for yet

another assault, those settlers who could still walk carried the ones who couldn't out through an irrigation ditch. Fourteen had survived, including the Old Boy, who came out on your father's back. They walked over five kilometers before they met up with a patrol from Moshe Dayan's forces, who had just pushed the Syrians back at Samakh."

"By the next day, the Syrian Army had fled the entire area, including the captured settlements, which they had gutted, leaving their dead behind to rot in the fields."

David stopped talking and threw another pebble. Beth sat beside him, a thousand thoughts and emotions colliding in her brain and in her heart. The only way she knew she was crying was when a tear hit her hand.

A shadow on the rocks made her look up. A family of vultures was riding the air currents high above them in a spiral, moving higher and higher - the ugliest, most repulsive of birds soaring with a grace and beauty beyond compare.

Her gentle, sweet father, mercilessly destroyed those men, fathers and sons of other women, and she was rejoicing at his courage, rejoicing at their deaths. The brutality of it. The honor, the thrill of it. The sounds of it coming to life in her memory. And the fear. The awful smell of fear.

Beth felt suddenly sick. She held her aching head in her hands until the feeling passed. When she opened her eyes, David was standing, holding his hand out. She took it and he pulled her to her feet.

"Let's go back," he said.

When they reached the car, he opened the glove box and pulled out a polished wooden box and a large white envelope.

"It's all in here." He handed her the envelope. "The eyewitness accounts, all of it." Then he opened the box.

Inside, embedded in deep blue velvet was a medal in the shape of the Star of David.

"Your father wouldn't accept this, but the Old Boy kept it for him anyway. Now, it's yours."

Beth's fingers ran over the Hebrew script engraved on the front. It read, Medal of Valor.

"He wouldn't accept it?"

"No. He said he didn't deserve it. I always thought it was because he was too modest. But maybe there was more to it than that."

"David, he loved Israel. I know he did."

"Yeah, I know."

He put his hand on the ignition then hesitated. "When are you leaving?"

"As soon as I can arrange it."

"I suppose you're still insisting on going to Germany?"

"Yes."

"I wish you would reconsider."

"Why? I'm certainly not going to learn any more here. Maybe if I go back to the beginning, find his family, see where he came from . . . It may be a waste of time, but I've got to try."

"I realize that, but until we find out more about the elusive Mr. Smith and whoever sent him, I don't think it's safe for you to be traipsing around strange countries by yourself, love."

"I'm over forty, David, I don't traipse."

"All right then, if you insist on going, I'll go with you. I know Germany quite well and I speak the language."

"I do not need a nursemaid. And besides, you know you can't leave your father again. Not now. What if something happened while you were gone? You'd never forgive yourself." David opened his mouth to speak, but she stopped him. "No, David. This is not your decision. It's mine. Please, let me make it."

"It's your neck."

"I'm glad you realize that."

"You call me at the first sign of trouble. Do you understand?"

"Yes."

"One more thing. Do you remember your *Krav Maga* training?"

"Of course, I remember. All those summers your dad drilled us repeatedly, how could I forget? Why?"

"When we get back, we'll go over a few moves, just in case."

"Oh, for Christ's sake, David, is that really necessary?"

"Absolutely necessary."

"All right, if you insist. Now, can we go? I have a million things to do before I leave."

He turned the key, rousing the Land Rover back to life.

"First on the list should be having my head examined for not stopping you."

When they got back, David insisted they work out before dinner, before anything. They did it outside in the cool night air, under her uncle's balcony with him yelling instructions at them the entire time.

"Inflict pain!" and "Never stop moving!" were followed by shouts of "Change direction, change direction."

Beth ended up on the mat again and again until her brain and her reflexes started to remember and improve her reaction time. Finally, after kicking David to the mat a half dozen times, she convinced him and her uncle above them on the balcony to call it a night so she could pack.

~~~~

Benny had pretended to be asleep when Beth came into his room early that morning to say goodbye. She had kissed him on the forehead, waited a moment, then left. That was it. He knew he would never see her again.

The nurse, the pretty new one, had seen him watching Beth leave, but she hadn't given him away. This one might last for a while. At least she had the sense to know he still had a mind.

That had been hours ago. He looked at the pocket watch then closed his eyes. Beth would be halfway home by now, and it was just as well. Some things should stay buried. It had been a stupid thing for Aaron to do, leaving those papers where she could find them. Aaron wasn't a stupid man, but that was stupid. For all his plans, she'd found out anyway.

"Well, Old Boy, you certainly managed to muck things up nice and proper."

The sound of David's voice brought Benny's eyes open only a crack--enough to see him standing at the foot of the bed.

"Piss off."

David motioned to the nurse to leave them alone, then crossed to the window and surveyed the desert.

"She could be walking into a trap, but you were too bloody high-minded to stop her. And too bloody stubborn. Do you have any idea of the danger you and your petty little secrets have put her in? What do you think we were doing down there last night, a little light exercise? I was trying to make sure she can protect herself."

"What the hell are you talking about? She's better off back in her classroom where she belongs. She should leave the past to the past."

"Is that what you think she's doing? Then you're a bigger fool than I would have thought. Beth has no intention of going quietly back to Los Angeles. She'll be landing in Munich in another hour."

"Munich?" He pushed himself up. "Why the hell would she go to Munich? She would never go to Germany."

"Think again, Old Boy. She's gone to dig up the truth about her father with the only lead you've left her, those papers. Do you really think whoever tracked Uncle Aaron down after all these years will sit idly by and watch while his daughter--?"

"Jesus Christ! Make sense, boy. What the hell are you talking about?"

"Dear God, you don't mean . . .? I don't believe it. She didn't tell you about the phone call, did she?"

"Phone call? What phone call? God damn it, David!

What the hell are you talking about?"

"You honestly don't know, do you? Well, in that case, Old Boy, it seems I owe you an apology. Maybe together we can figure out how to protect her."

~~~~

Christ! He was a bigger fool than Aaron. He should have stopped her. David should have stopped her. David kept saying they would keep her safe. He'd better be right.

But what the hell did David know about Nazis? A hundred years wouldn't mellow those bastards, not to mention forty-odd. If Beth got in their way, she wouldn't stand a chance.

David had connections and he still had a few of his own. Even in Germany, after all these years. He wasn't dead yet, by God.

"You," he barked, and the pretty nurse promptly put down the novel she was reading.

"Yes, sir? What can I get for you?"

"A telephone. I need a goddamn telephone."

"Yes, sir. I'll check on it right now." She went to the door but hesitated. "Is there anything else, sir?"

"You're goddamned right. I need some privacy. You got that?"

"Of course. I'll be right back."

He watched her backside as she stepped outside. Nice and round. She was smart, and she had a nice ass. She just might last awhile at that.

Half an hour later, he ordered her to get that goddamned telephone out of his room and forced himself out of bed, feeling vital again for the first time in months. The mere mention of his name could still open doors, and that pleased him. He was not going to die yet, by God.

Whoever the hell this was who'd dug up Peter Rolf's name had better not mess with Beth. He'd let her do what she meant to do; he owed her that much.

Munich. That's where it had all started. Started there and damn near ended there.

Suddenly, he laughed out loud. The nurse came to his side, but he waved her away.

"I was just remembering something." And he laughed again.

"It must be very funny," the pretty nurse said, smiling along with him.

"It wasn't at the time, but now that I look back on it, it was a hell of a way to meet a man."

Shadow of the Flag

CHAPTER
EIGHTEEN

Munich, Germany (American Sector) - 1946

Anna lay still, listening to the rhythmic beating of her husband's heart, their naked bodies still entwined. She moved her hand slowly across his chest, fascinated by every inch of his body, by the way it made her feel. At the thought of it, she pressed against him more. In his sleep, he pulled her closer still. Oh, how she loved to be wrapped in his arms.

She had cried out again tonight in her ecstasy. She'd tried not to, but she couldn't help it. He did that to her. She fervently hoped Ursula and her mother didn't think too badly of her, because she was sure they could hear. One day, when she was helping Ursula's mother, the old woman winked at her. Anna had blushed viciously, but inside, it had made her happy. Everything about Peter made her happy.

These last months had been like a dream, even though sometimes her horrible nightmares had returned. Somehow, Peter always helped them dissolve away. But Peter had nightmares of his own and there were times when he became very distant. She knew he was thinking about something dark and fearful, something he still wouldn't talk about. Thankfully, those times were becoming fewer and fewer, as if even that dark, fearful thing would finally leave them.

When Peter found work as a teacher, he had insisted that she quit her job cleaning for the officers, so she could gain back her strength. Since she was at home, she was able to watch after Mrs. Kahler while Ursula was at work. Ursula, in turn, brought them wonderful things like chicken and fresh vegetables. Anna had put on so much weight; she was getting quite plump.

The thought of food reminded her she was hungry and there was still cheese and bread left from their dinner, a dinner that had been interrupted by play that had led them to their bed. But she didn't want to disturb Peter; he was sleeping so peacefully.

Suddenly, Anna heard a noise, a footfall on the staircase outside their flat. In that same instant, Peter came awake, wide-awake. She felt his entire body, every muscle tense as he sat up beside her, listening.

At the first knock on the door, Peter plunged out of bed, motioning for her to stay where she was and to be still.

The knocking came again, exploding thoughts and fears in her mind. The SS pounding on their door in the dead of night, dragging them out of their beds, dragging them into Hell.

Peter grabbed the heavy iron skillet from the stove, and in one move positioned himself by the door, ready to strike.

A man's voice called out, "Anna Tauber. Is Anna Tauber here?"

Anna's breath stopped. Everything around her stopped. In an instant, she was out of the bed, wrapping her dressing gown around her, all with only the slightest awareness of the alarm on her naked husband's face, frying pan still poised to strike. Anna ran to the door and threw it open.

"Benny! Oh, my Benny!" Such joy! She thought she would burst. And as quickly, the pain and anguish of the horror they had endured exploded in her as she clung desperately to him.

"Mama and Papa?" The words left her in a soft sob. There

was no need for him to speak; she felt the truth pass from his broken heart to hers.

She finally released her hold long enough to look at him, to touch his tear-streaked face, trying to convince herself he wasn't an illusion. He was strong and healthy, and so much taller.

"My darling, darling Benny, you found me."

He took a breath and wiped his face with the back of his hand. "A friend saw your notice, and he . . . Anna, you look wonderful."

"Fat as a goose!" She tried to smile, tying the sash of her gown a little tighter.

"No. Beautiful." He beamed at her through the tears that still glistening on his thick black lashes. "How long have you . . . What was that?"

Oh, dear. She had forgotten Peter.

Before she could stop him, Benny stepped inside the flat, grabbed the door and swung it shut, revealing Peter, naked Peter, frying pan dangling at his side.

Benny looked him up and down for one awful moment, contempt growing steadily in his eyes, and then he turned on Anna. He yanked his arm out of her grasp and pushed her away.

"A *shaygets*, a Gentile? You whore yourself to a *shaygets*?"

In a flash, Peter's fist shot out and Benny dropped to the floor.

"If you ever speak to my wife like that again, you little worm, I will rip your tongue out."

Anna fell to her knees and gathered Benny in her arms.

"Peter, how could you?" She touched her hand to the red welt rising on Benny's cheek. A thin line of blood trickled from the corner of his mouth. "He's just a boy."

"I'm not a boy."

"He's not a boy."

Both men muttered the words simultaneously, one

squirming in her arms, the other looming over her like a great marble statue of righteous indignation.

"Oh, for heaven's sake! This is simply too much." She helped Benny off the floor and into a chair. "Peter, do put some clothes on. Have you no modesty?"

The statue grumbled his way across the room and grabbed his trousers from where they had landed when he'd stripped them off so hastily only a few hours before. He shot one last scowl at Benny and turned his back, jerking on one pant leg, then the other.

Anna ignored him and went to the sink to wet a cloth. This was the first time she had ever been angry at Peter, ever. She wrung out the cloth, took a bottle of iodine from the shelf, and rushed back to Benny's side.

"Please, darling," she said, dabbing the cloth at the corner of her Benny's frowning mouth, "don't be angry. Peter is such a good man, even if he is behaving like an ape."

She glanced back at Peter, who had taken to pacing. Barefoot, with no shirt, it was obvious he was doing everything he could to puff out his chest and make the muscles in his arms seem more formidable. He looked very much like a gorilla in a cage.

"Ow!" Benny twisted away from her. "That hurts."

"It's only iodine, darling."

"Well, it hurts. I can't believe you'd actually marry that Nazi swine--"

"Please, Benny. How can you say such a thing? Peter wasn't a Nazi. He was a soldier, yes, but--"

"A fucking Nazi soldier."

"Benny! Your language! Oh, Peter, do sit down. You're only making matters worse."

She watched him stomp over to the bed and perch himself on the edge, his arms defiantly crossed on his bare chest. He was being absolutely impossible. He could at least try to be civil.

"Anna, they gassed us. They put us in ovens, treated us worse than animals. German soldiers did that, fu--, all right, soldiers like him. And you let him put his fucking hands on you! Shit! It fucking disgusts me."

"I've had enough of you, you little worm." Peter started up, but one look from Anna and he sat back down.

"*Putz*," Benny muttered.

"Stop it! I've had enough of both of you. Peter, you sit there and do your best to behave like a civilized human being. And Benjamin, you hold this to your mouth until it stops bleeding, and don't say another word. Not another word. Do you hear? What would Papa say if he heard you?"

His black eyes blinked then narrowed at his adversary across the room, daring him to come closer. She half expected him to stick out his tongue.

"I am going to get dressed and fix something for us to eat--"

"I won't eat with that--"

"You will do as I say, Benjamin. Now, I will leave you alone and I expect you both to behave. Goodness, I feel as if I'm in a nursery with two naughty little boys!"

She picked up her dress from the chair and her underwear, which had fallen to the floor, catching the glare in her Benny's eyes. She ignored him, ignored both of them and walked into the bathroom.

When she stepped out again and saw them still sitting like stones, scowling at each other, it struck her that all the joy she had felt a few moments ago had shriveled up and blown away like dust. She loved these two men so very much, and they hated each other. Benny had every reason to hate the people who did such awful things, every reason. But she loved Peter, loved him above life.

Fighting back the tears, she moved quickly past them to the tiny kitchen. She took out the bread and cheese and started slicing it.

"Look what you've done," Peter said, rushing to her. "You made her cry."

"Me?" Benny looked up. "I--"

"No, Peter, stop." She wiped her face on a towel. "Don't you see? You two are all I have." She put the bread and cheese down on the table. "We should be holding each other, telling each other about all the happy things we almost lost forever, talking about Mama and Papa. Instead, look at us. It's like another war." She knelt by Benny's chair. "Darling, we cannot undo what has happened to us. But I love Peter with all my heart. I never intended to fall in love with a Gentile, but I have. Besides, Peter's not really like other Gentiles." She reached for her husband's hand, smiling up at him. "He already knew most of our prayers, in Hebrew even, and he says them with me. We do our best to keep Kosher. And the priest who married us performed a Jewish ceremony."

"I don't blame you for hating the sight of me," Peter said. "But I was never a party member and I never killed Jews."

"None of you did, did you? Ask any German. No one did anything. No one saw anything. So, what the hell caused millions of Jews to disappear from the face of the earth? Did they just decide to walk into the gas chambers by themselves like lemmings off a fucking cliff?"

"You don't think I feel responsible? *Scheisse!*"

"Enough!" Anna sat down at the table and directed Peter to do the same, but as quickly as Peter sat down, Benny stood up.

"No. I will not share food with him. I love you, Anna, but I won't do it. I'm not a child anymore."

"You're acting like one."

His chin moved a little higher. "I came here to tell you I'm going to Palestine. We Jews are building a homeland there. *Eretz Israel.*"

"Palestine? Oh, Benny, is it really true? You've always dreamed of this."

"How?" Peter asked. "I thought the British were turning

Jews away."

"I have friends who can get me papers. We'll be taking a group out in about a week, and I want Anna to go with me. *Next year, Jerusalem.* Remember, Anna?"

She had heard those words spoken all her life.

"I want to take you, Anna, but I won't take him. I won't take a fucking Nazi into Palestine."

"Oh, Benny, I can't go without my husband. My life is with him."

"Anna, are you certain about this?" Peter took both of her hands and pulled her to her feet. "You put up with so much here, the Frau Grübers, the lot of them. Anna, maybe you should--"

"Silly, of course I'm certain. Besides, Frau Grüber doesn't bother me that much. Truly. Let's not discuss it anymore. I will not leave you, Peter."

"Anna," Benny muttered, "you belong with your own people, not this--"

"No more, Benny, sh-h. Will you really be here for one week? Oh, please say I will see you again before you leave. I could not bear for you to go without seeing you again."

"I'll come back, but not when the *shaygets* is here."

Through her tears, she watched him go, watched the door close behind him.

A moment later, Peter had his boots on and was running out the door after Benny, pulling his shirt on as he went. "I'll be right back," he called over his shoulder.

~~~~

"What do you want, *putz*?"

"Look, you little worm, why don't you shut your filthy mouth long enough to hear what I have to say."

Benny kept walking. The street was dark and deserted; the only sound the hollow echo of their footsteps on the cobblestones.

"The only thing I want to hear out of your fucking mouth is that you'll let Anna go with me."

"I won't stop her."

That brought Benny to a halt. The loathing and suspicion in his face were undeniable even in the dim light of the single working streetlamp.

"Are you saying you want her to go?"

"That's exactly what I'm saying. As long as she's with me, she's not safe, no matter where we are."

"What do you mean, she's not safe?"

"It's a long story. All you need to know is that she won't go anywhere if she thinks she's leaving me behind."

"I told you before; I'm not taking a fucking Nazi into Palestine. I don't care if you've got the entire fucking dregs of the SS after you." Benny started off across the street.

"You'd better goddamn care, you little shit. Because if the fucking SS are after me, you can be damn sure they'll be after her, too, or hadn't you figured that out yet?"

Benny stopped again and scowled back at him, a struggle raging behind those angry black eyes. Peter doubted anything he said could penetrate that hatred, but still, he had to try.

"I'm not asking you to take me, but Anna's got to think I'm going, or she won't leave. She may be soft and gentle, but she wouldn't have survived the camps if she didn't have a will of iron. You of all people should know that."

"Well, she's not stupid either," Benny spat the words out.

"Then we'd better make our story convincing, hadn't we?"

Berlin - 1945

"Gitler kaputt! Krieg aus!"

The cadre had jumped down from a bridge above the Lehrter Bahnhof railway station into an entire platoon of bivouacked Russian infantry.

"Voyna kaputt! The war is over!" the Russians announced cheerfully, over and over again in a mixture of Russian and broken German. The Russians had taken the cadre for simple Volkssturm men, as tired of war as they were.

By a sheer stroke of luck, not ten minutes earlier, the cadre had shed the insignia from their uniforms. Bormann had even dropped the heavy leather coat he was wearing, and when he did, he remembered to grab his satchel back from Erich.

When the Russians offered them cigarettes and invited them closer to the fire, Erich slipped back into the shadows to keep his eye on Bormann, who was slowly edging away from the others. The Reichsleiter suddenly broke into a run with Stumpfegger close on his heels. The rest of the group panicked, scrambling away from the Russians as best they could.

Erich followed Bormann and Stumpfegger back up the slope into a stand of trees near the bridge. The Russians hadn't pursued them, but the two men had stayed hidden anyway. They were watching the bridge. Erich saw Bormann check his watch.

"Herr Reichsleiter," Erich whispered from his hiding place.

"Lieutenant!" Stumpfegger squeaked in relief as Erich showed himself. "The Russians . . .?"

"They aren't interested in us," Erich said, joining them. "Let's move on."

"No, look! They're here!" Bormann cried out and took off running toward the bridge. A Red Cross ambulance pulled to a stop beside the bridge and two men got out, both dressed in the medical uniforms of the Red Cross. They opened the back doors

of the ambulance, lifted out a body and carried it to a spot near the bridge.

When Erich drew closer, he recognized one of the men as SS-Gruppenführer Heinrich Müller, the head of the Gestapo. Then he recognized the corpse.

It was Martin Bormann.

For a moment, Erich thought he was hallucinating. The body looked enough like Bormann to be his twin, with the same short stocky frame, square head and, amazingly, the same scar beside his left eye. A doppelgänger. *He even wore the brown uniform of the Reichsleiter with the insignia removed, exactly like Bormann's.*

The scene was surreal. One man stood above the other, alive, panting from the exertion of the short sprint from the trees. The other lay dead stretched out neatly on his back with his arms straight by his sides, as if he had lain down to take a nap.

The touch was clearly Müller's. Erich had encountered his twisted and brutal sense of humor before.

Müller greeted the real Bormann with a warm handshake. "Has it been difficult, old friend?" he asked.

"You're damn right it's been difficult," Bormann said irritably. "I was nearly blown to bits."

"Well, it's over now, or almost." Müller laughed. "What do you think about my handiwork." He indicated the dead man on the ground. "I chanced upon this good fellow in one of the camps. I have had him pampered ever since. A Jew from a village very near your home, Martin. The resemblance is interesting, is it not? A relative, perhaps?"

Bormann scowled at Müller. "Half the Russian army is roasting potatoes underneath this bridge, and you make jokes? Are you getting me out of here or not?"

"In a moment, Martin, in a moment. First things first."

Müller turned to Stumpfegger. "Ah, Ludwig, how nice to see you again. And Lieutenant Fromer, isn't it?" He smiled at Erich. "I was not expecting you to join us, but of course, it causes us only a small problem."

"Thank you, Herr General," Erich said. "The Führer asked me--"

"No, no. There is no need to explain I assure you.

"Where is mine? Where is my double?" Stumpfegger demanded. "You promised--"

Müller cheerfully slapped the doctor on the back. "Ludwig, my friend, finding a Jew of your extraordinary stature wasn't so easy. We had to make a slight adjustment."

He brought up his hand and flicked what looked to be a pocket lighter directly under the doctor's nose. Instead of a flame, a small puff of gas shot out. Like cutting the strings on a child's puppet, Stumpfegger crumpled to the ground. In no more than three seconds, he was dead.

In a heartbeat, Erich knew he was next. Erich had seen death too many times to mistake its face, but this time, he was incredibly calm.

"Viktor, my friend," Müller said to the other man from the ambulance who pulled a Walther P-38 out of the holster under his arm and pointed it at Erich. "The good Lieutenant seems to have spoiled our plans. I counted on only one more to be rid of." Müller turned the pocket lighter over in his hand and looked at it, smiling. "A clever little invention, is it not? Cyanide, you know. But unfortunately, it holds only one dose." He dropped it into his pocket. "I am afraid all I can offer you is this." He nodded toward the gun in his companion's hand. "My apologies."

The shot hit Erich in the chest, sending him over the embankment. By the time he tumbled to a stop beside the tracks at the bottom, blackness had engulfed him.

~~~~

The ambulance headed out of Berlin with Müller and Bormann in the back. As Bormann changed into civilian clothes, Müller pulled the brown paper packet out of the satchel.

"Ah, so this is it, then?" he said. "A great deal rests on this one piece of cloth." He untied the string and reverently unfolded the paper. "What the hell is this?" he demanded suddenly.

Bormann, who was tying a shoe, looked up. "What are you talking about?"

"This! This!" Müller shook the dusty white cloth under Bormann's nose. "What kind of trick are you trying to pull? This is a tablecloth, a filthy tablecloth. Where is the Blood Flag?"

Bormann could only stare. Involuntarily, he reached out and took the tablecloth from Müller's hands. "I don't understand," he said feebly. "I don't understand."

CHAPTER
NINETEEN

Munich, Germany (American Sector) - 1946

Frau Grüber plunged the scoop into the sack of flour two more times before she was satisfied. She prided herself on knowing exactly how much flour it would take to make her loaves. Fridays she would need 40 loaves, but Tuesdays it would be only 25, Wednesday 27 or perhaps 28.

They were always perfect her loaves, unlike her husband's sloppy, inferior ones. Frau Grüber had no tolerance for the imprecise. None at all.

Her powerful arms worked the ingredients, turning them again and again until the dough began to form.

The years Herr Grüber had been away in the Army were the best years of her life. Finally, she had been in charge with no interference from her careless, sentimental fool of a husband.

Now he was back, making a mess in her kitchen, the clumsy oaf.

She slapped the great ball of dough onto the wooden counter and began to knead it with her strong, capable hands.

To make it worse, her husband acted as if they were rich, giving away bread to whatever beggar happened by.

Frau Grüber had never spoken the words aloud, but she

had thought many times how much better off she would be if her husband had been killed straightaway by that Russian bullet. Then at least he would have been a hero of the Reich.

But no! She punched her fist into the ball of dough. He had to come home with nothing more than a pitiful wound in the leg, just enough to limp about complaining of the pain, while she still had to do all the heavy work.

And of course, he wanted his "rights" as a husband. He was even clumsier in the bed than in the kitchen.

Frau Grüber separated the dough into neat round balls, covered them on the baking trays, and set them aside to rise.

It was then that she realized she was not alone. There was a man watching her from the backdoor of the kitchen. She liked to say that she was afraid of nothing and no one, but the truth was her stomach did a flip at the sight silhouetted in the doorway. The early morning sunlight behind him reflected off the black leather of his coat yet prevented her from seeing his face.

She knew in an instant that Führer or no Führer, this man was Gestapo.

There had been stories about the Allies using these men for their own purposes. Same men, different masters.

She wiped her hands on her apron. "Yes, what do you want?" she demanded. She knew better than to show any sign of weakness to a man like this, and politeness meant weakness to Frau Grüber.

He stepped into the room. Taking his time removing his gloves one finger at a time, he carefully pulled off the first glove, then the second. Neatly nesting them together, he folded them and placed them in his coat pocket. The brim of his hat was tilted down keeping his face in its shadow. Not that she wanted to see his face any clearer. She knew better than to seek familiarity with a man who dressed like that.

He still hadn't spoken.

Frau Grüber felt a cold trickle of sweat follow a slow path down her spine. She could feel herself losing her nerve and with it, her temper. She bit her lip, lest she say something she would regret.

"You are Frau Grüber?" he asked finally. "You are the wife of Grüber the baker?"

"*Ja.* What is it you want with my husband? The bakery is not open at this hour." But then, of course, he knew that already.

"Oh, it is not your husband whom I want, Frau. It is you."

"M-me?" she stammered and damned herself for her weakness. "I have done nothing. We buy nothing on the black market. Nothing at all. I have proof. I have receipts."

"No, Frau Grüber, you mistake me. I am not an official of the Occupation." She could see enough of his mouth to see the corners tick up into something of a smile as he glanced about the kitchen. "It seems we are quite alone, neh?"

Frau Grüber was no fool. "My husband is just above us in our quarters. I need only to call him," she added coolly.

"Then under the circumstances, I believe we can be ourselves." Suddenly, he snapped his arm out in front of him. "Heil Hitler!"

Frau Grüber gave a nervous little laugh and responded with naughty pleasure. "Heil Hitler!"

"I understand you have helped us in the past, and I have come to ask it again, my good woman." He glanced approvingly about her kitchen. "I see that you are a very efficient baker. Everything in its place. Commendable, yes."

"I pride myself in my work, Herr. . .?"

"Names only complicate matters. Don't you agree?"

"As you wish." She sat down on her stool and folded her hands in her lap. "Why have you come to me?"

"Ah, yes, straight to the point. You and I will do well together, I think." He closed the door behind him and turned back to her. "I am here to ask you about one of your customers, Frau Gruber, a young woman. A young Jewish woman. Can you help me?"

Shadow of the Flag

~ 186 ~

CHAPTER
TWENTY

Munich, Germany - 1990

Holocaust survivor once told Beth that when he was on a cruise ship and the passengers were asked to disembark onto German soil, he had calmly stepped off the gangplank, opened his fly and urinated on the ground in front of everyone. He then zipped up his pants, turned around and walked back on board.

Oh, how she wished she could do that. Instead, she stepped off the plane with the biggest, flashiest Star of David she could find at the Tel Aviv airport hanging around her neck. For once in her life, she wanted to proclaim to the world that she was a Jew.

Where were all the blue-eyed blondes? The only family she saw who looked Aryan had Boston accents. Even the logos on tee shirts were American.

Her next myth was blown as her taxi pulled out of the airport, a taxi driven by a Middle Eastern man: graffiti spray-painted on signs, on overpasses, and on the sides of buildings. Much more of this and she'd think she was back in L.A. instead of the middle of Bavaria.

The only comment on her choice of jewelry came from the clerk at her hotel who greeted her with a cheerful "Shalom."

So what? This is a tourist town. Would the rest of the country be so happy to have a Jew in their midst? It didn't matter; she had no intention of taking off her lovely new necklace, at least not yet.

Between sharing the elevator with an African-American couple from St. Louis and passing two Asian maids in the hall, Beth wouldn't have been surprised if the next person she saw was a Hasidic rabbi.

She saw him a few hours later in the *Untergrundbahn* station, the subway station. Black hat, *payot* or side curls, the whole getup, rushing to a train.

Had she really expected goose-stepping blue-eyed blondes parading through scoured streets, shouting "Heil Hitler" as they went? She didn't know what she had expected, but it certainly wasn't this.

The subway brought her to the Marienplatz, the bustling center of old Munich. Busy sidewalk cafes lined a plaza surrounded by high-end boutiques and tourist stops, all very colorful with the golden statue of the Virgin Mary atop a pillar in the center of the plaza.

Beth sat across from the famed Glockenspiel, reading her guidebook and waiting for the promised eleven o'clock hour. *"Central Marienplatz throbs with life . . ."*

It was throbbing now, painfully throbbing with blaring electronic pop music coming from a huge boombox surrounded by a giggling group of German teenagers. Eleven o'clock came and the mechanical dancers began to turn high above her head to their own music, which unfortunately could not overpower the boombox. Even so, it was beautiful and worth seeing, and she'd had enough.

She followed the dotted lines in her guidebook which led her a short distance away and up the steps of the red-roofed, onion-domed cathedral, the *Frauenkirche*.

Beth walked through the doors and nearly collapsed at what she saw. She had stepped straight into her own nightmare. The massive sanctuary was a duplicate of the one in her dream that night in Israel. She dared not move any closer to the altar, afraid there might be a casket there, just as there had been in her dream - afraid of what might be inside.

She picked an empty pew in the back. Most of them were empty, only a few scattered people sat here and there. None of them in Nazi uniforms. None of them shouting, "*Sieg Heil.*"

She knew dreams were messages from your subconscious, so it wasn't too big a leap to know why coffins and Nazis would show up together. The church must have been one she'd seen in the travel guides; and clearly, her subconscious had supplied the details - the statues, the crucifix, the painted blood.

She had planned to ask if the priest who married her parents might still be alive. But as a priest genuflected near the front of the chapel and walked toward the back where she sat, she let him pass by. At that moment, she and her subconscious had truly had enough. She rushed outside.

It took two blocks for her breathing to get back to normal and for her to admit to herself that no matter what, she wasn't ready to give up yet. She pulled out her street map once again determined to find her destination: Edelweiss Strasse, the address on the marriage certificate.

It didn't take long, and it wasn't far away. By the time she found it, she was calmer, calm enough to start questioning everything she remembered about the stupid dream. And calm enough to wonder why she had worked herself up into such a state in the first place.

She was standing on a neat, orderly street of tall, narrow apartment buildings, colorful facades lined up one after the next. Some with window boxes filled with red and pink geraniums and some with crisp white curtains tied back uniformly in every window. Number 30 was halfway down the block, a building with a statue of a saint perched in a niche on the corner.

Her parents had lived here? Right here on this lovely, bright clean street with each building neatly painted, flowers glowing in the sun?

Should she walk in and knock on someone's door or just leave. She'd read in one of the travel guides that Germans do not take kindly to people dropping in unannounced. It upsets their perfectly ordered schedules. Even if they're doing nothing, they've planned to do nothing. Actually, that wasn't so hard to understand. Beth felt like that herself quite often, but she doubted it would be so important to any American that it would end up in a guidebook.

As if some great hand of Fate was directing everything, at that moment the door to Number 30 opened and a fresh-faced young woman emerged. She could have stepped straight off a travel poster or, more likely, out of Beth's clichéd imagination: rosy cheeks, pert little nose, sparkling blue eyes, and of course, shining blond hair. But she was dressed like a typical American: jogging shoes, jeans and a short, light cardigan that hugged her youthful figure and showed off her tiny bare waist. Take her off this Munich street and plunk her down in L.A. and she'd fit right in.

The pretty Aryan poster child smiled sweetly and said, "*Guten tag.*"

"*Guten tag,*" Beth repeated, trying to pretend she'd hadn't been standing there rooted to the pavement. She started moving and kept moving, walking down one street after another until she'd gotten herself quite lost. Twice she made the nearly fatal error of wandering into bike lanes. Apparently, she was expected not only to know the traffic rules, but also to obey them or be run down by speeding cyclists.

More than once she had the feeling she was being watched. She even started to think she was being followed but realized this must be residue of the paranoia that had been gripping her since she got here. She also didn't have to analyze too hard to realize she was both exhausted and starving.

She finally stumbled onto a large open-air market of vegetable stands and small shops displaying their specialties, loaves of fresh bread, honey, and one with slabs of meat and strings of sausages hanging in the window. Beth headed for a crowded outdoor cafe where a buxom blonde waitress in a dirndl dress slammed a dripping mug of beer down in front of her and bullied her into ordering without the slightest idea what she would get. It turned out to be a hot plate of thick brown sausages and sauerkraut.

The disdainful laughter coming from nearby tables made Beth aware that the waitress was the entertainment and no doubt gullible tourists the joke. Whether it was the alcohol or the sausage or the distaste at being made the butt of a German joke, Beth walked away from the table ready to tackle Number 30 Edelweiss Strasse again.

The pretty poster child arrived back in time to find Beth staring at the building again. She greeted Beth in German.

"I'm sorry, I don't speak German," Beth said lamely.

"Oh! You are American? How wonderful! Are you looking for someone? Please can I help you?"

The smile that went with the rest of the perfect German face was irresistible. Beth hated it when people you are totally prepared to hate are unhateable.

"I'm not really looking for anyone. You see, my parents lived in this building when they were first married in 1946. I lost them both recently, and I thought . . ." Beth didn't know what she thought or why she was telling this young woman any of this.

"I, too, have lost my mother. It is very difficult, neh? But, you know, I think this street was mostly rubble then, after the war. Oh, no! That can't be so, because Frau Schreiter was here during the war. I remember her telling me so. Could it be that she knew your parents? Would you like to speak with her?"

Beth's heart jumped a little. "Shouldn't I call first or something?"

"Why? You are already here. Come in. Frau Schreiter loves to have visitors. Her English is not so good as mine, so I will help translate for you."

"I hate to impose on you."

"Not at all. It is so romantic, do you think?" She led Beth up the staircase. "I cannot help but to notice your necklace. Are you Jewish?"

"I am." Beth braced herself for what would follow.

"Really! I will have to tell my friend Dieter." She knocked on the apartment door on the second floor. "He is so much into Jewish everything. Last year, he traveled to Israel to work in a *Kibbutz*. I think his grandfather was a Nazi or something, and I tell Dieter that he does this just to make his parents crazy." She rapped again. "It does, you know. It makes them crazy. They are very, very old fashioned and very, um, Catolic, you say?"

"Yes, Catholic."

"I am myself nothing. At least, not exactly. Oh, dear, Frau Schreiter does not hear so well. I will just peek inside." She opened the door and called, "Frau Schreiter!"

Beth heard a responding, "Ja," followed by the appearance of an elderly woman in a plain beige skirt, crisp pale blue blouse, and sturdy leather shoes. The ensuing conversation was in German. Whatever was said, Frau Schreiter seemed delighted to welcome Beth into her home.

The room was bright and clean, heavy with trinkets and mementos of a lifetime. Crisp crocheted doilies and embroidered cloths covered every polished surface, with potted plants and cut flowers filling every otherwise unoccupied niche and corner.

With introductions all around, English to German, German to English and back again, Beth learned that her young interpreter's name was Karin and that Frau Schreiter had indeed lived in this building during part of the war.

A tall, slim woman in her eighties, Frau Schreiter glowed

with vitality, refusing Karin's offer of help in her small kitchen. She insisted that Beth and Karin both sit on the sofa while she prepared tea and *apfel streusel*, which she served on a handsomely carved tray.

"You will forgive my English. It is so long since I have used it."

"You speak very well, Frau Schreiter. I'm so grateful that you would see me. And this pastry is delicious."

"*Vielen Dank*. It was my mother's . . .*Rezept?*"

"Recipe, yes?" Karin offered. She spoke in German to Frau Schreiter and then said, "I told Frau Schreiter that your mother *und* father were from München. It is so?"

"Yes, they were married here after the war. "They listed this address as their home. That's why Karin found me outside your building. They left here and moved to Israel, or rather it was Palestine then in 1947." She pulled out the photo of her parents that she had carried in her wallet for years and offered it to Frau Schreiter. "This is their wedding photo."

Frau Schreiter looked at the photo. "I am sorry, my eyes they are not so good. I cannot see the faces. Karin, *Bitte bringen Sie meine Lupe aus dem Schlafzimmer?*"

"*Ja,*" Karen said jumping briskly to her feet. "She wants her magnifying glass. It is in the bedroom."

A moment later, the old woman squinted through the magnifying glass while holding the photo under the lamp. She let out a little gasp.

Beth sat forward, hoping.

The old woman looked again, moving the magnifying glass closer then farther away from the photo. Finally, she looked up, shaking her head sadly.

"At first, I thought. . .but, nein, that cannot be." She handed the photo back to Beth. "They were married in 1946, neh?"

"Yes. In April."

"My apologies. I was not here in 1946."

Beth suddenly felt herself sinking. "But you thought you recognized them. Please take another look." The hope she didn't even know was there was suddenly crumbling.

"Your father reminds me very much of my dear brother."

"Your brother?"

"*Ja*, but you see, Erich died at the end of the war, far from here."

"Oh, I see," Beth said. How could she have imagined it would be that easy? The first place you stop and, Voilá! here are your parents. All the secrets are unlocked so you can go home? Beth blushed at the absurdity.

"May I see it, too?" asked Karin. Frau Schreiter passed it over with one last mournful glance.

The old woman began to speak in halting English, with Karin helping her along the way. "When me and my Hans were married, we moved to München. That was 1938, right before the war. This was a tiny apartment then, but it was all we could afford. They have made two flats into one, so to make them bigger, yes?

"When the war started, my brother was called up, but we had hoped my Hans would not have to serve since he was a teacher. But in time they took him, too. He was not a very good soldier, I think, because he was killed in only three months' time. My poor brother survived only to be killed at the very end. He died in a wood where there had been fierce fighting. The Red Cross told me.

"But, you see, after my Hans was killed, my father was taken ill, so I went to care for him until he died. The bombings were very bad in the cities, so I stayed there until the war was over. Then it was not so easy to go from one place to another, so I did not come back for some time. When I did, a flat in my old building was available. It was nice, because here I have my memories of my Hans all around."

The eyes of this old woman shone with the love of a young girl, and Beth felt a pang of envy for that kind of love, faithful and enduring. The kind her parents knew.

When Beth said goodbye, she left Karin the name of her hotel where she could be reached, just in case Frau Schreiter remembered something, anything at all that would help.

That night, she fell asleep curled up like a child with the photo of her dead parents clutched to her.

Shadow of the Flag

CHAPTER
TWENTY-ONE

Munich, Germany (American Sector) - 1946

Anna could barely keep from giggling. No one could touch her happiness today. God had smiled on her at last. He had brought her beautiful Benny back to her. And as if that weren't enough . . .

"Good afternoon, Frau Rolf." Herr Grüber's blue eyes twinkled at her. He had dropped his voice to a whisper. "You are looking especially pretty today, I must say."

Anna knew she was blushing crimson, but she didn't care. She felt pretty. And she didn't mind being told that she was. Not one bit.

"Thank you, Herr Grüber." She lowered her voice, too. "It's a very special day. You see, my dearest friend has finally come home."

"*Wunderbar!*" The baker patted her hand across the counter; then his eyes darted toward the back room. "You must have something special for your celebration," he said in a voice so soft Anna could barely hear him. Then, quickly, he slipped three beautiful meringues into her sack and put a loaf of brown bread in on top. "The usual today, Frau Rolf?" he said at full volume. He winked at Anna.

Instantly, his wife appeared behind him.

"Oh, yes, *danke schön*." Anna took the sack Herr Grüber held out to her. "Good afternoon, Frau Grüber."

"Good afternoon, Frau Rolf." She punctuated her words with the tiniest snort of contempt, while her nasty little eyes darted from her husband to Anna.

Never mind, Anna said to herself, nodding and smiling to the others in line as she left. Never mind any of them. How could they bother her now? Not now. Not ever again.

Such a beautiful, warm autumn day. Her feet barely touched the ground as her mind raced from one happy thought to the next. True, she couldn't think about Mama and Papa, who were not there to share in her joy, but she knew they must be smiling down on her from heaven. She had to believe that. She had to believe that God was real, that heaven was real. Especially now, today, with such news! And wouldn't it be wonderful if Benny came back to see her today of all days!

Oh, yes! Oh, please, yes! Then she could tell them both together, both Peter and Benny. After so much death, she could tell them she was carrying life inside her.

She skipped up the steps, unaware that a man in a black leather trench coat followed her.

~~~~

Benny had told Peter to meet him at the Luitpoldbrücke Bridge at 4:00. It was 4:45 and Peter was tired of waiting.

The famous old landmark that crossed the Isar River had only been partially repaired from the Allied bomb damage. There were no shops, no places to sit, but there were plenty of American soldiers surveying Peter suspiciously. He'd wondered why Benny had picked this place to meet, but that had quickly become obvious - to make him as uncomfortable as possible.

Enough was enough. Peter rammed his hands into his pockets and set off toward home.

"You ought to learn patience, *putz*."

Benny stepped out from behind a tall hedge and fell into step beside Peter. He was shorter than Peter by a few inches with a slender body that looked positively underfed with his too large pants cinched at the waist by a shabby leather belt.

"And you're the one who's going to teach me, my friend?" Peter didn't vary his strides, which were easily longer than Benny's.

"I'm not your friend, you Nazi swine," Benny said, walking even faster, "so don't pull this shit with me."

"It's so comforting to know you're consistent, even if you aren't too bright." Peter stopped abruptly, grabbed Benny by the arm and pulled him up short. "Listen to me very carefully. I'll say this slowly so it has a better chance of sinking in. You and I must at least appear to cooperate, or Anna isn't going to believe any of this for one minute. Do you understand that much?"

Benny jerked his arm free. "I'm here, aren't I? I've got papers for both of you, just like we agreed. Aaron Rosen and his wife Anna, just like you said. She'll see them and she'll believe it. But if you want me to kiss your cheek and welcome you to the family, you are dead wrong."

"Fair enough. And you'll keep your temper under control, right?"

"You hit me, remember?"

"Yeah, I remember. I also remember what you called my wife, so consider yourself fortunate you're still breathing." Peter started walking again. "When do you leave?"

"We start for Italy in three days."

The words slammed into Peter like an iron fist, forcing the air from his lungs and the blood from his veins. He covered the next few blocks in silence only half aware of Benny trotting beside him. He forced one thought to rotate in his mind grinding away at the pain that tore his heart out of his chest. *Anna will be safe. Anna will be safe. At least, Anna will be safe.*

As they approached the last corner before their flat, the sound of his name whispered shook Peter back to awareness of the street around him and Benny beside him. Ursula Kahler stepped out of the shadows, clutching her handbag in her arms, her face pale and frightened.

"There's a man," she whispered frantically. "Oh, Herr Rolf, he's in there with Anna! I heard him."

In that first instant, terror froze Peter's brain into blind stupidity; but a movement beside him broke through the panic. He reached out instinctively and caught Benny by the shirt and dragged him to a stop.

"Get your hands off me, you fucking asshole?" Benny shoved him hard. Peter stumbled backwards, but he didn't let go. Benny came at him again. This time, Peter grabbed him by the collar and pushed him back against the crumbling building.

"We don't know what this is about yet; but whatever it is, if you want to help Anna, you foulmouthed piece of dung, you'd better get control of yourself now and stay calm."

"Calm. . .?" Benny croaked.

Peter tightened his grip at Benny's throat. "Calm," he repeated, staring straight into those fiery black eyes until they started to yield, then he let go. Benny stumbled free, coughing to catch his breath.

Ursula looked horrified. "Herr Rolf, this man? Who is he?"

"I have a fairly good idea. And if I'm right, I know what he wants. Ursula, tell me everything."

"I saw her coming home from the bakery, but she was too far ahead of me to catch her up. If I had done so. . ." She sniffed, as tears streamed down face. She wiped them away quickly with her crumpled handkerchief and took a deep breath. "When she got to our building, I saw him." She gave a little gasp of realization. "Oh! He must have been waiting for her, Herr Rolf. He followed right after her up the stairs.

I was so frightened. He looked like *they* used to look." The next word was almost inaudible. "Gestapo, Herr Rolf. He looked like Gestapo." She stared up at him, her eyes red and swollen, pleading. "But there can be no more Gestapo. How can there be? They're all gone. Please tell me they're gone."

"They're back. Aren't they?" said a voice beside him.

Peter turned to see Benny still rubbing his throat.

"I think one is," Peter said simply. "Did you see his face, Ursula?"

The tears were flowing unabated now. Her face had gone even paler than before. "Not his face. He wore a black leather coat with the brim of his hat was pulled down. I went inside the building after them. I could hear his voice coming from your flat. Then I came outside again to wait for you."

Peter turned to Benny. "If we rush in there without some kind of plan, we will get her killed." Then more to himself than to the others, he said, "I was a damn fool to drag her into this. I knew it was only a matter of time before they tracked me down. She's the bait."

"Oh, yeah, she's the bait all right. And you think you can fucking trade yourself and whatever they want for her. Is that your plan, you fucking idiot! He's not going to let her go when he has you. Why should he? She's nothing to him, less than nothing. She's a Jew. He's using her to get you and he's going to fucking kill the both of you," Benny glanced at Ursula, who was standing wide-eyed with her hands to her mouth. "And he'll probably kill us, too. No witnesses. Well, I'm not waiting for that. I'm going to get Anna if I have to do it with my bare hands." With a look of utter disgust, Benny pushed past Peter and broke into a run toward the flat. Peter let him go. He was going to get himself killed, and Peter would be right behind him.

Before he could move to follow, Ursula opened the handbag she had been clutching so tightly in her arms. "I brought you this." She reached inside and pulled out an ancient revolver. "It was my father's, from the Great War. My mother told me to give it to you. She put bullets in it."

Peter took the revolver, checked the chambers then kissed Ursula on her wet cheek.

"Wait here where you'll be safe. Will you do that?"

She straightened herself up, wiped the tears away again, and said, "Yes, Herr Rolf. I will. Please be careful."

Peter knew with certainty that Benny was right. They were dealing with someone so ruthless and calculating that the chances of any of them walking away from this alive were next to nothing.

He nodded to Ursula and ran after Benny.

Berlin - 1945

Erich came to under the bush that had stopped him from sliding onto the railway tracks. If anyone had seen him while he was unconscious, they would have taken him for one more corpse left to rot where it fell.

He sat up and examined the hole in his tunic, square in the center of his chest. The hole continued through his shirt and the thick folds of the cloth he had buttoned inside. He felt the skin on his chest and was amazed to find he wasn't bleeding. There would be a nasty bruise from the force of the bullet, but there was not so much as a scratch. He must have been unconscious for no more than a few minutes, and from the lump on his head, Erich guessed he'd knocked himself out during his fall.

He pulled the Blood Flag out and started to unfold it. Something rattled inside the folds. More carefully, he opened fold after fold of the flag, until he had reached the center of the bundle.

The orange-gray, smoke-filled skies offered no sun to reflect off the facets that lay before him, but still they glistened. Hundreds of diamonds, large, perfectly cut stones shimmered against the rough stained cloth, and amongst them lay the spent bullet that had been meant to take his life.

Erich sat on the ground still trying to catch his breath, yet as if hypnotized, unable to tear his eyes away from the diamonds and unable to make his mind move. The sound of voices in the distance shook him into action. They were coming towards him.

He folded the flag back onto itself, wrapped it in the paper again and stuffed it back inside his tunic. He stumbled away, sliding behind a concrete piling just as six ragged children came into view.

They were scampering along the railroad tracks and from the looks of it, scavenging for whatever they could find, food, bits of firewood, anything to help them survive. The oldest boy was about nine or ten, the youngest no more than four. They were filthy, scrawny with the hardened look to them Erich had seen take over on the battlefield. The oldest boy had a rifle slung over his shoulder. It was nearly as big as he was.

He'd heard rumors about these children, kellerkinder they were called, orphans of a bombed city left to make their own way or starve to death.

Alone, Erich doubted he could get past the Russians. He'd either be captured or dead by nightfall. These waifs knew the hidden alleys and tunnels of Berlin better than anyone. In a split second, Erich made his choice and stepped out from behind the piling.

"Guten tag," he said, smiling pleasantly.

The boy swung the rifle around like a seasoned soldier and leveled it at Erich. A matted-haired girl not more than eight years old pulled a knife, while the younger ones scattered for cover.

Erich put his hands in the air. "I am unarmed."

"Shoot him," said the girl.

A dirty finger moved menacingly on the trigger.

"Can you help me out of the city?" Erich asked, trying to keep eye contact with the boy.

"Why should we?" the boy asked, the rifle held steady. "You have rations?"

"No, I have nothing. But if I find you food, will you help me?"

"We can find our own food," snapped the girl with the knife. "Shoot him," she said fiercely.

"First, why not see if I can help you. If I don't, then you can shoot me."

In the end, it was what every kid wants that won them over – sweets. He promised them candy, or at least sugar; and it was through a ridiculous stroke of luck that he produced it.

Forget equality of the masses. Apparently, even Soviet

officers managed better rations than their underlings, including better vodka and an occasional sweet, in this case, pilfered German chocolate.

Erich slipped back to the campfire where he'd encountered the Russians earlier, kept out of sight until he spotted an officer and followed him. By evening, Captain Szechskovich was ready for his treat. Unfortunately, by then, Erich had it tucked safely away and was winding his way back to the railroad tracks.

The face of the little girl who had demanded they murder him outright lit up instantly at the sight of chocolate. Erich opened the vodka while the kids divided their bounty evenly between them.

"Well?" he asked as the last bit of brown was licked from the last finger. "Will you help me?"

The two leaders looked at each other and nodded.

"We'll get you to the edge of the city," the oldest boy said.

"Then you are on your own," said the bloodthirsty little girl, rubbing her knife on her filthy shirttail.

"When can we go?" He was tired, and he was hungry, but he didn't want to chance the city any longer than he had to. "Now?"

A flicker of fright showed in the girl's eyes for just one instant, but it was the boy who spoke.

"No. It's too dangerous at night. First light. We'll go then."

"First light it is then."

The children led him to a place they'd roughly concealed behind broken branches, an open drain, large enough for them to walk upright, but he was forced to crouch almost in half. It was dry, certainly, and relatively comfortable for the little mites – blankets twisted into individual nests.

Each child fell into its own space. Erich saw remnants of toys in some, a stuffed bear, a bald broken doll, whatever they could save or scrounge to make their miserable existence bearable.

Erich picked a space against the pipe wall and settled in

for the night. If he thought having an adult present would give some comfort to these waifs, he saw quickly that he was mistaken. They trusted no one, least of all adults. Their eyes stayed focused on him until one by one they lost their battle to remain awake. More than once, he was jolted awake by screams coming from one nightmare or another.

The blood-thirsty girl seemed to have taken on the role of mother to these children, going from one shaking, trembling child to the next, until they had all drifted to sleep again.

Not for the first time in that long day had Erich felt hatred boil up inside him – hatred especially for those who had created this hell where children paid such a terrible price.

~~~~

They were good to their word. The sky, that had never lost its orange hue, was just beginning to lighten when they headed out after a breakfast of stale biscuits.

They led Erich through a maze of storm drains, sewers, cellars, and once or twice, deserted subway tunnels. The fighting was still raging overhead, and occasionally they had to run in the open to reach the next leg of the trip.

Even the smallest urchin knew the route, probably blindfolded. They wouldn't get lost if they were separated. He, on the other hand, was quite lost most of the time. Occasionally, he saw a landmark that was unmistakable, but it wasn't often enough for him to keep track of where they were or where they were going.

Finally, they emerged from yet another sewer at the edge of a wood. Erich could hear guns not far behind them, but he was out of the center of it.

Without a word, the oldest boy started to turn back, his job done, but Erich caught him by the arm. The boy jerked free, glaring. The girl was glaring too, malevolently.

"We gave you what you wanted—"

"No, I just wanted to thank you. Thank you all."

"Oh." He seemed to relax just a bit.

"Look, I want you to have something that might help you. But it carries a certain amount of risk. You'll have to find someone you can trust to help you with it, but it could give you all a chance to survive."

"We're doing all right without your help," the girl said defiantly.

"Yes, I know you are. But the Russians are unpredictable and dangerous. If you must, get yourselves out of the city and go west. Find the Americans or the British – not the French, understand?"

The boy nodded. He seemed to know what Erich was telling him was true enough to pay attention.

"Here." Erich took the boy's dirt-blackened hand and placed one shining diamond in the center of it. "Do you know what this is?"

The diamond's brilliance was instantly reflected in the boy's eyes. He knew. Looking over his shoulder at the small glistening object, the girl's eyes dazzled even more.

"It will give you a chance, all of you. But don't show it to anyone unless you can trust them completely. Do you understand?"

"Yes," the boy said gravely.

Erich left them standing there in the opening of the sewer pipe, all circled around that little piece of hope. One of the little ones waved goodbye to him as he ran into the woods.

Erich didn't wave back.

Shadow of the Flag

CHAPTER
TWENTY-TWO

Munich, Germany - 1990

Beth sat in bed, watching the morning news and nursing a cup of the black coffee room service had brought her. She hadn't had the courage to face a café full of strangers, especially German strangers.

The news anchors could have been interchanged with their counterparts in Los Angeles: a distinguished looking man graying at the temples with a pretty young thing at his side, showing more than enough cleavage. The only difference was the language. Beth could understand enough to figure out that the one topic centermost in their minds and their newscasts was *Deutsche Wiedervereinigung*, German reunification. Would it happen? Wouldn't it happen?

The totally unbigoted part of her applauded it. The daughter of Anna Rosen, Holocaust survivor, found herself horrified at the prospect of a united, affluent and unilaterally powerful Germany.

Just as Beth was about to turn off the television, a video clip came on that needed no translation. The pictures were of a mob of skinheads, their arms outstretched in the Nazi salute, marching down the middle of a street in Leipzig.

Beth suddenly felt quite ill. The paranoia was back with

Shadow of the Flag

a vengeance. She had been insane to let this unreasonable compulsion about her father drive her this far. She was going home on the next plane. To hell with the truth. To hell with all of it. She was getting out of here.

She picked up the phone and dialed David's number. Three of her cousins answered the phone in turn before she heard Rivka's voice.

"David is away for a few days, darling. Shall I have him call you?"

No. She didn't need him to call. She needed him to be there to talk to her NOW!

She punched in a series of numbers from her phone card again. It was nine in the morning. That meant it was midnight in L.A. Surely, Rachel would answer. On the fourth ring, she heard, "Hi, this is Rachel. I'm not here right now. You can leave a message, or if you really, really need to reach me, call my mom. She always knows where I am."

Well, Mom hadn't a clue where she was. And she really, really needed to reach her. Besides, how many times had she told her daughter not to announce to the world that no one was home? It was like handing a key to the nearest stranger and inviting him to rob you blind.

Beth took a chance and dialed her own number. Rachel answered almost immediately.

"Mom! Where are you? Uncle David said you went to Germany. I told him that can't be right! You would never go there, but he said you did. Are you really in Germany?"

"Just for a couple days, honey."

"Wow!" then a large silence.

"I have to take care of some of Papa's business, that's all. Rachel, why are you at my place this late?"

Rachel ignored her question. "Papa had business in Germany? I don't know, Mom, first you run off to Israel on the spur of the moment then you end up in Germany of all places. And then the other night--"

"What about the other night?"

"Nothing, it's nothing. What kind of business did Papa have in Germany, anyway?"

"Rachel, what happened the other night?"

"Oh, it was probably nothing. Really."

"Probably nothing? What happened? Why aren't you at home?"

"It's just that Itz and I have been coming over every day to check on things, and the other night, Itz thought he saw someone sneaking away from the house. I didn't see anything myself, but we checked all the doors and windows. Everything was shut tight, and the alarm hadn't gone off or anything. But Itz still swears there was someone, so he called the police. They said they'd have a patrol go by once in a while. Anyway, we decided it's probably best if we stay here while you're gone. Just in case."

Beth caught the "we" but let it slide. It wasn't as if she didn't know they were sleeping together. What the hell did she expect?

"Are you sure that won't be a problem?"

"It's a long walk to Temple on Shabbat, but the exercise will do us good. Don't worry, Mom. Really."

"No, I won't worry. Thanks, honey. And thank Itzhak for me."

"Sure. But, Mom, you didn't tell me why you had to go to Germany."

"Later, honey. I don't want to use up all my minutes on this phone card. I'll call you again in a couple days, okay?"

"Okay, I guess, but--"

"I love you, honey. Bye."

Beth hung up the phone and walked to the open window. It was raining, a delicate rain that somehow seemed different than at home. Maybe it was the smell; maybe it was the lack of acid in the rain. She held her hand out the window, letting the cool raindrops slide over it.

Everything about this country screamed at her to leave. Maybe she should come to her senses and drop this whole thing. David was right - her father was almost a rabbi. Should she negate the evidence of a lifetime over what? A few ancient papers? A phone call?

She picked up the manila envelope again, pulled out the papers and spread them out on the bed. They were over forty years old. How was she supposed to find out anything from information that old?

Her father looked up at her from a world she knew nothing about. His name, birth date, place of birth.

Feldenhausen, Bavaria. She would start there.

~~~~

Where the city had intimidated Beth, the idea of driving on the Autobahn where there was no real speed limit scared the life out of her. Her alternative was the train. The following morning, she boarded the train.

Beth had traveled in Europe before, but never alone. Brian had been there. Brian had handled all the travel arrangements, the tips, the luggage. Brian had kept her safe. Now, she was on her own, in a country she hated, surrounded by the harsh language and stern manner that awakened some kind of primal fear in her.

With just what she could stuff in her carry-on bag, Beth curled herself up on a seat by the window. She tried to ignore the other passengers and tried not to think about the obsession that had compelled her to be on this train in the first place. The quaint Bavarian countryside sped by, with houses straight out of "Heidi," long white buildings with dark wooden balconies and brightly painted shutters, where the families once lived in one end and the farm animals in the other, and maybe still did. All of this against a growing Alpine backdrop of jagged granite peaks.

The young woman in a business suit, who sat frowning

across from Beth, kept checking her watch. Finally, she spoke to Beth in German.

"I'm sorry," Beth said, "I don't speak German."

The young woman's face lightened immediately.

"You are on holiday?" she asked in English this time.

"Yes. On holiday."

"How nice. I am rushing to a meeting with a very important client and these trains," she looked at her watch again, "they are never on time." Then she laughed. "You would think we Germans could run our trains on time, wouldn't you? I think we only pretend to be efficient, but we really don't do things very well." She laughed again. "You're American? I would love to live there. I've been several times. Do you know San Francisco? I have friends there."

Beth took a deep breath and gave up any hope of remaining invisible.

The girl reminded Beth of Rachel at her best: energetic, opinionated, ready to conquer the world. Rachel before Itzhak.

The girl heard her station announced and got up to leave. When the new passengers filed in and took their seats, Beth found herself a little sad the girl had left. She realized she missed Rachel, really missed her. Maybe she was worrying more than she'd realized about the incident with the house. *Christ! Why don't you give up this ridiculous quest and go home?*

"*Verzeihen Sie! Ist das Ihre Zeitung?*"

Beth looked up to see a man now seated where the young woman had been, and he was obviously expecting an answer.

"I'm sorry, I don't speak German."

"Then I take it you don't read it either." He smiled a disarming smile and held up a newspaper. Graying hair, late forties, early fifties, and quite good looking. "I assume this is not your paper. It was on the empty seat." The accent was West Coast, U.S.A.

"No, it's not mine. You're American?" she said.

"German by birth, actually, but I grew up in the States, went to UCLA before I came back home to live." He leaned forward to shake her hand. "Cristof Neumann." He had amazing blue eyes.

"Beth Samuels. I teach at UCLA."

"A pleasant coincidence." His hand was warm and strong, and he held hers a little too long before releasing it. "What brings you here, Beth Samuels? No one vacations in Germany. It must be business."

"Yes, business." *A moment ago, it was a holiday, now it's business. Good Lord, Beth, make up your mind.* "What about you?"

"I travel abroad most of the time, Italy, Egypt, Middle East and so forth – I'm probably one of the few people you'll see around here with a suntan in the spring," he laughed looking at his own bronzed hand, "so I usually spend my holidays in Germany. I'm taking a few days off to do a little fishing, a little hiking."

Two chattering teenaged girls took the aisle seats next to them, which made further conversation more of a challenge. Cristof smiled and shrugged, opened the newspaper, clearly not wanting to compete with the increased noise level.

A few miles later, Beth heard her station announced and stood up to gather her things.

"This is my stop," she said, when he closed the paper. "It was nice meeting you."

"Another coincidence, I'm off here as well. I'm booked at a local inn." He followed her down the aisle with his own suitcase and a long narrow bag, which he tucked under his arm. "Perhaps we will see one another in the village."

"Yes, perhaps."

"Auf weidersein."

He hesitated for a moment on the platform; she assumed waiting for some encouragement from her to linger. She smiled politely and said goodbye. He walked away with the other passengers from the train, and Beth was left alone on the platform.

In that moment, Beth knew for certain she should get back on the train and go home, and that she was surely mad not to do just that. But just as she felt her sanity start to return, the train began to move away leaving her there. She let out a deep sigh, not knowing if it came from resolve or submission to what lay ahead. Either way, she was committed now, whether she liked it or not. She picked up her suitcase and walked into the station.

The rosy-cheeked stationmaster cheerfully suggested an inn a short distance away. It was up a steep grade, too steep to drag her overstuffed bag, so he telephoned a local taxi to drive her there.

His kindness was enough to convince Beth to ask his help. "I have recently learned that my father was born in this village. Could you tell me how I can find out if his family is still here?"

"*Ja*? This is so? So wonderful for you to visit your father's birthplace! People do not do such things anymore. Vat is the family name?"

"Rolf," she said with a sense of revulsion that surprised her.

"This is not common this name." He rubbed his chin vigorously. "For a Christian name, *ja*, but as a family name, not so. No, I do not know of it. You are sure it is from this village?"

Beth felt her stomach take a lurch. Was this the end then?

Her disappointment must have been only too obvious, because the station master said encouragingly, "Oh, do not give up, please. I am a newcomer to the village. Only 25 years have I lived here. You must speak to the priest. He will know. There will be records in the *Kirche*, *ja*."

The village set in the steep Alpine foothills was a travel

poster come to life, down to the *lederhosen* and *dirndls* worn by the people in the streets. The taxi went around so many turns; Beth knew the driver was running up the fare. She would have had the taxi wait to be sure there was a room available, but that would have run the fare up even higher. Apparently, they got enough tourists to think nothing of cheating them.

Inside, she was greeted by a middle-aged woman in a *dirndl* who beamed and gushed with delight as she assured Beth they had just the room for her, one with a scenic view of the village and the mountains.

An hour later, after a stroll through the village, Beth was being dressed down in the middle of the lobby by the same woman for the horrific sin of breaking the rule against bringing food back to her room from the village market. Beth had made the mistake of asking for a knife to cut the bread and cheese and a corkscrew for the wine.

"Is there a problem?" Cristof Neumann stood in the doorway. "Perhaps I can help." He spoke soothingly to the innkeeper in German, which didn't seem to help much. The woman railed on and on, clearly expounding on Beth's criminal nature. The word "American" was used enough for Beth to know it wasn't a compliment.

Cristof tut-tutted, shook his head in shock and embarrassment, and otherwise groveled until the woman had vented enough of her spleen to stop threatening to toss Beth out on the street. Then he turned to Beth with a wink.

"Frau Huber accepts your apology and says she understands that things are different in America."

"Thank her for her understanding," Beth said through gritted teeth. "She is most kind." When Cristof had translated this, Frau Huber bowed stiffly and walked away, giving an audible snort as she turned the corner into the back office.

Cristof laughed. "Now that we've narrowly averted an

international incident, why don't you invite me to share your bread and cheese, and I will take you out for the best apple strudel in this part of Bavaria."

"You've certainly earned it. I think she was about to call the police if you hadn't walked in. Are you staying here?"

"I am indeed. This is our third coincidence today, but this one doesn't count for much. This is a very small hamlet with only two inns to speak of. Now, where is this feast I've just defended?"

They had reached her door when Beth remembered she still didn't have a wine opener.

"Never fear, my dear lady, I come equipped with a Swiss Army knife." He promptly produced said implement and unfolded the corkscrew. "The only army in the world prepared for either a French Merlot or a German Riesling. Which is it, madam?"

"Why, German Riesling, of course!"

They settled down on the balcony with their makeshift meal, the Swiss Army knife providing all the implements needed to cut the cheese and serve the wine in the two glasses from the bathroom.

"I'm sorry. I just can't believe that woman's reaction. What is it with Germans and their rules?"

"It's so deeply ingrained we don't even realize how ridiculous we must appear to the rest of the world. We justify it by deluding ourselves that we have a nice clean orderly society – which simply isn't true, of course."

"On the plane, I had the gall to ask for a glass of water to take a pill. The flight attendant snapped, 'You vill sit down now und vait for the beverage service!'"

"And did you sit?"

"Like a meek little puppy in training. For an American, all this obedience goes against the grain. How can you stand it?"

"Ah, but even though I grew up in the States, my parents were very, very Old World. So, when I returned to Germany,

I fell right into step. But at least I have the perspective to see what caricatures of ourselves we are."

"I am quite sure Americans are the same to other countries."

They chatted, sipped wine and laughed, as they watched the village sink into darkness with the mountain backdrop changing through hues of pink and deepening purples, until at last, they too disappeared. There were few lights from the village to reflect against the black velvet sky, leaving it twinkling with a blanket of diamonds.

By the time the wine was gone, the temperature had dropped substantially, driving them back indoors. Before Beth even fully realized how awkward she felt to be alone in a hotel room with a handsome man, Cristof bid her goodnight with the excuse of an early morning date with a fishing pole.

He hadn't even tried to kiss her on the cheek. And when Beth gazed at her reflection in the bathroom mirror with her toothbrush protruding from her mouth, she had to admit she was disappointed.

Oh, for heaven's sake, you're a woman of a certain age, and what self-respecting man of a similar age would think twice about you as an object of lust? Give it up, girl. No one above Rachel's age would interest a man like Cristof.

~~~~

People in Europe walk a lot. People in Bavaria walk excessively--uphill, downhill, like mountain goats, and they have the sturdy bodies to prove it. Beth, on the other hand, was a Southern California girl and even though UCLA boasted some mild slopes, it had nothing to compare to downtown Feldenhausen.

She left the hotel after a breakfast of the same dark seedy bread she'd had at her hotel in Munich, topped with hazelnut butter and fresh jam and a soft-boiled egg with a deep orange yoke, but she passed on the assortment of sliced cheeses and cold cuts that seemed to be a staple at German breakfasts. For the entire time, Frau Huber scowled at her from the dining room door, watching her every move as if she expected Beth to stuff her pockets full of rolls and silverware to sneak back to her room.

Beth bid her a cheery *"Guten Morgen"* as she grabbed her jacket and left. She received a grunt in response.

By the time she reached the church that rose up in the center of town, Beth wasn't exactly gasping, but she was certainly vowing to exercise more when she got home. She gave the massive doors to the chapel a pull. They didn't budge. The place was locked up tight. Apparently, it was against the rules to pray on Wednesday mornings.

She stood there contemplating what to do next when she noticed a tall gate at the side of the old stone structure. She wondered how many rules she was breaking when she opened the latch and stepped into a walled cemetery.

A stone path lined the neat rows of rectangular plots. Unlike American cemeteries where few graves are ever decorated with artificial flowers or a wilted potted plant, most of these plots were beautifully tended and each one was unique. Some had little picket fences, some bordered with flowers or shrubs, and some were covered with massive, engraved stones.

A round peasant woman followed Beth into the cemetery and started tending one of the graves, pulling weeds from the pretty little garden that covered the space. Beth could hear the woman carrying on what seemed to be a one-way conversation with the occupant of the grave. The woman paid no attention to Beth at all as she walked along the path to the wall that surrounded the cemetery.

The wall surprised her. It was not merely a wall but was a series of memorial plaques to the fallen soldiers of the village. Along with the names and dates, many of the plaques had pictures, engraved cameos of proud young men in uniform.

Some were from the First World War, some from the Second. And some had one from each - father and son, she wondered - both having given their lives for the Fatherland. Beth assumed from the fact that there were no graves nearby, the bodies of these young men had never come home.

There were so many of them. Two wars had cost this one small village dearly. The pictures showed young enlisted men, some still teenagers by the dates, with the invincibility of youth captured in the moment. Alongside were older men, some with the Nazi eagle and skull and crossbones of the SS on their caps, arrogant pride frozen on their faces. Had they lived long enough for that pride to have been shattered? Beth certainly hoped so.

Beth could feel sympathy for the children caught up in a war waged by adults and for their families. But for the SS, who had also left behind loved ones, Beth felt only contempt.

She moved on down the wall, studying the faces, reading their names and the dates, finding herself wondering what had happened to the Jews of this village. Where were their graves? She wondered if some of these young men had terrorized them long before marching off to war.

She had almost walked away, having seen enough to know why she didn't like this place, when she saw the name Rolf. Peter Rolf. She already knew the birth date; it matched the paper in her purse. The plaque read: *26 März 1921 - Unbekannt 1945*.

Then suddenly, a cold wave of nausea moved up her body. Her knees turned to rubber. She sank down onto the path - not with grace, but clumsily with a thud. She didn't feel it. She didn't feel anything except the growing need to vomit.

The face of a young man looked back at her from the cameo in the center of the plaque, a young man who had not come home. Round, fair, with a short round nose and a jolly mouth that looked quick to laugh - a happy face, the face of someone who clearly enjoyed life and would even find a way to enjoy the army.

It was the face of a total stranger. Not one feature was familiar. Not one.

She dug in her purse for the picture that had propelled her on this journey. There was no mistake. Even as she sat there on the gravel path, trying to imagine how the years of deprivation and misery of war would change that jolly young soldier, she knew it could not make the two faces match.

She was looking at Peter Rolf on the wall - Peter Rolf who was missed and mourned by his family; Peter Rolf who had not come home. This was not the Peter Rolf who had been de-nazified and married to Anna Tauber. This was not her father.

What twisted nightmare had she dropped into?

Shadow of the Flag

Germany - 1945

Erich had no idea how long he'd been walking since he'd left Berlin. However long it had been, two days, three days, he was too exhausted to care. He only knew he had to keep moving – away from his own and into the arms of the enemy. Being taken prisoner by the Americans or the British was his best hope to survive. It was sheer instinct – instinct to survive - that pushed him forward step by painful, impossible step.

He was somewhere deep in a forest that had been decimated by recent fighting - fierce fighting by the looks of it. Everywhere on the forest floor, bodies or parts of bodies were still half-buried in the mud. No one had bothered to collect them and probably never would.

The only way he knew he was still moving in the general direction of the Allied lines was because of the orange glow of the setting sun that shone now through the ever-present smoky haze. Mortar rounds exploded relentlessly beyond his line of sight. Sporadic rifle fire sounded closer, but so far, he had seen no other living being. Clearly, even animals knew better than to be in this place of death.

Earlier he had come across the shell of an abandoned farmhouse but had been reluctant to get too close. He knew from long experience that any structure no matter how badly damaged could be booby-trapped by either side. Explosives didn't discriminate as to which side you were on. Dead was dead.

He had slept a few hours in the trunk of a hollow tree. It was there that he'd left the bundle, marked it in his mind as best he could, and walked away.

Mile after torturous mile, he forced his legs to move forward, forced his body to remain upright when all it wanted was to lie down and stay there forever. Erich trod on, his eyes almost closed.

His foot struck something buried on the forest floor that sent him sprawling. Slowly, as he pushed his aching body up to his knees, he saw one blank gray eye staring up at him. The other half of the forehead had been blown away, leaving only that single eye and the gaping mouth frozen in a silent cry.

Erich heaved in a ragged breath and stared at the dead man. Every horror he had seen, every nightmare he had experienced in the last years of his life lay there before him in that mangled face. A life like his own, blown apart, left to rot in a nameless place, no one even knowing he was dead.

Did this man have a family? Did he have a wife, a mother, children? Would they wait in vain to hear what had happened to their son, their father, their lover?

Erich had passed hundreds like him in this nightmare forest. He'd turned away from them, marching on toward his own life. But this screaming dead man staring up at him grabbed at his insides and tore them open.

Suddenly, Erich was clawing frantically at the man's pockets. He had to know who this faceless soldier was. He found the papers tucked in the inside pocket of the tunic.

Erich looked through them, turning them over in his hands as if that would somehow bring meaning to what he was doing, staring at them without really seeing them. Why did he even care? He had seen hundreds, no, thousands of dead men before.

Then Erich realized they were born the same year. They were same height. They had the same color eyes. The same color hair.

The idea came to him so fast there was no time to question it. He fished in his pockets for his own papers, shoved them into the dead man's tunic, and started to run. He ran until he could no longer breathe, never looking back.

~~~~

The explosion came close; the impact blew him into the air. He landed face down on the forest floor, too dazed to move, *every inch of his body screaming the fact that death had not yet come. Then slowly through the pounding in his ears, he made out voices.*

He lay motionless, feigning death, as the voices drew nearer. They were not speaking German or Russian or French. Yes, it was English. He had no idea whether they were British or American, but it was definitely English.

If he moved too quickly, they might shoot. If he didn't move quickly enough, they might be gone, and he would miss the chance.

"Help," he cried in English. "Help me! Please."

At the sound of approaching steps, he turned his head and looked up into the barrel of a rifle.

"Sarge!" called the freckled-faced boy above him. "I got a live one here."

They marched him with his hands on top of his head to a holding area about a mile away where a dozen other German soldiers squatted in the dirt, waiting to be processed. The sergeant shoved him down beside them.

When his turn finally came, he stood in front of a makeshift desk in a large green tent. Behind it, the lieutenant didn't look up from the pile of papers spread in front of him.

"Name?" the American asked in German.

"Rolf," he answered. "Sergeant Peter Rolf."

Shadow of the Flag

CHAPTER
TWENTY-THREE

Feldenhausen, Germany – 1990

"*Bist du krank?*"

A hand touched Beth gently on her shoulder. It took a moment for her to focus on the concerned face of the elderly woman who bent over her.

"I'm sorry, I don't speak German," Beth finally managed to say.

"Are you ill, young woman?" the woman asked in perfect, softly accented English.

Had she fainted? She wasn't even sure. She only knew that she'd had enough. She was going home. She pushed herself to her feet.

The woman steadied her as she began to sway.

"Please, why don't you come inside and rest a few minutes."

Beth blinked at the church behind them.

"It's locked," she said lamely.

"Then perhaps we can sit over here. They seem to have provided a lovely bench for us."

Beth followed her obediently to the stone bench and sat.

"Are you feeling better?" the woman said after a moment, her hand still resting on Beth's shoulder.

"Yes, thank you."

"Very good. When you are up to it, we will walk to the village for a cup of tea. That will be nice, yes?"

Beth tried to focus on the woman beside her. Elderly, slender and very stylish, perhaps in her seventies, perhaps older – her hair and makeup perfectly done, her clothing simple and elegant, obviously expensive. She clearly was not the same robust peasant woman who had been muttering over one of the graves earlier. That woman was nowhere in sight. Remnants of the weeds she had pulled lay strewn untidily over the grave she'd been tending.

Since Beth had seen no one come or go, she wondered just how long she had been sitting there in a daze. There was nothing more Beth wanted to see in this graveyard. That was certain.

"A cup of tea sounds perfect," Beth said as she got to her feet. "I'm fine now. Thank you so much for helping me."

"Do not mention it. I know a very nice tea shop not far from here. I will enjoy the company."

"You are so kind. I'm Beth, by the way."

"My name is Gertrude Bräden, but I insist you call me Gertrude."

~~~~

Elsa followed behind just far enough, so she could still see her mistress walking ahead of her with that *Amis* woman. Elsa did not like Americans. No, not at all. And she didn't see why her mistress had to bother with this one.

Elsa had been told to go back to the car and wait with the chauffeur, but she didn't want to be that far from her mistress. She certainly didn't want to wait alone with that foul man. He was not at all loyal and, as Elsa had learned, could be very cruel.

She shuffled along behind the two women, keeping out of sight as best she could. She would be punished for disobeying, but she didn't care, not this time. Elsa knew she was not very bright, but she had a very bad feeling about this young woman. She dared not speak out about her feeling. Her mistress would not allow that, but it was there all the same. Something bad was going to happen. Something very bad. Elsa knew it deep in her heart, and she was very frightened.

When the women ahead of her turned right down a small lane, Elsa held back, afraid to be seen so close to the tea shop. She heard the chime on the door as it opened.

They would sit and enjoy cakes and tea. Elsa would stand in the darkest shadow she could find and wait.

~~~~

Beth took a seat opposite Gertrude Bräden at a little round table next to the window. The tea shop was nicely decorated with blue ruffled curtains, lace tablecloths on tables set with matching rose-patterned tea service and linen napkins.

"Good, we are in time for high tea. I recall they serve a very adequate English tea here."

"That would be fine," Beth said automatically, not really caring what she had and doubting she could eat anything at all. She felt more than a little sick to her stomach.

The older woman ordered in German and then turned back to Beth.

"Now, my dear child, do you want to share with me what has upset you so badly? Something surely did. You dropped like a stone to the hard ground. It gave me quite a fright."

"I'm sorry. I didn't mean--"

"Of course, you didn't. You had a terrible shock." A thin, veined hand reached across the table and patted Beth's cold hand. "Something you weren't expecting?"

"Yes, you could say that." Beth stared at the roses painted on the gold-trimmed plate in front of her.

"I couldn't help noticing that the memorial plaque was for a young soldier. Was he a relative?"

Beth looked up.

"No, he was a stranger to me." As was my father for that matter, she added to herself, a total stranger.

"But you are troubled about this stranger, this Peter Rolf." Gertrude had obviously registered Beth's reaction to the sound of that name because she quickly added, "As a family name, it has rather an unusual spelling, you see. Ah, here we are."

The waitress had arrived with a cart loaded with a cozy-covered tea pot and a three-tiered tray of finger sandwiches and miniature pastries. She made a little ceremony of pouring their tea with Gertrude translating as she explained each of the sandwiches and pastries.

"Lovely. *Danke*," Gertrude said and added a few more words in German, dismissing the woman. "We will serve ourselves, shall we? More privacy this way. Ah, these fruit tarts are lovely. You must try one."

Beth felt grateful for the interruption and for the switch in topic to a discussion of the food, as far away from Peter Rolf as they could get. But after a few moments, Gertrude brought the subject back.

"These plaques that you saw serve instead of proper graves. You see, after the war, many families here never knew what had happened to their loved ones."

"Yes, I thought that must be the case."

"Of course, one as young as you would have no idea how difficult it was. The war left so many questions unanswered." Gertrude sipped her tea then dabbed delicately at the corners of her mouth. Somehow, the look in Gertrude's eyes didn't quite match the smile on her face.

"I imagine so," Beth said, suddenly feeling a twinge of discomfort. For a fleeting second, Beth caught a flash of an almost primordial hunger, like watching a tiger sensing the vulnerability of a prey.

"Surely," Gertrude went on quite pleasantly, as if she were discussing nothing more disconcerting than the weather, "they would want to know if their loved one had died in honor on the battlefield, or had they been taken away by the Russians simply to disappear forever in some horrible Gulag."

Gertrude refilled her own teacup then Beth's, the heavy tea pot trembling a little in one long thin hand while a manicured fingertip steadied the lid.

"Excellent tea, isn't it?" she asked as she set the tea pot down and selected three lumps of sugar with ornate silver tongs.

"Yes, it's--" Beth began, but Gertrude continued as if she hadn't noticed.

"There were so many who were accused of horrible things." She slowly stirred the sugar in her cup, all the while smiling across the table at Beth, who was growing more and more uncomfortable. "Of course, false or true, all Germans were considered guilty by the world, even the most innocent."

It was as if a switch had been thrown inside Beth's head. Her growing sense of discomfort was real and palpable now.

"My mother was in Auschwitz," she said bluntly, not caring one bit if she was being rude to this stranger who had so kindly come to her rescue.

But if Beth's intention was to shock the woman, to force her off the subject, it failed miserably. The tiger-eyes narrowed but the smile did not flicker; if anything, it became indulgent, as if she were dealing with a small child of less than normal intelligence.

"That is unfortunate, my dear child, but you must agree that the British and the Americans imprisoned their own citizens in internment camps as well. Surely, you understand it is common practice when a country is at war."

Stunned by the sheer insensitivity of the statement, Beth started to sputter a response, but Gertrude held up her hand and continued on forcefully, her tiger's eyes now burning. "And after the war, our fathers and our sons were treated no better than common criminals at their hands."

"Excuse me? If you are talking about the trials, those men were criminals. They were murderers, brutal hideous murderers."

"Criminals? Murderers?" All pretense of calm had left the woman now, her eyes on fire with obsessive passion. "When all they were doing was serving their country as they had been ordered?" She was shaking, her pale face crimson with rage. "My father was not a murderer!"

Nothing in Beth's life had prepared her for this twisted surreal moment. She didn't know what to do or what to say, and she was too stunned and too frightened to move. As much as she wanted to run away from this elegant woman across the table who had suddenly sprouted fangs, some force compelled her to stay put.

"Your father?" she asked as calmly as she could.

Then, as if a sinister spell had magically been broken, those fierce eyes began to brim with tears. In one heartbeat, Gertrude Bräden's gaze shifted to the window, as if transporting her to another place, another time.

"Yes," she gasped in barely a whisper. "My dear Papa was persecuted for nothing worse than trying to preserve the human race for the future – a man who had never hurt anyone, not a living soul. He was hunted down, dragged before a tribunal and hanged. Hanged!" Abruptly, her voice became shrill. "Innocent!" she cried, turning every head in the shop. "You speak of murderers. What about my Papa who was murdered by our conquerors? Murdered!"

And just as suddenly, she crumpled into sobs.

Beth knew every eye in the café was on them now. She was afraid to move, not knowing whether to comfort the sobbing woman in front of her or to turn tail and run out the door.

At that moment, Gertrude's perfectly coifed head shot up, her long fingers shot out and grabbed Beth's wrist. The red, tear-filled eyes held Beth motionless.

"He was not a criminal," Gertrude said in a strangled voice.

"Look," Beth twisted her arm free and stood up, "I appreciate what you did to help me, but I really do have to go now."

"No! You must not!"

"I'm happy to pay. Please, I insist." Beth motioned to the stunned waitress, who had obviously been hanging on every word of the intense little drama playing out at her table. "This should cover the bill." She laid fifty Deutsche Marks on the table – more than enough, surely.

"No!" Gertrude pleaded again. "You must not leave yet."

Beth looked at her with a mixture of pity and abhorrence. "Goodbye," she said and walked out of the café.

The fresh air felt like an elixir to the toxic scene she had just experienced. After one deep breath, she started walking as fast as she could go, but she only made it a few steps when Gertrude's fingers dug into her arm.

"You must not go. If you don't give it to me, they will take it. Do you understand? And they will not serve you cakes and tea. They will take it by force. They will kill you if they must, kill those you love. It is nothing to them."

Suddenly, as if she had appeared from nowhere, another woman ran up and grabbed Gertrude by the shoulders. Beth recognized her instantly. She was the peasant woman who had been in the cemetery tending the grave.

"*Frau Bräden, bitte, bitte, komm mit mir,*" she said gently.

Gertrude's fingers loosened their grip on Beth's arm. She seemed to sag into the arms of the round woman, who turned her away and slowly led her down the narrow lane.

"Wait!" Beth cried after them. "What do you mean, they will kill me? Who? What is this about? I don't understand."

Ignoring the urgings of the other woman, Gertrude stopped and turned back to face Beth.

"The *Blutfahne*, Frau Samuels. Bring it to me before it is too late."

"What? What are you talking about?"

The woman shrugged slowly, almost agonizingly, and allowed herself to be guided away.

"Stop, please. Who are you? How do you know my last name?"

The peasant woman glanced back with a look of such pure hatred that Beth stopped where she was.

"This is insane," Beth said as she watched them walk away from her. "Insane." There was no other word for it.

~~~~

In the shadows of a recessed doorway nearby, a man with the remnants of a deep tan watched the retreating figures of Gertrude Bräden and her faithful servant Elsa. Then he turned his attention to the other woman still watching them from the middle of the narrow street. He stepped deeper into the shadows, and for the briefest moment when she passed by, a satisfied grin stole across his face.

CHAPTER
TWENTY-FOUR

Munich, Germany (American Sector) - 1946

eter took the stairs three at a time, each step a prayer in sound reverberating up to the open door of their flat, climaxing in the crack of a gunshot and Benny flying out through the doorway. He landed on the floor with a thud as the door swung shut again.

"He missed me!" Benny looked up triumphantly to see the revolver in Peter's hand and grinned. He scrambled back to his feet.

"Idiot," Peter said. He slid the gun into the pocket of his jacket and rested his finger on the trigger. "Stay back or you'll get us all killed."

"He's straight ahead. He's holding her in front of him."

Peter nodded then yelled as loud as he could, "Anna, go limp! Faint!" as he kicked the door open again.

He had no idea if his wife's startled, frightened eyes that greeted him meant that she understood and would respond, but he had no choice but to trust that she did.

He knew the face of the man twisting her arm behind her back and holding a very familiar Walther P-38 aimed at her head.

"The next one's for her," the man said coldly.

"Not if you want what you came for. Because if you harm her, you'll have to kill me and you'll never find it. Viktor? That's what *he* called you isn't it? Viktor. The last time he told you to kill me. I don't think your boss will be happy with you if you come back empty handed. Do you?"

The man called Viktor laughed and twisted Anna's arm tighter, making her cry out in pain.

"If you hurt her, I'll tear your throat out. I promise you that."

"I think not, *schwein*. Give it to me now or she'll scream a lot louder."

"You let her go first then I'll give it to you. It's right over here." Peter stepped toward the tall cylindrical masonry heater in the corner of the room.

"No, it's not. I looked."

"Then you didn't look hard enough. Let her go and I'll show you where it is. Hurt her, and you'll never find it.

"Oh, I know many ways to make you tell me, *saumensch*, none of them pleasant. Shall I start by showing you what I'll do with this *schmutzig Jüdin*."

Suddenly, Benny leaped through the door like a panther. Startled, Viktor fired at Benny. At that same instant, Anna sagged in the man's arms, pulling him off balance. The shot Peter fired ripped through the pocket of his jacket and into Viktor's forehead, jerking his head back against the window, shattering the glass. His body slid to the floor as Peter gathered Anna into his arms.

"You did what I said," he whimpered into her hair. "You understood."

"Of course," she said softly, "I trust you."

~~~~

"You are the luckiest man I have ever met and the stupidest." Peter paced back and forth in the small space left to him.

"I gave you the chance you needed, didn't I?" Benny sat propped against the wall with both Anna and Ursula fluttering over the flesh wound in his arm.

"What do we do now?" Anna asked, looking up from the makeshift bandage that had already turned pink.

"Benny will take you to Palestine," Peter said, still pacing. He dared not look at Anna. "I'll deal with this and then I'll join you."

"I will not leave without you, Peter, and that's final."

"Anna, don't you see? I can't put you in this kind of danger ever, ever again. They're after me, and it's not going to stop here. If they tracked me to Munich, they can track me anywhere."

She stood up and went to him, taking hold of his hand.

"Peter, I'm pregnant."

What little air that remained in his lungs left him in a long low moan. And then he broke down and cried. Sliding to the floor, he clung to her, burying his face in her sweet body and sobbed.

"We all go," Benny said. "I have the papers. I've already made the arrangements."

Peter knew the arrangements. Benny was right. They would trick Anna like they had planned.

"Yes, my darling husband, we will all go together."

He couldn't look up. He couldn't bear to see her face. His hand was on her belly, on his child. The child he would never see. The child he must keep safe.

"That's right." Benny's hand clasped his shoulder. "We *all* go together."

Peter looked up then. Benny and Anna helped him to his feet. He felt like an ancient old man, a rag, as he watched them embrace and Benny pat Anna's belly.

"A baby? A baby!" Benny grabbed her around the waist and twirled her around. Then he hugged Peter, almost knocking him over in his unmitigated glee.

Peter had to sit down while everyone hugged everyone, while the body of Viktor lay ignored at their feet where it had fallen. Someone even kicked the foot aside as if it were nothing at all.

Then, as quickly as it started, the joy jolted back to reality when Ursula asked, "Won't we have to tell the police about the body?"

"No!" Ursula's mother stood in the doorway, leaning on her cane. "No police, Ursula. And Herr Rolf must get his wife away from here as quickly as they can."

Benny looked at him. "She's right. We can't wait for the others?"

"Peter, what about Father Josef?" Anna said. "He will help us, surely."

"Yes, my dears," the old woman said smiling, "Father Josef is the man to ask. He will help you while my daughter and I will deal with *that*." She gave a repulsive nod at the body.

"But Mother, how?"

"It's all right, Frau Kahler," Peter said. "We will find a place for it tonight."

The old woman thought this over for a moment. "Yes, I think a block or two over. They will not start clearing there for some time. By then, who will care?"

"By then," said Anna, "we will have our baby and will be happy and safe in Palestine on a *Kibbutz*!"

~~~~

Herr Grüber had noticed the change in his wife almost as soon as he entered the bakery that morning, and it made him nervous. For years after their marriage, he had lived in hope that underneath her stern exterior might lay a heart of gold. But that hope had long since dissolved.

If he was truly honest, which he seldom ever allowed himself to be, he had been happiest when he was in the Army. Even with all the miseries that had brought to him, arriving home after he had been wounded was one of the most miserable moments of his life.

Away from Frau Grüber, he could be a happy, cheerful, man. He could be brave and strong and proud. With her, he was primarily sad. He tried to sneak a little kindness here and there when she wasn't looking. But instead of making him feel better, each time he succeeded made him feel more of a failure. Why should a man have to sneak to do a small thing that might bring a smile to someone else?

The answer was simple enough: his wife.

Today, as he stood at the counter handing out loaves of bread and taking money and ration stamps, he could hear her humming to herself, and it troubled him very much.

She was pleased with herself. Why?

He had always thought the only thing that would make his wife happy enough to hum a tune would have been his own demise. But since he was still very much alive, at least for the moment, something else must have delighted her. Whatever it was, it couldn't be good.

The day wore on and the humming grew louder. No, thought Herr Grüber as he nodded and smiled at his customers, this was not good at all.

Perhaps she had a new customer, someone who would pay the highest price. Yes, that must be it. But what customer? He knew of no one.

At the end of the day, after he had closed and locked the shop, he went to the back room and watched her setting up for the next day, watched her moving from one chore to the next in perfect order, happier than he had seen her in years. And then he knew.

"What have you done?"

She ignored him.

He moved across the room and grabbed both of her beefy arms in his hands.

"I asked you a question. What have you done?"

Her eyes were wide. She was afraid. He had never seen her afraid before, certainly never of him. Her fear stoked his anger, his disgust of her.

"I—I--," she stammered.

"You what?" he demanded.

She pulled out of his grasp. "I did my duty," she said defiantly and turned back to her chores.

He grabbed her again and made her face him. "Your duty to what?"

"To the Führer, of course!" she said, her chin thrust out, her head held high.

"You're insane!" He let go of her, as if he had been burned, as if the touch of her had scalded his hands. "Your precious Führer is dead."

"No, he's not!" she screamed. "That's a lie!" She pushed him away. Her eyes were wild now, her face red. "He's in hiding. I know it. He's coming back. The Party is coming back. The Gestapo is already here. They came yesterday. And I gave them what they wanted. I was valuable to them before, and they remembered me!"

Herr Grüber stumbled backwards. He couldn't believe what he was hearing. It made him sick to his stomach. So sick he thought he would retch then and there.

She was evil. She was mad. She'd always been mad. Always been evil and he'd simply refused to admit it to himself. Now, as if someone had pulled a ripcord and released him, he felt freedom rise in him in an intoxicating rush. He yanked his apron off over his head and threw it to the ground.

There was nothing to be said to her. Nothing.

Without a word, he left her there with her ovens, with her loaves of bread and walked back into the shop, while she screamed after him. He opened the till, stuffed everything in his pockets, unlocked the door and slammed out the shop.

He had no idea where he would go, no idea at all; but he knew he would be fine wherever he went as long as it was far away from her.

He would be fine, he thought to himself, quite happily. He would be just fine.

Shadow of the Flag

CHAPTER
TWENTY-FIVE

Feldenhausen, Germany – 1990

Beth raced down the hill, hoping it was the right direction to take her back to her hotel. She didn't care what she had to do to get out of this hideous place; she was going to do it. These people were crazy. Certifiable. And so was she for pursuing this stupid quest of hers. She had been threatened. Her family had been threatened.

She gasped, stopped in her tracks with both hands clasped to her mouth. Rachel. The prowler. Was it all connected? What the hell was going on?

She could see the train station two blocks ahead and broke into a run.

Five minutes later she was still trying to catch her breath, sitting on a bench in front of the station, waiting for a taxi. She'd missed the train to Munich and there wasn't another one until noon tomorrow. Her choice was to wait until then or rent a car and chance driving back on the Autobahn. She opted for the train – again. She would use the time to book her flight. One more day and she'd be on a plane back home. Enough. The quest was over. And she'd failed.

"Well, hello. We meet again."

Beth looked up into the smiling blue eyes of Cristof, who

had magically appeared beside the bench.

"May I join you?" he asked and sat without waiting for her reply. "You look all done in. Is everything okay? Why don't you let me buy you dinner, then we'll take you home and tuck you up for the night."

"To be honest, I don't think I could eat anything. And I've got a taxi coming."

"Good." He smiled again, rubbing her cold fingers between his warm hands. "Then I'll just do the tucking part."

She was all done in. Completely so. And the kindness in his voice and eyes made that fact physically apparent. She felt crushed, flattened, as if she'd been rolled over by a giant asphalt compactor. Perhaps because she was so exhausted, perhaps because she was tired mulling it all over endlessly in her head, suddenly she blurted out the whole sordid incident to this handsome stranger.

"My God, Beth, how horrible for you. I'd like to say she's an aberration, but the chances are there are plenty from that generation who are still trying to justify what happened. I'm really sorry you had to run into one of them like that."

The taxi pulled up in front of them before she could answer him, and she didn't want to talk further until they were alone. At the inn, Cristof accompanied her to her room, and they picked up where they left off.

"That's just it. I don't think it was an accident that she was there. I think she had followed me. She knew my name. I hadn't told her, but she knew it."

"Wow! Beth, at this point, maybe I should be asking if you're in any kind of trouble and can I help?"

That did it. She didn't know if it was the look in those crystal blue eyes or the kindness of his touch, but she spilled it all. Every detail, including the phone call that brought on her father's death, his dying words, the papers, Peter Rolf's plaque in the cemetery, even Jacob Smith, and finally the disconcerting encounter with Gertrude Bräden.

"She kept demanding that I give her something, and I have no idea what she was talking about. What the hell is a 'blootfawn' anyway?"

"No clue." He shrugged then thought for a moment. "Well, maybe a small clue. In German, *Blut* is blood and *fahne* is flag, so I suppose together it must mean blood flag. The old woman was going on about her Nazi father, right? Maybe it's some Nazi relic. Look, you look exhausted. Tomorrow, we'll see what we can find out."

"I'm taking the train back to Munich tomorrow. I forgot to tell you."

"I'm sorry to hear that. What time's your train?" he asked.

"Noon."

"I'd like to see you again before you leave, if that's all right."

"I'd like that."

"Okay, I'll take you to the station. Get some sleep."

"Thank you, Cristof."

"*Gute Nacht*, my dear Beth." He kissed her on the forehead and left.

The first thing she did was call home to make sure Rachel and Darling Itzhak were all right. They were. She tried to reach David again; but, no, he was still away. So much for call me if you need me, cousin dear.

Beth woke before six in the morning, and there wasn't much point in trying to go back to sleep. The train would take her back to Munich in a few hours anyway.

She set about making her travel arrangements, all the while ignoring the questions rolling around in her mind, "What on earth is this blood flag? And who would want it so badly that they would threaten to kill me and my family to get it?"

With her desire to get out of Feldenhausen, out of Germany driving her, she threw everything into her carry-on and headed downstairs to settle her bill and have breakfast. She wasn't hungry, but it would waste time. Then she would head to the train station to wait there.

No, she remembered, she had to wait for Cristof. He said he would take her to the station, and that thought cheered her up a little.

Frau Huber eyed her suspiciously as she crossed the lobby after she'd paid her bill. It was perfectly clear she would not be missed. Ignoring the woman's stares, Beth settled herself down in the adjacent dining room and did her best to eat. Her first bite made her realize she hadn't eaten anything last night.

Frau Huber continued to glare at her when Cristof arrived with a taxi to pick her up. He was so cheerful, and she was so happy to be leaving this place that for the few brief moments it took to deposit her at the train station, Beth didn't give the mysterious flag another thought. In fact, it wasn't until her train was nearing Munich and she was having a pleasant conversation with two "middle-aged" British ladies, who were clearly having great fun practicing their German that she remembered at all. So, she asked.

"Blood Flag? Absolutely, we know what that is!" said the taller, more robust of the two. "Don't we, Lucy?" She elbowed her friend jovially.

"Absolutely, Annabelle," agreed Lucy, who was round and cherry-cheeked. "Hitler's Blood Flag."

"We grew up in the Blitz, you know," said Annabelle. "You couldn't help but know everything there was to know about the Nazis and good old Adolf since they were bombing the hell out of us most of the time."

"I taught History at a girls' school until I retired last year," said Lucy, "and I liked to make those little monsters learn as much about the War as I could squeeze into their tiny little depraved brains. I always thought it should be a question on the A-Levels, but one has so little control of these things."

"I'll wager Lucy can quote it to you right out of the textbook!" Annabelle beamed, showing a good bit of gum above her somewhat yellowed teeth.

"I'd love to hear it," Beth said. In fact, she needed to hear it – desperately needed to hear it.

"Well, if you insist." Lucy grinned, wiggled and sat up very straight in her seat. "The *Blutfahne*, or Blood Flag, was a Nazi swastika flag used in the Beer Hall Putsch in Munich, Germany 1923. It became one of the most revered symbols of the Nazi Party."

Lucy's friend, Annabelle, reached across the space between them and smacked Beth on the knee. "You see, that's where old Adolf got sent to prison and wrote *Mein Kampf* - the start of the whole thing."

"As I was saying," Lucy continued, "the flag was covered in the blood of Hitler's comrades who were killed and because of that it was treated as a holy relic."

"Honestly, can you imagine?" Annabelle said cheerfully. "A bunch of nutters!"

"What happened to it?" Beth asked, trying her best to stay calm.

"No one knows," said Lucy. "It disappeared at the end of the war. I don't think anyone ever found it."

"Just as well," said her friend. "You wouldn't want those skinheads you see nowadays getting their grubby hands on something like that! They'd try to start the whole thing up again."

"Not much chance of that," said Lucy. "It's probably a souvenir in some soldier's attic, long forgotten."

"That's my guess," said Annabelle. "Oh, look! Here's Munich just up ahead. I can't wait to try their strudel. We're trying every recipe we can find all over Germany to see who has the best!"

Shadow of the Flag

CHAPTER
TWENTY-SIX

Munich, Germany – 1990

"Shalom, Mrs. Samuels. We are so happy to have you back with us." The same cheerful young woman who had welcomed her to her hotel the first time greeted her again at the front desk with the same very wide grin. "Your room has been waiting for you. Everything is as you left it. And you have a letter."

"A letter?"

"Yes, a young woman delivered it yesterday. She asked that we hold it for you."

"Thank you. That's very kind." The sweet Alpine face of Karin flashed into her memory as soon as she opened the envelope and read the name at the bottom of the note.

"*Dear Beth, Frau Schreiter would like to see you if you have the time. Would you be so kind as to telephone me at this number if you can come? Thank you very much. Your friend, Karin*"

With all that had gone on since she'd left this hotel only two days ago, this felt sane and even encouraging. Sanity – what a lovely thought. Were there really sane people left in the world? Beth had begun to doubt it. "Is there a phone I can use for a local call?" she asked.

"Of course, you may use the one in the sitting area. Just explain to our operator."

When Karin answered, she sounded beside herself with excitement. Since Beth had planned to fly out the following day, of course it would be perfectly wonderful for her to visit this evening. Did Beth remember the way? Yes, how lovely. They would see her soon. And please bring the photo you showed us before.

Beth hung up, went to her room to freshen up, and headed out of the hotel for the walk along the River to the *Untergrundbahn*. A few minutes later she looked up at the street sign to Edelweiss Strasse and took a deep breath.

Karin came bounding out of the building. She had clearly been watching from the window.

"I am so happy you could come. Frau Schreiter is so happy, too." She linked arms with Beth as they made their way back to the flat where Frau Schreiter stood in the open doorway.

Every space in the neat living room was covered. Old photographs were spread out on the coffee table, on the polished sideboard, and even on the floor.

"You can see we've been very busy. Frau Schreiter thought about everything you said and about the photograph you showed us, and she realized that because her eyesight is so bad and so much time has passed, she thought it might be good to try again. And she brought out all her old photographs. Some of them go back way before the War. They're amazing. We've been having such a good time looking at them."

"Please have a seat, Mrs. Samuels," said Frau Schreiter.

"And I will make us tea," chirped Karin, bustling out of the room.

"When you were here before," Frau Schreiter spoke hesitantly, making sure she had each English word correct before she said it, "I thought the photograph you showed me looked familiar, but you see, my eyesight. . ."

Beth pulled the photo out of her purse and handed it to her.

"Thank you. And would you be so kind as to look at these?" She gave Beth a small stack of photos along with her magnifying glass. "Some are of my brother Erich before the War. Here to please look closer?"

Just to be polite, Beth took the glass from her and looked at a few of the photos. She recognized Frau Schreiter, some clearly from before she was married as she was quite young, a schoolgirl. In some a boy stood with her, her brother no doubt, younger than his sister, shorter in some, growing taller in each successive shot.

"And here is one of him in his uniform after he was conscripted."

Beth's hands had begun trembling before she touched the photo, almost as soon as she realized whose face she was looking at after the third or fourth picture. The trembling of her hands merely reflected the violent quaking that had gripped her brain.

"Erich?" she said, looking up into the tear-brimmed eyes of the old woman beside her.

"Yes, that's my dear brother Erich, Erich Fromer."

Karin came back with the tea tray. "When you left, we looked through all of these, but we couldn't be sure until we looked again at your photo, too." She shoved some of the pictures aside and nestled the tea tray on the table in front of them. "It's him, isn't it?" She knelt beside Frau Schreiter and took her hand.

All the breath went out of Beth as she sank back against the cushions. All the breath and all the strength.

"Oh, my dear!" Frau Schreiter patted Beth's hand. "Pour the tea, Karin. *Du armes Kind*. You poor child. This has been a shock. To me, as well." She took the cup of tea and wrapped it in Beth's hands. "I had been told my brother was killed. They said they had found all his papers with his body. But there must have been a mistake."

As the old woman spoke, the mystery of her father's life

became suddenly so clear to Beth. This dear woman was her aunt. Her father was Erich Fromer growing up in these photos. A German soldier conscripted, forced into an army to fight a war he couldn't possibly have believed in. What fearful awful things had happened to make him shed that identity and don another? To become Peter Rolf, to marry his beloved Anna and then again to remake himself into Aaron Rosen, the hero of Israel, the devout Jew, the man she loved so deeply even their differences had not shaken it?

Beth set her cup back on the tray and wrapped her arms around Frau Schreiter. Karin's arms engulfed them both as all three women cried.

Hours later Beth waved goodbye to the two women who had so lovingly welcomed her into their lives and wound her way back to the *Untergrundbahn*. The sky was black with only the sliver of a moon and twinkling stars to give it light. There was a glow and sound coming from the Marianplatz, but she skirted by it and headed directly to the subway.

Beth wasn't the least bit tired after her long day that started in utter confusion and ended with the beginnings of closure. The air was crisp. The night suited her. So many questions had been answered, and so many more remained. But at least it wasn't still the void of not knowing.

Her aunt – she'd never had a real aunt before – Rivka would never have been comfortable with that title – her Aunt Elisabeth told her stories about her father as a boy, as a young man, as the best friend of a neighbor boy named Aaron Rosen – a Jew. It was clear that her father had loved him like a brother – no wonder he had chosen that name. Had the real Aaron died in the camps? The answer was most likely yes; so few Jews had survived. Had he taken that name to let his beloved friend live on? Or was she just romanticizing a choice of convenience. She would never know for sure. And if Uncle Benny knew the answer, he probably wouldn't tell her.

But even her frustration with the stubborn old so-and-so couldn't shake away the lightness she felt as she trotted down the steps to the train. The station was almost deserted. Only a few gaggles of young people, arms around each other, heads together, wrapped in the selfishness of youth, waited on the platforms for their trains home after an evening of frolic.

She felt invisible to them. An adult. An alien. It made her think of Rachel and that thought made her miss her like mad.

Her train whooshed to a stop in front of her. The doors slid open and she stepped in along with a few others farther ahead in the cars. Then just as the doors started to close, two men stepped in and sat together directly across from her.

One man, well-dressed and the taller of the two, ignored her. The other sat watching her with a look on his face she could only describe as a leer. He was not an attractive man in any sense of the word, pink and flabby with a shaved head, but clearly taken with his own charm and virility. Her first inclination was to move to another seat. There were plenty. Then her feminist sensibilities took over and she refused to be unseated by his behavior. Besides, she only had two more stops and she would be out of the train and into her hotel. Safe and sound.

A few minutes later, she climbed the last steps to the street, realizing she was more tired than she'd thought. She'd sleep well tonight, especially after the walk to her hotel. It wasn't far, just a few blocks along the Isar River and across the bridge, and it was well lit - for the most part.

The sound of footsteps behind her coming closer at first made her politely step to the side to let whoever was in such a hurry pass her by, but they didn't. She glanced quickly over her shoulder and saw the same two men from the train closing in behind her. She knew at once this was no coincidence and she felt a rush of fear.

As if a recording clicked on in her head with her uncle's

voice narrating, every self-defense technique she had ever been taught flashed in her mind. First, she knew she had to take control of the situation, put distance between her and her attackers. She could see lights and a few people exiting a museum not far ahead. She picked up her pace. So, did the men behind her.

She broke into a run, screaming for help, but a powerful arm grabbed her around the waist, lifting her into the air.

Inflict pain! her uncle's voice in her head shouted as a hand clamped over her mouth. She bit down hard on the flesh of the man's palm.

"*Scheisse!*" the man growled.

She grabbed two fingers of the hand that held her and jerked them back. His grip gave way just enough for her left foot to find the ground. She stomped her right foot down on his instep.

"*Schlampe!*" he yelped. She swiveled further out of his grasp and rammed her elbow into his diaphragm. The blow knocked the wind out of him; she slammed her fist back into his nose.

He stumbled back away from her as she ran screaming.

She raced toward the lights, toward the people in the street. Suddenly, she heard a yell and a loud splash from the river. She looked back and saw a bald head bob to the surface spewing water. The second man, the taller one from the train, rushed to the water's edge to help his friend, then just as quickly changed his mind and broke into a run back toward the subway. The man in the river swam away as fast as he could.

Surrounded by the people in front of the museum, Beth caught her breath. They offered to call the police, but she said no. The last thing she wanted was to deal with the German police.

Two young men, both about the same age as Rachel, using their best English, told her in turns they had seen a stranger coming out of nowhere and heaving her attacker into the river. This shadowy stranger just as quickly disappeared into the night. They insisted on escorting her to the hotel all the while telling her repeatedly in their stumbling English, then in German to each other, all about her rescuer and how impressed they were with her fighting skills. She knew this by the way they kept reenacting the moves she'd used on her attacker. She had to admit, she had impressed even herself.

At the entrance to her hotel, she shook their hands and kissed each of them on their cheeks, but they still refused to leave her until they had delivered her safely to the hotel clerk. It was then that she saw David.

~~~~

"It was you, wasn't it? Wasn't it, David? You threw that man in the river."

"You could have been killed! You do know that, don't you? Good God, Beth." David paced back and forth in the hotel room.

"How long have you been following me?"

"These people aren't mucking about, Beth."

"How long, David?"

He pushed both hands through his hair at once and turned to pace back the other way.

"Since you got here, if you must know. I had some friends keeping an eye on you – for your own safety – until I could get here. And what the hell were you thinking walking around Munich in the dark by yourself? Jesus! Of course, I was following you. Have you no sense at all?"

She watched him about-face again but said nothing. He was right, of course, and she was grateful. But how does someone go from a simple, quiet, dull life to THIS in an instant? Danger at every turn?

She was too tired to think about it. The adrenaline that had charged through Beth a few minutes ago on the street was gone. She flopped back on the bed feeling like a wet dishrag. Besides, David was making her dizzy. She closed her eyes.

She felt him sit down beside her on the bed.

"We have to sort out what we're up against," he said, flopping back beside her. "And if they are starting to get this aggressive, we need to do it quickly."

"Your father probably knows most of it," she said, "if not all." She opened her eyes and stared at the ceiling.

"He says he's told me everything he knows." David rolled over, propping himself up on one elbow to look down at her. "But the truth is your dad was better at keeping his secrets than my dad will ever hope to be. The Old Boy knew he had taken something; and whatever it was, it was dangerous."

He brushed a strand of hair from her face.

"And he knew someone was pretty motivated to get it back. Failing that, he thinks they would have been quite happy having your father's head on a pike as a substitute. The good news, at the very least, is that the Old Boy has managed to figure out *who* was after it."

"Who?" Beth sat up.

"Heinrich Müller, head of the Gestapo."

"Oh, God, David. Even I know who Heinrich Müller was."

"I'm not so sure 'was' is the accurate tense."

"How can that be true? Dad was a young man at the end of the War. Müller was running things. He'd have to be--"

"Ninety, yeah, but that doesn't mean there aren't others, younger ones who are very much alive who'd gladly carry on his vendettas."

Beth just stared at him with her mouth quite literally hanging open. Then she took in a deep breath.

"I think I know what they're after."

Now she was the one pacing. She told him everything she had found out about who her father really was, about Elisabeth and Gertrude Bräden and the whole outrageous incident. And about the Blood Flag.

"Jesus!" David exclaimed, "No wonder they want it back. Do you realize how valuable that would be in the wrong hands?"

"But even if my father stole it from these people, why would he have kept it all these years? Why not destroy it if he didn't want them to have it?"

"Insurance?" said David.

"Well, that really worked well, didn't it?"

"Yeah, well."

"Wait a minute. Those two men tonight, did they really think I'd be walking around with something like that in my purse?"

"No, but they probably figured you have it stashed somewhere or at least you know where it is. And Beth, these men know how to get answers."

"So, their plan was to kidnap and torture me until I told them? But why wait until now? Why didn't they go after it when my father was alive? He'd be the one to tell them where he'd hidden it, if he'd hidden it? Not me."

"That's just it," David said. "They did."

"Of course, how stupid of me. The phone call. That's why it upset him so badly. Oh my God, David! The prowler. Rachel said they saw a prowler around the house. My flight isn't until 8:00 tomorrow morning and then there's another, what? 16 hours until I get home? I have to call her right now. I don't want her in the house if they come back."

She picked up the phone, punched in the numbers from her phone card and waited.

"Hello, this is the Samuels residence."

"Oh, God," she looked at David in panic, "it's the answering machine."

*"No one is available. . .*Mom?" Rachel's voice cut in, "is that you?"

"Oh, thank God. Rachel, I need you to listen to me very carefully and do exactly what I say. Promise me?"

"Sure, Mom, but you're scaring me. What's wrong? What's going on?"

"I'll explain it all later, honey. Please just listen. I want you to go back to your apartment right now. Do you understand?"

"Sure, but why?"

"And Rachel, I want you to go into my bedroom, look in the back of the second drawer of my dresser. Do it right now. I'll wait."

"Okay?" Beth heard the receiver being laid on the table and Rachel answering Itzhak's questions in the background. A moment later, she was back on the line. "Mom, I don't understand."

"I know you don't, but you must trust me on this, honey. That's Papa's gun. You need to load it. The bullets are right there. Load it and take it with you."

Beth could hear Rachel shushing Itzhak. "Okay. I'm loading it right now."

"Now, get your things and leave immediately. Promise me?"

"I promise, Mom. We'll leave right now."

"Keep that gun with you, Rachel. Papa left it to us for a reason."

"I'm really scared, Mom. When are you coming home?"

"I'm leaving in the morning. I couldn't get a non-stop flight, but I'll be there soon. I'll call you and let you know when to expect me. I love you, honey."

"I love you, too, Mom."

Beth looked up at David through her tears. He gathered her into his arms.

"You're not going anywhere alone," he said.

She pushed herself out of his cocoon. "David, how can you go with me? Even if you did, you'd have to go back in a couple days.

"Beth--"

She put two fingers up to his mouth. "I have people there

who can watch over me, too. Rachel and Darling Itzhak and Brian, if I have to. If anything happens, I'll call you. Okay?"

"Oh, for Christ's sake, Beth. How well did that work for you this time?"

Vienna, Austria - 1990

The flames consumed the body of the round woman who lay face down on the floor of the kitchen first then snaked up the staircase of the stately townhouse, following the track the gasoline had laid for them to the grand bedroom on the second floor.

There they danced over and around the body of another woman before igniting the bedclothes and the draperies. The windows exploded from the heat as the structure began to collapse in upon itself.

Sirens and screams of neighbors filled the night air as a tall man moved away satisfied.

He had another place to be now.

Shadow of the Flag

CHAPTER
TWENTY-SEVEN

Geneva, Switzerland – 1990

"Show them in."

He sat back with his veined, spotted hands laced across his chest, waiting for them, counting his breaths, marking his time.

Otto walked in first with Werner letting him take the lead. Always so brave, our Werner. A burgundy bruise was shaping nicely on the side of Otto's face and an adhesive stretched across the bridge of his nose. Werner showed no scars of battle, but he wouldn't, of course.

They snapped to attention in front of his desk; their arms shot out in salute, allowing him to see the bandage on Otto's hand.

"Heil Hitler!" they barked in unison.

He waited, letting them stand there like two rather pathetic statues with their arms jutting out, waiting for his response so they could relax. He drew this part out enjoying every second of their discomfort.

"At ease," he said finally, but did not return their salutes.

"Uncle," said Werner nervously, hopefully. "You wanted to see us?"

"No!" he blared back, pushing himself to his feet and

walking around his desk to stand in their faces. "I did NOT want to see you. I want to see the *Blutfahne*, you stupid imbeciles! I gave you one task, to follow Johann's instructions, and you--"

"We tried," whimpered Otto.

"DO NOT INTERRUPT ME AGAIN!"

He felt his strength falter. Feeling suddenly weak, he caught the edge of the desk. He wasn't finished yet.

"You tried to capture the woman and failed? She wasn't even a young woman, as I understand it. Still she got away."

Werner started to speak, to defend himself, but at one sharp glance, the old man made him think better of it, and his mouth clamped shut.

"Did you think she would carry the *Blutfahne* with her? Bring it to Germany to make it easy for you? She may not even know where it is! *Dummköpfe*, both of you. Idiots!"

His right leg suddenly went numb. He moved back around to his chair using the desk for support. Werner moved to help him, but he waved him back. He flopped into the chair to catch his breath then looked back at them, one then the other.

"I warned you. I WARNED YOU!"

"But, Uncle, please let us help you," Werner came around the desk beside him.

"Get away!" he shouted, but the words didn't sound right. He reached his arm out to buzz his secretary, but it didn't follow his command.

He saw a blurred Otto rush out of the room as Werner bent over him, loosening his collar.

He wanted them punished, but they swam away from him into a haze.

CHAPTER
TWENTY-EIGHT

Los Angeles, California – 1990

The plane was late leaving Munich and even later arriving in Los Angeles after another delay in New York. Beth had not slept at all and her chest felt as if someone had put a large heavy stone where her heart should have been. She'd felt this kind of extreme exhaustion once before in her life when she and Brian had been delayed in a snow storm in some God-awful airport when they were too young and too broke to afford a motel room.

As hard as she tried, she couldn't think, couldn't reason, and quite honestly couldn't care less about anything but a bed. And on top of that she didn't know if she would ever feel safe again after these last few days. At least she knew that Rachel was safe and not a sitting duck if someone came back to the house. She doubted Darling Itzhak would have offered her much protection.

She saw Rachel waving at her from the crowd of waiting friends and relatives in the terminal when she finally walked off the plane at LAX. Since she'd done customs in New York, this part was easy. Rachel scooped her up and chattered her to the luggage carousel and to the car park. Itzhak, it seemed, had been too busy to come. Itzhak allowing Rachel to go anywhere by herself – now that was interesting. Did Beth sense a crack in Paradise?

Once they were alone in the car, Rachel demanded to know everything, especially why she wasn't to stay at the house. The phone call had really frightened her, plus she had been enjoying her privacy, away from her cramped apartment and her roommates and hated giving it up.

Too tired to explain in detail, Beth gave her the best cursory explanation she had come up with during her long hours on the plane, putting off the inevitable as long as possible. But when they pulled into her driveway, it became obvious that the nightmare had now been foisted on Rachel as well.

Beth knew something was wrong as soon as she saw the house. The front door stood ajar, the doorjamb cracked where the door had been kicked in.

Even seeing this did not prepare her for what was inside. Every inch of every room lay before her in chaos - cushions, upholstered furniture, bedding, clothing - all shredded. If someone had been looking for something, their search must have turned to a frenzy of rage when they didn't find it, because amidst the layers upon layers of torn fabric and stuffing covering the floors lay ripped books and papers and the broken shards of Beth's every possession.

While they waited for the police to arrive, surrounded by utter disaster, Beth sat on the floor with Rachel's head on her lap and told her the story from beginning to end. Everything she had learned, everything that had happened.

Later, when the police had come and gone, she called David. It would take hours and hours, but he would be here soon. She didn't even know what he could do to help, but he was the one person she truly wanted to be here with her. He'd been so right about that.

Beth and her daughter ended up sleeping curled up together on a pull-out bed in Brian's spare room, next door to her ex-husband and Betty Boop. Beth didn't care anymore. She didn't care about Brian and his need to prove he wasn't growing old, and she didn't care if every goddamned Nazi on the planet came marching down Wilshire Boulevard. She was too tired, and her beautiful home had been turned into a garbage dump and her father had died and she was in the middle of a nightmare.

The next day, they all pitched in together to pick through the remnants of Beth's life, filling the large dumpster Brian had rented. Even Itzhak showed up to help for a while. Beth tried to make light of it all, saying she had always meant to de-clutter and redecorate, but no one laughed.

Finally, when Brian headed to the airport to pick up David, Itzhak and Rachel went to get Kosher take out, and Betty Boop – damn! Sabrina – was happily puttering in the kitchen, Beth allowed herself to enter her father's room on her own. She'd waited as long as she could before going in, not being able to bear the finality of it.

It was clear that one of them had tackled this room already. The shredded bedding had been removed. And since Beth had already cleared out most of her father's clothing a million years ago, before she'd left for Israel, there hadn't been much left for anyone to destroy. To her surprise, three ties, two shirts, and a sweater were neatly folded and stacked on the dresser. Somehow, they had survived the hurricane of rage that had destroyed everything else.

"This is where it all started, Daddy," she said to her father. "If I hadn't found that key, would we be here now?"

But, of course, Beth knew it hadn't been the papers from the safe deposit box that had led her to this point in time. It had been her father's courageous act of conscience so many years ago. He had not taken the Blood Flag as a souvenir. He'd taken it to stop anyone from using it ever again. She didn't know the details of how and when, but she knew the why. And she knew why her mother had been complicit in his plan.

As she stood there with her hand on the small stack of her father's clothing, she remembered something. Something small. Something she'd tossed into a corner in a fit of anger and frustration. Something she had seen every day of her life and had grown to resent - her father's last words to her embroidered on a small satin pillow.

Suddenly, that pillow became vitally important. She scrambled around the room, but she couldn't find it. Had it gone in the things she'd sent to the rummage sale? Had it been destroyed along with everything else? If not, where was it now?

She had dropped onto her hands and knees to look under the bed when she heard the front door open.

"Rachel, are you back? Remember that little pillow that my mom embroidered? I can't find it."

A loud noise from the other room made her stop.

"Sabrina?"

No one answered. She called again as she got to her feet and walked into the living room.

Cristof stood in the entryway. Sabrina sat on the floor slumped against the wall

"Hello, Beth," he said.

"Cristof! Oh, my God! Sabrina!" Beth started forward; then she stopped. "How'd you get in here?"

"That pretty daughter of yours let me in." He glanced down at Sabrina on the floor.

"What's happened to her?" She wasn't her daughter, but he wouldn't know that.

"She's taking a little nap right now."

Every inch of Beth wanted to rush to Sabrina to see if she was okay, but she stood frozen to the spot. What was he doing here? How did he find her?

His eyes gave her the answers in a hideous jolt of knowing. All the kindness of those crystal blue eyes had gone, replaced by an icy look of pure contempt. It was as if a frightening beast had stripped off the shell of the kind, attractive man who had befriended her only a few days ago.

"Where is it, Beth? That little pillow you just asked about? I heard you." He strode across the room toward her, kicking aside the remnants of trash still strewn in his path. "It was in that bedroom when I saw it."

Instinctively, she backed up as he came closer. "I don't know what you're talking about," she said, trying her best to keep the crushing panic she felt inside out of her voice.

"Oh, I think you do. I think you know exactly what I'm talking about."

"No, I don't!" She jumped back into the bedroom and slammed the door shut behind her, knowing full well she'd left Sabrina out there alone with him. So frightened she could hardly breathe, she turned the lock on the handle. It would never hold him.

From the other side of the door she heard him laugh.

"Did you forget, Beth? You told me the whole story including his last words."

She looked around frantic for something to block the door. She shoved at the dresser, but it wouldn't budge.

"After I made sure he hadn't hidden the flag somewhere in your house, it came to me." His voice came through the door loud and clear. "He was telling you where to look. You figured that out, too, didn't you?"

She grabbed the desk chair and propped it under the doorknob.

"I didn't put it together as quickly as I should have, but fortunately I know Hebrew, and Arabic for that matter. I'm pretty good at it, too. 'Though He slay me, yet I will trust Him.' A stupid idea when you think about it."

With a crash, the door flew open; the chair tumbled away.

He stood in the doorway, smiling, glancing around the room, taking it in slowly, confidently. He walked toward her. She had nowhere to run. He stopped so close to her she could feel his breath as he glared down at her.

Suddenly, he backhanded her, hitting her so hard she flew backwards. Pain shot through her body as she hit the bed and tumbled to the floor. For a second, she blacked out but came to just as quickly.

He had her straddled on the floor next to the bed, holding her down. She tried to fight back, to kick, to push him off, but she couldn't move under the weight of him.

In that instant, just as she had heard her uncle's commands in her head on that street in Munich, she heard another voice. This one so dear to her the sound of it brought a deep calm. It was her father's voice saying one word - *Trust*.

Her hand brushed a piece of metal. The broken blade of her father's cane. She stretched out her fingers as he closed his hands around her throat.

"I hadn't bothered with it because it was so small," Cristof said with the same calm voice, as if he had all the time in the world, "but what if it holds the key?"

And then he tightened his hands, choking her, cutting off all air and all thought. Beth's mind ceased - only instinct remained.

She plunged the blade into his thigh.

He bellowed with pain, releasing her neck as his hand flew to the shaft sticking out his leg.

"You bitch," he spat and yanked the blade out. Blood spurted from the wound, but he ignored it and turned the bloody spike on her, straight to her throat.

Beth closed her eyes; she knew it was over.

But suddenly, she heard an awful crack and felt the weight of him fall off her. She didn't dare open her eyes, but she could breathe. She was still alive.

"Beth," said the loveliest voice she had ever heard. She opened her eyes and saw David standing over her. Cristof lay motionless in a crumpled heap beside her; his head turned at an odd angle.

David lifted her into his arms.

"Damn!" he said and buried his face in her hair.

CHAPTER
TWENTY-NINE

They all sat together in the living room on white plastic deck chairs arranged in a tight little circle, watching her intently. Brian held Sabrina in his lap. She was fine other than having a bruise where her head had struck the wall. David said Cristof must have just cut off her air supply enough to render her unconscious and tossed her aside.

Rachel sat close to Beth, like she had as a child. Itzhak had left on the pretext of studying, but Beth believed he'd been deeply upset by the whole situation and was trying to find a way to wiggle as far away from this family as he could get. And Rachel didn't seem to mind.

David was on Beth's other side, touching her - his hand on her back, on her shoulder, or stroking her hair, as if he had to make sure she was real and alive.

He'd called someone, who called someone else, who came and took Cristof's body away. The men who came confirmed that this had been the Austrian national they'd been watching. A man named Johann Schmidt on at least one passport. No one seemed particularly interested in notifying the police. They just made his body disappear, which was fine with Beth.

Rachel had been the one who'd taken the little pillow, rescued it when it was about to be tossed into the dumpster.

She'd recognized it as her grandmother's work and, as such, considered it precious. She'd forgotten all about it until her mother described it to her when she and Itzhak had returned with their take-out meal in hand to find that the drama of Beth's near death and rescue had just ended.

Now, as everyone watched, Beth carefully snipped open the stitches along the side of the satin fabric and eased it open. She unfolded the batting inside revealing a fat sealed gray packet, a small red cloth pouch that closed with a little button, and a folded sheet of paper, yellowed with age. It was addressed to Beth.

"*My precious daughter, Elizabeth,*" it began. The handwriting was her mother's most careful script.

"*If you have found this, you will already know some of what has transpired. I will tell you a story like I did when you were just a little girl.*

"*Once upon a time, there was a handsome and brave soldier who saw the most terrible things done by evil men of great power. God gave to him a chance to help stop these men – a chance, if he chose to take it, that would mean grave danger forevermore.*

"*This man is your dear father, my darling Beth. I have never known such courage as I have seen in him.*

"*During the war, he fought in Russia and saved many of his fellow soldiers from certain death but was very badly wounded. The evil men of power wanted men who were so brave as he to protect them. When the war was over, these cowardly men ran away, taking with them an awful thing, a thing called the Blutfahne, the Blood Flag, to use again one day to reunite and rise to power once more when the time was right.*

"*Your father stole that flag and kept it hidden, knowing he would be hunted. He changed his name and disappeared. It was then that we found each other. I was so weak and sad after the camps, but he brought life back to me. We fell so deeply in love. But we were not to be safe. The men found us, but we escaped. With my dear Benny's help, together we changed our names and made our way to Palestine, where you were born, my dearest darling.*

"Before we left on our journey, your father told me his great secret and showed me this horrible, evil flag. He also showed me a great many diamonds that had been hidden inside the flag. We vowed that night to use them only to help those in need. These diamonds that had been stolen from so many dead Jews would be used only for good. Those that are left are here for you to carry on."

Beth opened the red pouch. Inside were at least fifty glittering diamonds, each a caret or two in size. She passed the pouch around the little circle to gasps of amazement. When it came back around, she read again.

"That night, we took this horrid, filthy flag that had cost so much of so many and made certain no one would ever see it or use it again.

"We trust that you will know what to do now, my love."

Beth stared at the letter, tears streaking down her face. "She's signed it, '*We love you so, your mother and your father.*'"

~~~~

Beth locked her classroom door and headed across campus toward her car. The UCLA campus was green and lush and shimmering this time of year. Spring was in full bloom and summer on its way. It was hot but not too hot, bright but not too bright. And she loved it here.

It had been over a week since David had left. He'd said he'd be back as soon as he possibly could, and even the ambiguousness of that had made Beth's heart flutter more than she liked to admit.

David had taken the little satin pillow to his father. Beth still couldn't quite grasp why her parents had kept it – other than the feeling of triumph over profound evil, it must have given them a constant reminder of what? Their good fortune?

Their ordeal? What? She wondered if she would ever really understand.

But Beth had begun to understand the whole Trust thing, at least a little. And who was this God who would stand by and allow his children to face such horrific nightmares as the Holocaust and thousands of other instances where pure evil had won the day? Then she remembered that sense of calm that had taken over when she faced her own death. The panic had left her and something she could only describe as profound peace had taken its place. Where did that come from?

It wrapped itself around in her mind back to that word again. Trust. Whom do you trust? When do you trust? And again, the question: how do you trust a God who would slay you for your trouble?

Even that brought her back to that sense of peace.

Beth zigzagged through the parking lot to her car, climbed in and headed home as the 3:00 news came on the radio. She started to click it off when she heard that the East and West German governments had just signed their treaty of reunification.

She listened to the report then turned it off. Surprisingly, she was okay with it. She wished them well. She thought about her aunt Elisabeth and the letter she'd received just yesterday. Lovely little Karin must be ecstatic.

Rachel's car was in the driveway when Beth got home. Beth found her in the kitchen eating a bowl of ice cream.

"Hi, Mom," she said and took another bite.

"Hi, honey." Beth set her briefcase on the chair by the kitchen table. "Where's Itzhak?"

Rachel licked the spoon and looked up.

"I've been meaning to talk to you about that."

"Oh, yeah?"

"Here, I'll get you some ice cream." Rachel got up and pulled the tub out of the freezer. Mocha chocolate chip. As she busied herself scooping a bowl out for Beth, she talked, and Beth tried her best to listen without jumping up and down with glee after hearing her first words.

"We broke up," Rachel said matter-of-factly. "Actually, he dumped me. He said in his position it just wasn't going to work for his future with my family having been associated with Nazis and all."

"He what?" Beth almost tipped over her bowl when she jumped out of her chair.

"Oh, Mom, don't get yourself all worked up. I felt the same way as you for about one second. But the truth was, I was ready to break it off with him. Itzhak is such a twit. I feel like I've just been released from prison. I can see my friends – my non-Jewish friends again. I can go where I want and do what I want." She swirled her spoon one last time around the bowl to get the very last drop and looked up. "I'm not even sure I want to do the whole Kosher thing anymore, you know. I've been thinking about going to maybe one of the Conservative temples, like Rabbi Pressman's. What do you think?"

Beth burst out laughing.

"And what's so funny?"

"Well, I have been contemplating whether I should start keeping Kosher again or whether maybe I should just start by going to temple once in a while. You know, figure out just exactly what this Jewish thing is all about. What do you think?"

They both laughed.

CHAPTER
THIRTY

Geneva, Switzerland – 1990

The full moon reflected itself in a thousand wavelets created as the motorboat rocked silently to a stop in front of the serene villa overlooking Lake Geneva. Six shadows stepped out onto the wooden dock, a seventh climbed out more slowly, assisted by the others.

Sitting in the wheelchair they had unfolded for him, Major General Benjamin Klaus ignored the persistent pain in his dying body while he waited alone on the dock, watching the others move silently across toward the sweeping lawn. Shadows shifting through shadows, they covered the distance to the villa in seconds.

Maybe this burst of energy he felt would be his last, but he wasn't complaining. He felt almost young again in the cool night air. One last mission. One last chapter to close.

David trotted back to his father's side on the dock.

"Any trouble?" Benny asked.

"No. There were two men playing cards who put up a bit of a fight, but nothing we couldn't handle. I think they may have been the men who attacked Beth in Munich."

"Okay, let's get this over with, son."

The wheelchair took the journey up the drive easily, but

Benny was anxious, tempted to get out and walk, but he didn't. He would conserve the strength he'd been given for the end.

"Look," he said with a smile as they reached the stately reception hall with its grand staircase, "he's even provided me with a lift. How considerate." He clicked a switch on the wall, and a motorized chairlift descended slowly to his side. Benny left his wheelchair and climbed onboard the lift, pushed a button on the arm of the chair and rode to the top of the curved staircase. "I need to get one of these," he said cheerfully.

David followed him up.

At the top, Benny pushed himself to his feet and walked through the door, no cane, no walker for this. He stepped past the inert form of a baldheaded man inside the entrance of the outer room. A second man lay slumped in the far corner. Benny walked through another door into a large bedchamber.

A tall bank of windows along the back wall covered floor to ceiling with heavy brocade draperies closed off the night sky. Lights turned low along the walls lit the room with a soothing amber glow.

In the center of the room, a skeletal shell of a man lay on a hospital bed, hooked to and surrounded by machines and beeping monitors, his mouth and nose covered in a clear plastic breathing mask that fed him each regulated breath. His alert concave eyes darted to the door and back to Benny, accurately registering what was happening.

"Good evening, Herr Müller," Benny said in German, just to make sure there was no misunderstanding. "I don't think we've ever been introduced. I'm the dirty little Jew who's going to ruin your day."

From the other room, the frantic sound of a buzzer drew Benny's glance over his shoulder. He laughed. "I don't think that's going to help you much, my friend." He walked over to the bedside and easily forced the buzzer out of Müller's hand. "You see, there's no one out there who gives a damn."

Benny stood back and watched as the old man tried to wiggle himself as far away from him as his narrow bed and all his tubes would allow.

"Nowhere to run? Yes, our misdeeds have a way of catching up to us in the end. Mine will too, no doubt very soon. But not today. No, not today.

Müller's boney veined hand pulled down the breathing mask as he attempted to gasp out words, but they were unintelligible. Benny replaced the mask.

"You're going to need that a little longer." Reaching into his shoulder bag, Benny added conversationally, "I've brought you something to cheer you up."

He pulled out a small square satin embroidered pillow, no more than six inches across. "Isn't it pretty? Do you like it? Oh, well, you probably don't read Hebrew, do you?"

Fear and curiosity battled each other for dominance in the faded blue-gray eyes. Benny was amused.

"It's a little too biblical for my taste, but the woman who made it believed it. Her husband came to believe in it, too – lived his life by it." He turned the pillow over in his hands. "Oh, I apologize. You probably want to know what it says, and I'm just rattling on. It says, 'Though He slay me, yet I will trust Him.' That's from the Book of Job, you know. Or maybe you don't know. I doubt you read the Scriptures. I certainly don't."

Benny sat down on the foot of the bed and leaned closer. "Just look at this delicate work. She took so much trouble; I was quite sure you'd appreciate it."

Benny twisted slightly to reach into his pocket and pull out a small pocketknife. "She did this all those years ago just for you, Müller, especially for you. It's true." He opened the knife.

Müller flinched; fear had clearly won over curiosity in those ancient eyes.

"No, no," Benny said reassuringly. "Trust me, if I were

going to stab you, I'd pick something more significant than this toothpick."

He took the knife to the stitching along one side of the satin. Stitch by stitch, he cut through then jabbed the small blade deeper into the pillow.

"That will do, I think. Yes." He looked up again and smiled. "You see, SS-Gruppenführer Heinrich Müller, I've brought you what you've been searching for all this time. You chased a good man to his grave for it. So, I've brought you your precious *Blutfahne*. Just think, Hitler's Blood Flag right here in this pretty little pillowcase." Benny stood up beside the bed, so Müller had a clear view and tipped the pillow over, letting a stream of ashes rain onto the floor.

The expression on Müller's face made Benny laugh out loud.

"You didn't really think he would let you have it back, did you, you son-of-a bitch?" With that, he ground the ashes into the carpet with his heel. Then he folded the embroidered fabric and slipped it back into the shoulder bag.

"Oh, and don't bother calling for help. No one will hear you. You've got your monitors to keep you company. They'll let you know when you're dead."

Benny clicked off the lights, took one last satisfied look at the dark room, at the red and green indicators racing on the monitors, and closed the door behind him.

The End

ABOUT THE AUTHOR

Milana Dietrich is an award winning author who was born in the Sandhills of Nebraska, grew up in South Dakota, graduated from high school in Alaska, married and moved to Florida – then found her forever home in Southern California. Following in the adored footsteps of her father, she was an artist since childhood; but she found her real  passion when she studied writing with the late Marjorie Miller of UCLA.

ACKNOWLEDGEMENTS

To my dear friend Elaine - brilliant writer and even more brilliant friend. Guarding and guiding me, even quite literally paving the way. You are, without a doubt, a gift from God. Thank you.

To the angels who are my friends and coworkers, even though I'm a writer, I have no words to express the love and gratitude I feel for each one of you. You have always supported me, encouraged me, stood beside me, protected me, helped me, and shielded me with your wings. Thank you. Thank you. How can I even express the gratitude I feel every single day for such amazing angels?

To my beloved family, Larisa and Michael and my sister, Nancy, thank you for your tireless support and faith in me. You are the solid ground I stand on. You are the cloud I ride into the sky. You are my laughter and my joy. Thank you.

To Cherry Hepburn, my publisher, to Connie and Megan, the angels at her side – what you have done is a miracle in itself. All I can say is I am the luckiest girl in the world.

My final word is to PY, who has supported me, held me in loving arms, watched over me in every single way imaginable for my entire life. Thank you for finding me. Thank you for everything, everything, everything.